Night of the Cupid

A Quirky Cozy Mystery

Kirsten Weiss

misterio press

About the Book

Roses, chocolate, and a completed to-do list. Is that too much to ask for Valentine's Day? When you own the Sierra's best UFO-themed B&B, it might be. Because murder is about to collide with all of Susan's carefully laid plans...

The Valentine's special at her B&B has attracted all the wrong guests—a group of Bigfoot seekers and the ex-con who shared the worst night of Susan's life in a small-town jail. At least she's got her boyfriend Arsen for moral support.

Or does she? Because as the big day approaches, Arsen's acting even more unpredictable than usual.

And when she discovers the body of a woman with a bevy of boyfriends, she learns that love gone wrong, means nothing goes right. But will Susan's determination to set things straight land her on the wrong end of Cupid's arrow?

If you love quirky heroines, twisty mysteries, and laugh-out-loud humor, you'll love Night of the Cupid, book seven in the Wits' End cozy mystery novels. Buy Night of the Cupid and start the hilarious caper today!

Acknowledgments

Thank you to Amy Rosen, who provided a much-needed continuity edit and has a marvelous eye for detail!

Copyright

This book is a work of fiction. Names, characters and incidents are either the product of the author's imagination or are used fictitiously. Any resemblance to actual persons, living or dead, is entirely coincidental.

Copyright ©2022 Kirsten Weiss. All rights reserved, including the right to reproduce this book, or portions thereof, in any form. No part of this text may be reproduced, transmitted, downloaded, decompiled, reverse engineered, or stored in or introduced into any information storage and retrieval system, in any form or by any means, whether electronic or mechanical without the express written permission of the author. The scanning, uploading, and distribution of this book via the Internet or via any other means without permission of the publisher is illegal and punishable by law. Please purchase only authorized electronic editions, and do not participate in or encourage electronic piracy of copyrighted materials.

The publisher does not have any control over and does not assume any responsibility for author or third-party websites and their content.

Visit the author website to sign up for updates on upcoming books and fun, free stuff: KirstenWeiss.com

Cover art by Dar Albert. Interior UFO art licensed via DepositPhotos.com.

misterio press / print edition October, 2022
ISBN-13: 978-1-944767-88-4

Contents

Chapter One — 1
Chapter Two — 11
Chapter Three — 19
Chapter Four — 29
Chapter Five — 37
Chapter Six — 45
Chapter Seven — 55
Chapter Eight — 63
Chapter Nine — 69
Chapter Ten — 77
Chapter Eleven — 86
Chapter Twelve — 92
Chapter Thirteen — 99
Chapter Fourteen — 106
Chapter Fifteen — 114
Chapter Sixteen — 121
Chapter Seventeen — 130
Chapter Eighteen — 136
Chapter Nineteen — 144
Chapter Twenty — 151

Chapter Twenty-One	159
Chapter Twenty-Two	164
Chapter Twenty-Three	171
Chapter Twenty-Four	180
Chapter Twenty-Five	186
Chapter Twenty-Six	195
Chapter Twenty-Seven	202
Chapter Twenty-Eight	208
Chapter Twenty-Nine	215
Chapter Thirty	222
Chapter Thirty-One	229
More Kirsten Weiss	236
Get Kirsten's Mobile App	240
Connect with Kirsten	241
About the Author	242

Chapter One

Nothing says romance like red roses.

I stepped back and admired the petals scattered artfully across the white coverlet. True, the flowers were *not* a gift from an admirer. My admirer knew I had plenty in my garden, even if it was February in the Sierras. (I have strangely behaving roses. I can't explain why they bloom all year. It's definitely not because of magic, as townsfolk have joked.)

I scanned the room one more time. The UFO photos on the walls were straight. The window curtains were neatly tied back. Chocolates sat centered on each pillow.

The Victorian smelled of vanilla and cinnamon. Bottles of champagne were chilling in my refrigerator. Every single room was booked. My B&B was as ready as it was going to be for our Valentine's special.

Pleasure bubbled in my chest. If the rest of the year continued this way, I might have the money to finally repair Wits' End's aging roof. Also, I love romance as much as the next girl.

A door closed downstairs, and cheerful voices floated from the foyer to me. I checked my watch. It was precisely one o'clock, the start of check-in. I frowned. Hardly anyone ever showed up on the dot.

It was as good a foreshadowing of trouble as I was going to get. But I shrugged, assuming I had delightfully punctual guests, and strode into the green-carpeted hallway.

At the top of the stairs, I tugged down the hem of my blue blouse and smoothed my slacks. "Valentine's romance or bust," I murmured and hurried down the steps. I stopped short on the third stair from the bottom.

The foyer was packed with couples. They were bundled in identical hunter green parkas and scarves and hats. Piles of luggage blocked the front door and spilled toward the dining area.

My hand clenched on the banister. They'd all arrived at once? And color coordinated?

"Hi, I'm Susan Witsend." Bemused, I descended the remaining steps. "Welcome to Wits' End."

A rosy cheeked older man stepped forward smartly. "Good afternoon. I'm Carl Carter, with the Bigfoot contingent." Colored light from the stained-glass transom slanted across his wrinkled face.

My neck tensed. "Bigfoot...?"

Oh, drat. Small-town Doyle was attempting to introduce Bigfoot as a tourist attraction. Most of my guests were still UFO aficionados (or Unidentified Arial Phenomena, i.e. UAP aficionados, as it had become fashionable to call them). But we did get the occasional Bigfoot hunter. I'd even introduced Bigfoot-UFO socks and t-shirts on the shelving inset into the stairs beside the front desk.

But the B&B was booked for the Valentine's special this week. My heart thumped unevenly. Had I messed up the bookings?

I hurried around the scarred wooden desk and checked my computer. Carl Carter had indeed booked a room, and my stomach plunged. *Bigfoot hunters.* My special *hadn't* attracted pairs of hopeless romantics. My advertising for the special had been a complete waste.

A rosy-cheeked white-haired woman stepped to the man's side. "We're so looking forward to the Valentine's Special."

"But no champagne on the job." Her husband wagged his finger playfully at her. "I'm afraid for my wife this is a bit of a working vacation. She's a writer."

Maybe my advertising hadn't been a total fail after all. "What do you write?" I asked.

"Romance," she said. "I'm hoping to get some inspiration."

I straightened from the computer. "And the rest of you are here for a Bigfoot hunt?"

"We prefer not to call it a hunt," Mr. Carter said. "We're not actually hunting one down to mount his head on a wall."

"That would be impolite," his wife agreed.

"We call ourselves seekers," he said.

"Of course." I shook myself. It didn't matter. They were guests. They were here to enjoy the Valentine's Day special and search for Sasquatch. Bigfoot might not shriek *romance*, but it took all sorts to make the world go round. "I like your uniforms."

"Carl owns an outdoor-wear company." His wife beamed.

"It's not all me." He slid his arm around her waist. "You're part of marketing. And contributing gear to our team was the least I could do."

I did a quick headcount. I was short one couple and a solo traveler. I hoped she wouldn't feel overwhelmed by the Bigfoot fans when she arrived.

A middle-aged woman with frosted hair pushed her way forward. "I've booked a double room."

A man of the same age, with sunburnt cheeks and his arm in a sling edged beside her and glared. "Me too."

The rooms were all doubles, but I smiled. "And you are...?" I checked the computer.

"Brooke Piper," she said.

"Finley Nicholson," the man said.

"Yes," I said, "I have you both down for rooms with queen beds." If they were each on their own, I wasn't short a couple after all. "How many keys would you like?" It was the polite way to get at how many people were staying in a room, but the trick didn't always work.

Brooke raised her chin. "One. I'm on my own. At last."

"Same here," Finley said. "And about time."

"Divorcées," Mrs. Carter murmured.

"Do we get the Valentine's special too?" she asked. "I was really looking forward to those chocolate-covered strawberries."

Her ex-husband eyed her curvaceous hips. "Maybe you should lay off the sugar," Finley muttered.

"What?" Brooke asked.

"Nothing," he said.

"Because I'll eat as many chocolate strawberries as I want," she snapped.

"Yes, they're included," I said before the tension could grow any thicker.

I checked everyone in without further incident and got them to their rooms. My cousin Dixie had inconveniently made herself scarce. Fortunately, the men insisted on carrying the heaviest luggage. I guessed it was full of delicate equipment for their Bigfoot search.

Finally, I trotted down the stairs to the empty foyer and sat behind the desk. I was still waiting on one solo traveler.

The kitchen door creaked open. Wagging his tail, Bailey trotted over and sat beside me. I bent to scratch behind the aging beagle's ears.

The swinging door creaked open again. Dixie peered out, her curling dark hair tipped with pink. "Are they gone?"

"Yes," I said testily. "No thanks to you."

"I can't believe you're stooping to the old Valentine's Day lure." She made a face and strode into the foyer. In her Army-green Henley top and cargo pants, she could have been part of the

Bigfoot group. "It's gross. I don't know how you can stand all the pink hearts and flowers."

Said the woman who'd switched her hair dye of the month to pink. "You're in luck then," I said. "They're not romantic couples. Well, some of them are. They're a group of Bigfoot hunters. Seekers," I corrected. I flipped through my planner on the reception desk.

She rolled her eyes. "Even worse. Do they know this is a UFO B&B?"

"I expect that was part of the attraction." In my experience, there was a lot of overlap when it came to interest in the supernatural. Though I still wasn't sure if UFOs fell under the supernatural or super-science classification.

The front door bumped open. A man wearing a navy fleece jacket and jeans walked into the foyer. His face was hidden behind the wooden crate he carried. "Ice sculpture?" he asked.

I bounced from my chair and closed the computer window. "That's us." I'd never ordered an ice sculpture before. The box was a little taller than I'd expected.

Dixie huffed a laugh. "An ice sculpture? Are you kidding me?" She squinted. "Victor? Is that you?"

He grunted an assent. "Where do you want it?"

"Right this way." I led him into the kitchen and into the laundry room, where I had a small extra freezer.

He set the crate on the floor and straightened.

Whoa. Brawny shoulders. Chiseled cheekbones. Wide azure eyes a girl could drown in. Not that I would. I was madly in love with the best guy in town. But still. I wasn't blind.

"The crate won't fit inside your freezer," Victor said. He looked to be about Dixie's age, in his mid-twenties. "We'll have to remove the sculpture. I'll get the crowbar." He strode from the cramped room.

Dixie appeared in the doorway. "Don't you think you're going a little overboard with this Valentine's Day business?"

I leaned against the industrial washing machine. "I wanted a chocolate sculpture, but it cost too much." Also, the ice sculptress was local. I believed in supporting my fellow Doyle business owners when I could.

She arched a dark eyebrow. "They're Bigfoot hunters."

"Seekers, not hunters. And I promised a romantic Valentine's special." I folded my arms. "So that's what the guests are getting." I believed in the power of the planner *and* in keeping my word. Even when I don't want to.

"I dunno. This kind of reeks of desperation. You sure you're not compensating for something?"

I sniffed. What was that supposed to mean? "I'm not desperate for romance. My relationship with Arsen is perfect."

"Sure."

It wasn't a cheerful, confident *sure*. There'd definitely been a *tone* in her voice. "What d—?"

Victor reappeared in the doorway, and she edged aside to let him pass. "So when did you become a deliveryman?" she asked him.

"The things we do for love," he said.

"Ah..." She nodded wisely.

Clueless, I shrugged. What the ice sculpture delivery man did in his free time was none of my business.

He pried off the top of the box. The four sides fell away.

Dixie and I stared. It was... This was... *Oh boy.*

"Want me to put it in the freezer for you?" He pulled a pair of work gloves from the rear pocket of his jeans.

"That's, ah, not what I ordered." I pointed at the sculpture—a naked man posed like Michelangelo's David. But this guy was better looking than the famous Florentine statue. And better... er... well.

"Whoa." Dixie gaped. "Is that to scale?"

Victor glowered at me. "Kelsey told me to deliver the sculpture. I delivered the sculpture. It's your problem now."

I stepped backward and bumped against the dryer. "But I ordered a swan inside a bed of roses," I said. "Not a..." *centerfold*. "I mean. He's... It's..."

"All yours." He stomped into the kitchen.

"No, wait." I hurried after him, my hands clenching spasmodically. "You have to take it back."

But he was already through the foyer and outside. I pushed through the double porch doors and stopped at the top of the steps. My breath steamed the air. Snow lay in drifts, icing the lawn and dotting the rose bushes beside the picket fence.

"But what am I supposed to *do* with it?" I called after him.

"Watch it melt, like every other ice sculpture." He climbed into his red van, slammed the door, and backed from the driveway.

I stamped my foot, and an icicle plunged from the far end of the porch to shatter on the hard ground. "Well, that's just..."

Shivering, I retreated inside and fumed. He had a lot of nerve dumping a pornographic ice sculpture on me. Now I'd have to take it back myself to get my swan. I stormed through the kitchen to the laundry room.

Dixie circled the sculpture. "You know, if you don't want it, I'll keep it."

"No, you will not. I'm returning it for my swan." I picked up the top of the crate. Belatedly, I realized I'd have to reconstruct the entire thing. But it looked simple enough.

Thirty minutes later, I was cursing at six wooden slats. They refused to stay together. What kind of fiend made a crate that couldn't be easily assembled? What was the point?

"We'll just have to take it back without the crate," I told Dixie.

She wrenched her gaze from the sculpture. "We? I've got an online UFO seminar in twenty minutes."

"I thought they were UAPs now."

She jammed her hands on the hips of her cargo pants. "Calling them phenomena rather than objects implies they may be non-corporeal. And calling them aerial rather than flying implies no one is actually flying them. They're UFOs."

"Gotcha. Now help me get it out to my car, will you?"

"Whatever."

We bundled up. I took the head and shoulders, and Dixie grabbed the base. We lugged the sculpture down the porch steps.

Its icy sides slithered in my gloved hands. My heart gave a lurch, and I grasped the shoulders more tightly.

Something crunched on my right, and I glanced over my shoulder. My neighbor Sarah pulled her daughter on a plastic sled across her yard, clotted with children's toys.

"Oh, hi Susan." Sarah waved with her free hand.

Her daughter bounced off the sled. She toddled to the fence between the properties. "Hi, Susan. What's that?"

Her mother's eyes widened. She clapped her mittened hands over the girl's eyes.

"A mistake," I said, cheeks burning, and duckwalked backward to my blue Crosstrek. One stupid mis-delivery, and I was contributing to the delinquency of a minor.

I opened the passenger door one-handed. Carefully, we laid the sculpture on the passenger seat where I could keep an eye on it.

"Okay, bye." Rubbing her arms, Dixie trotted into the Victorian.

"But—" My mouth pinched. *Never mind.* I could get it back to the sculptress without my cousin's help.

I returned for my purse and planner, got into the SUV, and backed from the driveway. Snow still clung to the pine branches and eves of the modest neighborhood homes. Though the skies were mercury, the streets were clear of ice as I drove into Doyle.

Paper valentine hearts and twinkle lights brightened the shop windows on the old-west Main Street. Snow frosted the tops of the wooden buildings' false fronts.

I slowed, anticipating a stop sign, and cast another glance at the sculpture. So far, it hadn't shifted much, which was good because

I needed to get it to the studio in one piece. I gnawed my bottom lip and hoped the sculptor hadn't given my swan to someone else.

I drove over the humpbacked stone bridge. A blur of brown darted in front of my SUV. I sucked in a breath and slammed on the brakes. Tires screeched. The sculpture flew forward. I grabbed blindly. "Don't, don't—"

Plink.

Horrified, I rocked back in my seat and stared at the piece of ice in my hand. My gaze ping-ponged from the sculpture to my palm. "No, no, no..." I muttered.

I'd broken it.

Maybe Kelsey wouldn't notice?

My shoulders slumped. Who was I kidding? It was the *first* thing anyone with eyes would notice about this sculpture.

The squirrel bounded across the other side of the road and over a split-rail fence. It flicked its tail at me and vanished up a nearby pine. My jaw tightened. I was starting to understand Bailey's dislike of the furry rodents.

A horn blared behind me. Glancing in the rearview mirror, I waved an apology. I drove on, turning up a narrow, winding road. Deep in a wooded hillside, I turned down a long dirt driveway to a cheerful red barn.

I parked and hurried to the door in the barn's side. Stamping my feet, I knocked. The door swung open.

"Hello? Kelsey?" I stepped inside and closed the door behind me, but my attempt to keep the cold air out was foolish. The barn was freezing. Of course it was. How else would she keep the ice cold?

"The door was open," I hollered and walked deeper inside.

Straw covered the floor, as it should in any good barn. Tall blocks of ice stood sentry. I wove between them like an explorer in an arctic Stonehenge.

"Hello?" I called. "So it turns out I got the wrong sculpture." *Slightly damaged.* Would she try to charge me for it? But she couldn't. It was her mistake. Or her deliveryman's.

I rounded a corner of ice and the tension between my shoulders released. My ice swan sat amid a bed of carved ice roses on a wooden table. An electric hand saw lay beside it.

"There it is," I said loudly. And now to give her the bad news. I swallowed. "Ah, I'm afraid there was an accident with the, er, David. Or whoever it was..." I turned and stumbled backward into the table.

Kelsey lay on the straw beside a massive ice sculpture—a cupid inside a starburst of ice. Red darkened her thick vest, a spear of ice jutting from her chest.

Chapter Two

"You should have got the chocolate." Sheriff McCourt stood outside the barn, her breath clouding the air.

"I should have got the chocolate," I repeated dully. I studied the ice sculpture, melting on my passenger seat. Deputies moved purposefully in and out of the nearby barn.

"What's that extra little piece there?" The sheriff motioned toward the broken bit inside a cupholder.

"Ah... The sculpture slid forward on the seat when I hit the brakes too hard. I wasn't looking and grabbed for it, and it... snapped off."

"Oh." She adjusted her broad-brimmed hat, her blond curls spilling from beneath it. The sheriff was petite, with a Shirley-Temple air. A lot of criminals underestimated her because of it. "So you gelded him?"

My face warmed. "It, not him."

"You gelded it."

"It was an accident," I said, flustered.

"That can't be to scale," she muttered.

"It might have melted a little on the way over," I admitted. "More than the rest of the sculpture, I mean."

"You mean it was bigger?" She gazed speculatively at me. "How are things with Arsen?"

I shifted my weight. "Great. He's amazing." Though he had been a little jumpy lately. "His security firm is doing really well." I think his sudden success might have surprised even him.

But my love life was neither here nor there. A murder had been committed. And it was lucky I'd been the one to discover the body. After all, I had experience in such matters. The sheriff and I had worked together on several cases. I was kind of her secret weapon, a sort of citizen-insider.

She sighed, her breath pluming. "Your sculpture doesn't really matter much now. I think you're out of luck for that refund."

"Actually, the swan sculpture I ordered was right there on the table. You wouldn't mind if I...?"

Her cornflower eyes took on a chilly glint. "It's a crime scene."

I sighed. "Right. It's just that the ice sculpture wasn't cheap."

"You should have got the chocolate."

"I should have the got the chocolate." We stared at the sculpture some more. A trickle of water ran down its brawny chest. "But I wanted to support a local business." The nearest business supplying chocolate sculptures was two hours away in Sacramento.

"And I appreciate your civic spirit. Well. Let's get it out of your car." She reached for the sculpture's head.

"Is it evidence?"

"Not if it melts."

The statue was even slipperier now. I've no idea how we got it out of my Crosstrek without dropping it. We set it beside a sledgehammer leaning negligently against the barn.

I rubbed the back of my neck. "Her death couldn't have been an accident, could it?"

"No. But the ice was already melting in her chest. If you hadn't come across her so soon, we wouldn't have had any evidence to preserve."

"So it *was* murder." Like I said. *Lucky me.*

"You said she had a helper drop your sculpture off?"

I nodded. "It's not mine, but yes. He's someone named Victor. He's in his mid-twenties? I think Dixie knows him."

"Oh, goodie," she muttered, and I grimaced.

Once, in a fit of youthful exuberance, Dixie had stolen a sheriff's car. It had happened years ago, but there was still some bitterness between the two women. And I got it. It's hard to trust someone who was once arrested.

A red van squelched wetly up the dirt drive.

"I think that's him now," I said.

The van pulled up behind my SUV. Victor stepped from the car in his blue Henley top and jeans.

The sheriff sucked in a breath. "Whoa."

"I know," I muttered. I was in an amazing relationship, but not even I'd been blind to Victor's good looks.

He caught sight of the sculpture and frowned. Victor strode to the barn. He hefted the sledgehammer.

"Wait," the sheriff barked. "Stop!"

Muscles bunched beneath his shirt. In a single swift movement, he swung the sledgehammer, smashing it atop the ice sculpture's head. The sculpture cracked and scattered into hundreds of pieces that rocked on the dirt.

"Whoa, whoa, whoa!" The sheriff drew her gun from her belt but kept it aimed low, at the ground. "Put that down. Right now."

He dropped the sledgehammer, and it thudded to the earth.

"What the—" I sputtered. "I wanted a refund on that!" Okay, yes, that was impossible now. But *he* didn't know that. Unless he was the killer. My jaw set.

Victor shrugged. "Never liked that sculpture. I suppose the neighbors complained about the noise again. Look, Kelsey can't help it. When inspiration strikes, it strikes."

The sheriff strode toward him and holstered her weapon. "That's not why I'm here."

"Why *are* you here?" he asked.

Deputy Owen Denton stuck his blond head out of the barn door. "The coroner's on his way, Sheriff."

Victor paled. "Coroner?"

Sheriff McCourt glared at her deputy. The young man's mouth puckered, and he ducked back inside the barn.

"Coroner?" Victor repeated more loudly. He turned to the barn.

The sheriff grabbed his arm. "I'm sorry to inform you Ms. Delaney is dead."

Victor staggered and braced one broad hand on the barn. His brow furrowed, his eyes widening with confusion. "No. She can't be. She was alive this morning."

"When did you last see her?" the sheriff asked.

The skin bunched around his startling blue eyes. Muscles corded in his neck. "But she can't be dead. I saw her."

"When did you see her?" she repeated more quietly.

He swallowed. "At eleven thirty. I picked up some sculptures to deliver, and she was alive. She was right here. Alive." His hands fisted. "Enrique." He glanced at the shattered sculpture.

"Who's Enrique?" I asked.

"Let's speak privately," the sheriff said to him. "Over there. I'll see you later, Susan." She led him to the far corner of the barn.

"Oh," I said. "Yes. Of course. You need space." I pressed my lips together. How was I supposed to hear Victor's testimony now? Pretending I wasn't part of the sheriff's investigative team was often a real challenge.

Rummaging in my oversized purse, I pantomimed a search and pulled out my phone. I put it to my ear, as if I were on a call, and edged closer to the sheriff and Victor.

"...jealous," Victor was saying.

"Witsend," the sheriff barked.

I jerked, dropping my phone. "Yes?"

She scowled. "Go home. Denton!" she bellowed.

The young deputy hurried from the barn. "Yes, Sheriff?"

"Escort Ms. Witsend home."

"Oh." I picked the phone off the ground. "That isn't necessary. I have my own car."

Her jaw clenched. "Follow her home," she ground out, "and make sure she gets there."

"Yes, ma'am." The deputy touched the rim of his hat.

Fine. She'd no doubt tell me all about the interview later. After all, it was no good being her secret weapon if everyone *knew* I was her secret weapon. Though after that incident with the stolen garden gnomes last year, the town was aware I tended to get involved.

The deputy's black and white SUV trailed behind me as I drove back to Wits' End. I pulled into the gravel driveway, stepped out and waved.

The deputy's car just sat there, idling at the end of my drive. I huffed a breath. Denton was taking his escort job seriously. I walked up the Victorian's porch steps and waved to him again from the first screen door.

Finally, his SUV pulled forward. It glided down the court.

"Took you long enough," Dixie said from behind me, and I jumped. "Did you have to beat the refund out of her?" she asked.

I let the screen door swing shut, edged past her on the closed porch, and opened the door to Wits' End. "No, it was terrible. Kelsey was dead."

Dixie blinked. "Dead? Why was she dead?"

I walked into the foyer and stopped in front of the reception desk. In his dog bed beside it, Bailey yawned.

"I have no idea," I said. "I found her dead with an... icicle like thing through her heart. Someone had broken it off one of her sculptures. I think they stabbed her with it."

My cousin stilled. "You're *not* kidding." Leaving the front door open, she trailed after me into the foyer.

I crossed the faux-Persian rug and shut the door. "Of course I'm not kidding. Why would I kid about that?" I studied her. "Are you okay?"

She shook her head, her pink-tipped hair quivering. "Yeah. Yeah. I'm just... I saw Kelsey last week. I can't believe she's dead."

A dull, foggy feeling settled in my chest. Dixie was so self-sufficient she'd crossed into hermit territory. I didn't think she had many friends. "I'm sorry. I didn't know you two were close."

"Remember the moment," she murmured.

"What?"

"It was a sort of *momento mori* saying she had. Not *remember you will die*, but *remember the moment*. That's what she always used to tell me."

I set my leather-bound planner on the desk and opened it to a blank murder investigation page. Arsen had given me the planner, tailoring pages to our investigative lifestyle. We hadn't used them in quite some time.

I found a mechanical pencil. "What can you tell me about Kelsey and Victor? And someone named Enrique."

Dixie folded her slender arms. "Here's the deal. Kelsey and I weren't friends. I was just her wingman sometimes. She had, like, three guys on the string—Victor, Enrique, and Anselm. I got to know them better than I did Kelsey. She was just using me."

I noted the names in my planner. "That doesn't sound like much fun for you." I straightened.

Dixie shrugged. "Kelsey paid for my drinks. The guys are all decent dancers. It wasn't bad."

"No, but..." My heart pinched. Wouldn't Dixie have liked a real relationship?

"It was fine," she said shortly.

And none of my business. "Would you make a list of the contact info for everyone you mentioned? I'll need to know where they work, and whatever else you know."

"Does Hannah know yet?"

"Hannah who?"

"Hannah Delaney. Kelsey's sister."

"Oh." *A sister. The poor woman.* I stared at my shoes. I was an only child, but I could imagine what she was about to go through. "I don't know," I said quietly. "Probably not yet. The sheriff will have to tell her."

Dixie gnawed her bottom lip. "This bites. Hannah's pretty cool."

"Were you two close?"

"No, but she's got a friend who works with the DOD. Sometimes she gets me good UFO intel."

The door to the kitchen swung open, and Arsen stepped into the foyer. Catching sight of us, he pulled up short. Arsen pivoted on his heel, as if to return inside the kitchen.

"Arsen?" I said.

He froze and turned to me, a broad smile on his face. "Oh, hey Susan. I didn't see you there." His khaki-colored tactical Henley strained against his broad shoulders.

And this is why Victor—attractive as he was—hadn't sent me into a girlish tailspin. I had Arsen, one of the handsomest men in town, and definitely the best.

"Have you heard?" Dixie said. "The ice sculptor, Kelsey Delaney, was killed. Murder. Susan found the body."

"Whoa." Arsen strode across the foyer, his tanned brow furrowed with concern. He ran his broad hands down my arms. This close, I could smell the fresh, clean scent of his soap. The light from the chandelier glinted off his whiskey-colored hair. "I'm sorry. Are you okay?" His hazel eyes darkened with concern.

"I'm fine," I said. "I just finished with the sheriff, and I barely knew Kelsey. But she was Dixie's friend."

"We weren't friends," she said flatly.

I shook my head. "But—"

The exterior screen door slammed.

Arsen frowned. "Are you expecting someone?"

"There's one more guest checking in today," I said.

The door swung open. A big redhead with frizzy hair strode inside. She dropped a massive sky-blue suitcase on the Persian carpet with a thunk. The woman spread her arms, the fabric of her longish pink parka crackling. "Witsend! You came to greet me!"

I blinked. Did I know her? She did look familiar... "I—uh—what?"

She ambled farther inside, craning her neck at the chandelier. "I thought I'd take you up on your offer to stay." Bailey rose from the dog bed. He shook himself and came to sniff the newcomer's thick-soled shoes.

"To stay?" I parroted, recognition dawning. Red hair. Broad shoulders. Desperado grin. No. This couldn't be happening. This could *not* be happening.

"Is this a friend of yours?" Arsen asked.

"The best kind of friend." The woman reached out and grasped Arsen's hand, pumping it enthusiastically. "We met in jail."

Chapter Three

"Jail?" Dixie's green eyes widened with delight. "You were in jail, Susan?"

"Yup," Sal said. "In Nowhere, Nevada. It's a bonding experience." The big woman scratched the armpit of her pink parka. "Jail, I mean. Not Nowhere."

Bonding? My cheeks burned. Jail had been one of the worst moments of my life. The lack of control. The smell of disinfectant. That sheriff had even taken by planner away. Plus, it was *jail*.

"But she wasn't in for long." Sal leaned against the reception desk and crossed her legs. She wore matching pink ankle boots. "Susan had to get out to catch that killer."

"Were you a... deputy?" Arsen asked her, frowning.

"What?" Sal reared backward against the desk. "Deputy? No way. Susan, you didn't tell him about me?"

"No, no," I said. "I mean, I did. It's just—I never knew your full name. We never introduced ourselves properly. You remember." I turned to Arsen. "The woman with the, er, chalk?" With it, she'd created an impromptu murder board on the jailhouse wall. It had actually been rather helpful.

Grinning, she socked me in the shoulder, and I winced. "I was instrumental in helping solve that murder."

"You were?" Dixie asked.

"Sure," Sal said. "We did that whole... thing. You know. Deducting whodunit. Using the gray cells. Like she said, I supplied the chalk and the organizational skills." She tapped her head.

Bailey sighed and slumped against her foot. She bent to pat the beagle's head.

"What were you in for?" Dixie asked.

"Dixie," I hissed, rubbing my shoulder. "That's a little rude." But my stomach lurched. What *had* Sal been arrested for? I didn't recall discussing it in jail, but I'd had a lot on my mind at the time.

"Nah, it's okay." Sal unzipped her thick parka. "I was in for assault."

My stomach plunged to the fake Persian carpet. "Assault? You attacked someone?"

"Not someone." She scowled. "I decked a guy. He was hassling my ex—an excitable, tense kind of guy. Reminds me a little of you, Susan."

"The guy you hit reminds you of Susan?" Arsen asked.

"No, no, no," she said. "He was a big guy, about your size. My *ex* reminds me of Susan."

"So he was hassling your ex, and you punched him," Dixie said gleefully.

"We-ell," she said. "I told him to knock it off. And then he called me fat, and the red haze came."

"The red haze?" I asked in a distant voice.

"It's like this wash," Sal said. "This red haze comes over my eyes. I can't be blamed for what happens next."

"Cool," Dixie said. "What happened to your ex?"

She scowled. "He's my ex, isn't he? How should I know?"

"What does he do?" Dixie asked.

"It's not important," I said quickly. "He's her ex. No one wants to talk about their ex."

Sal shrugged. "It's no biggie. He's a money man."

"For... the mob?" I whispered, horrified.

"Nah, for Tesla. He's an accountant. It's good pay."

"Your timing is *amazing*," Dixie said. "Susan found another dead body just today. A murdered woman."

Sal's chin jerked backward. "You're kidding. We've got another case? Good thing I brought my chalk."

"Sal's in room seven, right?" Dixie picked up Sal's suitcase and grunted. "You're going to love it. A guy was killed in there a couple of years back. It was the sheriff's ex-husband."

We didn't usually mention that detail to our guests. "That's—"

"No kidding." Sal braced her hands on her broad hips. "Think it's haunted?"

"Oh," my cousin said. "Totally." She staggered toward the green-carpeted stairs. "And did Susan tell you about Bigfoot?"

"Nuh-uh." She followed Dixie up the stairs. "We were pretty concentrated on our murder case back then." On the first step, Sal pivoted. She pointed a finger at the shelf beside the reception desk with its rows of souvenirs. "I want to get one of those alien bobbleheads before I leave though. Be sure to save one for me."

"Of course," I said distantly. We watched the two women disappear up the steps.

"I don't know about this new guest." Arsen rubbed his chin, his five o'clock shadow making scratching noises against his palm. "She looks a little rough."

"I can't turn her away. She has a reservation."

"If she's going to make you or your guests unsafe, yes," he said, "you can."

"I don't think she will." With the toe of my shoe, I flipped down a corner of the rug that had turned up. "I mean, she was nice in that jail. And she's out now. How is she going to be rehabilitated if she's not allowed to rent a room in a B&B?"

"Why'd she come here? And how'd she know how to find you if you didn't introduce yourselves?"

"She must have heard we cracked that murder in Nowhere after the sheriff let me go. And when the deputy came to release me, she might have said my last name out loud. Witsend. Wits' End. It wouldn't have been hard to put those two together."

Arsen raised a skeptical brow. "You're a soft touch." He smiled. "It's one of the things I love about you. But you need to be careful."

"I'm sure it will be fine." I laughed unevenly. "She was dating an accountant, not a member of a motorcycle gang. And it's not as if she's come to Doyle to pull off a caper."

Unless... *Nah*. She'd been arrested for assault, not grand theft. Not that assault was a good thing. In fact, it was pretty bad. Really bad. Maybe I should gently direct Sal away from the other guests?

Steps thundered on the stairs, and Dixie and Sal returned to the foyer. Sal was still bundled in her thick parka.

"No one's ever put rose petals on my bed before. Thanks, Sue. I mean, it's a little weird since we're just friends, but okay. I get it. You do you." Sal rubbed her hands together. "Now, what's the first step?"

I plucked a map from the brochure stand beside the door. "We've got hiking trails, and downtown Doyle is charming. Most of the sights are on Main Street, but it's still worth a look. There are tasting rooms and even a cute old jail—" I clamped my mouth shut.

Oh. Maybe not the old jail.

"I meant next with the investigation," Sal said, seemingly unperturbed by the jail reference.

"Usually," Dixie said, "Susan takes a casserole to the bereaved. Then she grills them for intel."

Sal's round face scrunched in consternation. "We have to bake a casserole?"

"Not a chance," Dixie said. "This is a B&B. Susan's got half a dozen breakfast casseroles in the freezer. She always makes extra. She drops one off a week to these nice old guys she found some stolen gnomes for. And you know, other casserole-related stuff comes up."

Sal nodded, her red curls bouncing. "Got it. The old *here's a casserole, now spill your guts* ploy. I find alcohol more effective, but this is your show."

"It might be a little too soon for casseroles," Arsen said.

"He's right," I said quickly. "The sheriff probably hasn't had a chance to inform Kelsey's sister about the murder. We need to wait until tomorrow, so we don't step on the sheriff's investigation." *Or wait until never.* After all, I could hardly assist the sheriff with Sal in tow.

Sal's lip curled. "Cops."

"In the meantime," I said, "have you eaten? Doyle has a fun collection of restaurants." *Far away from Wits' End and my other guests.*

"It's a little early to eat," Sal said. "But thanks."

Sweat dampened my forehead. I needed to get her out of here before she encountered the Bigfoot group. "Or there's—"

The front door opened. Rosy-cheeked, Carl and Clara Carter trooped into the foyer. "Tracks," Carl said, grinning. "We found possible Bigfoot tracks. Where are the others? Are they back yet?"

"Ah, no." I cast a quick glance at Sal. I doubted Sal would mind if I didn't introduce them. "I thought your group was sticking together?"

"We decided to break into pairs to expand the search field," the older man said. "And who's this? Another seeker?"

Oh, damn. "We were just leaving," I said repressively.

"I'm Sal." She stuck a plump hand out, and they shook. "You found Bigfoot tracks?" she asked.

"I think so. Look at these photos." He pulled his phone from the pocket of his parka, fiddled with the screen, and handed it to her.

She whistled. "You put the quarter next to it for scale?"

He nodded. "Exactly. You're familiar with the technique?"

"I know a thing or two," she said modestly. "I was instrumental in helping solve a murder once."

"Really?" Mrs. Carter asked, her voice burbling with excitement. "Would you like to see the tracks? I'd love to hear about your murder."

"Sure. It looks like I've got time to kill." Sal cracked her knuckles. "Lead on, Macduff."

The trio strolled from the B&B. I watched the front door swing shut. So much for keeping Sal away from the Bigfoot seekers. "This will be fine," I said uneasily. *Just fine.*

The next morning, Dixie leaned against my butcher-block kitchen counter and sipped coffee. "I don't see what the big deal is," she said. "The guy called her fat. What was Sal supposed to do?"

"Exercise some self-restraint." I set a dish in the washer. "And have you seen my cast-iron pans?" How could they have vanished from the cupboard? They weren't the sort of things I typically misplaced. I'd had to use a pair of ancient metal pans this morning. I didn't *like* those pans.

"Some people exercise too much self-restraint," my cousin muttered into her mug.

My eyes narrowed. "What was that?"

"No, I haven't seen your pans."

I slung the drying towel over my shoulder. "Well, they didn't walk out of the kitchen on their own."

"I didn't take your stupid pans. And why didn't you tell me you'd been in jail?"

"I wasn't accusing you, and it was all a misunderstanding," I said in a rush. "I wasn't charged with anything." Also, it was humiliating. I checked the drawer beneath the oven. No cast-iron pans. Where the heck had I put them?

"Oh, well. You never lorded my arrest over me. I guess I can cut you some slack."

"Thank you." I banged the drawer shut and straightened. "But since the charges were dropped, an arrest basically never happened."

"Yeah, no. I don't think it works that way."

Was I losing my mind? Had I put them away in the wrong place? I opened a random cupboard. No cast iron. "Did you get a chance to call Hannah and Anselm?"

"Yeah."

I wiped my hands on the dish towel and hung it on the stove door handle to dry. "And?"

Dixie was being more helpful than I'd expected with my investigation. But you should never underestimate people. We've all got hidden depths. Besides, these were Dixie's friends. Of course she wanted to help them. "Can we see them today?" I asked.

"Yeah, I said we'd be stopping by this morning. They're not going anywhere."

Sal burst into the kitchen, and I tensed. The kitchen was off limits to guests for good reasons involving hot stoves, damp floors, and other household hazards. Also, it was my private kitchen.

"Super breakfast, Sue. You don't mind if I call you Sue, do you? Great. Are we ready to go?" She wore red boots with fur at the top. A raspberry sweater covered her thick black leggings at her thighs.

"Go?" I asked blankly.

"To talk to the murdered woman's sister. You said ten o'clock, right Dix?"

"Yup." Dixie nodded like one of the bobbleheads on the shelf behind the reception desk. "Ten."

I clenched my fists. *Dixie.* Why was she encouraging this?

"Cool," Sal said. "I've got to do something before I go crazy. This place is quiet. Like, *Night of the Comet* quiet. Like humanity has been turned to dust after going through the path of a comet's tail, and we're the only survivors quiet. I'm going to get my jacket. Oh, and I'll bring you back your pans." She pivoted and strode into the foyer, the kitchen door swinging behind her.

"You told Sal?" I asked, outraged. *Wait. Pans?*

My cousin shrugged and blew on her coffee. "She asked. What was I supposed to do?"

I exhaled slowly. Dixie was right. I wouldn't lie to my guests, and I couldn't ask Dixie to either. Though a little bit of misdirection wouldn't have gone amiss.

I finished cleaning up and double checked my planner to make sure I hadn't missed anything. Naturally, I hadn't.

Sal strode into the kitchen brandishing my cast-iron pans. "Thanks for these."

"I didn't—What did you need my pans for?"

"I forgot to bring my free weights." She handed me the two pans.

That was... I shook my head. *Never mind.*

I returned the pans to their proper place. We piled into my Crosstrek. Dixie climbed into the back with Bailey and the casseroles.

"So tell us about Hannah," I said with forced cheerfulness. I backed the car from the drive.

"She couldn't stand her sister," my cousin said. Bailey woofed.

"Sisters," Sal said wisely. "It can be the best or worst relationship of your life."

I pulled into the court. "Why did she hate her?" I was a single child, so I didn't get sibling dynamics. But in my experience, most families at least tried to get along.

"Because Kelsey stole Hannah's boyfriend, Anselm," Dixie said.

"In my experience," Sal said. "Most stolen boyfriends want stealing. My ex—" She stopped herself and sighed.

"Maybe," my cousin said from the back. "But I think it bugged Hannah because Kelsey already had two other guys."

"Two others?" Sal asked.

I had enough on my hands managing one. I frowned. Arsen hadn't dropped in for breakfast this morning like he usually did. He must have been really busy.

"Three boyfriends does seem greedy," Sal said.

We drove down Main Street, and I pointed out the sights in Doyle to our guest. Finally, we turned up a small hill to a newish luxury condominium complex. Its manicured lawns were dotted with snow. With its stone walls and peaked rooflines it looked more appropriate for Aspen or Vail than funny little Doyle. But California was changing—even in the foothills.

Sal whistled. "This Hannah got money?"

"Sort of," Dixie said. "It's in her family. It kind of comes and goes."

"What's that supposed to mean?" I asked.

"Her parents cut Hannah off when she started seeing Anselm. And then when they broke up, she got back into her parents' good graces."

"And the money came back?" I asked. "What happened to Kelsey when she started dating Anselm?"

"Nothing. Kelsey had already told her parents to pound sand. She's been on her own for years. She said she didn't need their money."

"I'm liking this girl," Sal said. "Too bad she's dead."

We parked in the lot. I took the casserole, and Sal and I followed Dixie along a paving stone path to the glass front doors. They opened automatically, and we walked into the foyer. A curving security desk stood in front of one stone wall. Bailey looked around, interested.

Bernie, the complex's uniformed guard and our sometimes handyman, looked up and grinned. "Hey, Susan, Dixie, Bailey. What's up?"

"Hi, Bernie," I said. "We're here to see Hannah Delaney."

He smiled at Sal. "I'll call up." He phoned. "Susan and Dixie and a friend of theirs are here to see you... Okay." He hung up. "You can take the elevator up."

I nodded. "Thanks." We got into the elevator and the doors closed. "Anything else you'd like to mention about Hannah and Anselm?"

"Nope," Dixie said.

The elevator dinged, and the doors opened. We walked into a hallway with gleaming wood floors. Modern—and possibly original—art hung on the sand-colored walls. We approached Hannah's door and heard raised voices inside.

"—too late," a woman shouted. "Just get out."

The door flew open. A tall, auburn-haired man in a fleece-lined denim jacket and khaki slacks backed from it. A near-black, geometric tattoo curled across the back of his neck. "Hannah, I'm so sorry. This isn't what I wanted."

"Get out," she shrieked and slammed the door.

Heat crept from my chest to my neck. *Awkward.*

The man turned, his brown eyes mournful. He had the bad boy looks of a Hollywood star. What was going on? I'd never noticed so many attractive men in Doyle before.

"Hey, Anselm," Dixie said brightly. "How's it going?"

Anselm? One of Kelsey's boyfriends? *Even more awkward. And intriguing.*

Chapter Four

Anselm's face sagged. "Um—it's..."

Embarrassing? I shifted the frozen casserole in my arms. The complex's hallway, which moments ago had seemed wide and welcoming, was now cramped and cold. Bailey shook himself, his collar jingling.

"Hannah take a bite out of you?" Dixie nodded to the bandage around his index finger.

"Paper cut." He ripped off the bandage, exposing a thin, red line on the side of his knuckle.

"Meh, big deal." Sal sneered. "The lady told you to go. You gonna go or hang around her door like a bump on a log?"

My face grew hotter. We needed to build rapport with him, not run him off. He was a suspect.

"I'll just, er, go." Anselm hurried down the hallway. He pressed the elevator button.

Dixie laughed, and I rang the doorbell. "It's not funny," I whispered.

"Men," Sal huffed. "Nothing funny about 'em when they've betrayed you. That's for sure."

The door flew open. "I told you to—oh. Sorry. I didn't think you'd get here so quickly. I guess I was..." The young woman's brown eyes blinked and then widened.

"Hey, Hannah," Dixie said.

Hannah's hair was thick and brown. Her eyes were red and splotchy. Her face was tanned and freckled. She wore an oversized cream-colored sweater and matching leggings. Her feet were bare, the toenails painted pink. The color matched her long nails.

I sighed. If I tried for nails that long, they wouldn't last a week.

"We heard about your sister," Dixie continued, "and we're really sorry. We wanted to check in and see how you were doing. My cousin brought one of her famous breakfast casseroles, if you want it." She jerked her head in my direction.

"That's..." Hannah's shoulders crumpled inward. "That's nice. Thanks. Come in."

"We brought Bailey," I said, angling my head toward the beagle. "Is it okay if he comes in too?"

"Sure."

We trooped into her condo. She closed the door behind us and led us into a blue-gray living room. Rolled carpets lay on the hardwood floors. Moving boxes were stacked in the corners of the room.

Picture windows looked over the eastern mountains, lost in a bank of slate-colored clouds. Silver-framed photos stood on a grand piano in one corner of the room. Given the length of her nails, I guessed the piano was for decoration rather than playing.

I paused beside the piano and studied the photos. One picture lay outside a frame—a photo of Hannah and Kelsey at the lake. The sisters wore matching white tanks and blue headscarves, though Kelsey had broken with the theme, adding a gray coral pendant. Hannah's neck was bare.

Hannah motioned us to the couch, and we sat, jostling each other. She dropped into an oversized armchair. The condo smelled like chocolate-chip cookies. Though it was still well before lunch, my stomach growled.

"Anselm's back sniffing around, I see," Dixie said.

Hannah's lean face tightened. "Now that Kelsey isn't around to take care of him anymore. It's either me or his parents. And it's not going to be me."

Ouch. She obviously hadn't gotten over the earlier breakup.

"Would you like some cookies?" she continued. "I had them delivered. They're still fresh."

"I won't say *no* to that," Sal said. Bailey's nose twitched.

"This is Sal." I motioned to her. "A friend of ours from Nowhere, Nevada. She's visiting for the week."

Hannah rose and padded across the throw carpets to the open kitchen. Its glossy gray wall tiles glittered. "Nowhere? Where's that?" She returned with a pink bakery box and set it on the glass coffee table between us.

Sal leaned forward and opened the box, grabbed two. She slipped one into the pocket of her parka, and I smothered a wince.

"It's just on the other side of those mountains." I pointed at the windows. "It's really fun. They've got all these record-breaking big things."

"Nowhere's okay," Sal mumbled through a mouthful of cookie. "What's with the dude? He giving you trouble?"

Hannah flushed. "Dixie knows the whole story. We were together for a year. I thought—" She swallowed. "I thought we'd be together forever. I even—my parents didn't approve." She laughed bitterly. "So much so they finally cut me off, but I didn't care. I was in *love*." Her upper lip curled. "And then he met Kelsey, and two months later it was all over."

"Hold on." Sal leaned forward, bracing her elbows on her knees. "And now that little weasel is trying to get back in your good graces?"

"Maybe." Hannah turned her head to stare out the window. "I don't know."

I cleared my throat. "I heard, er, that your sister was seeing other people too."

"Kelsey had this weird magnetism." Her tone was bitter. "She always did. Men got sucked into her orbit like she was a sexy black hole."

"Who do you think could have done this?" I asked.

Her hand curled, her pink nails brushing her palm. "Pick a guy. Enrique. Victor."

"Anselm?" I asked, taking a cookie.

She looked at the throw carpet. "I don't think so," she said softly. "He came by my company last week. He seemed... I don't know. Sorry. Like he had regrets about the way things went down." She shook her head. "I don't know. Or maybe Vida finally did it."

"Vida?" I asked.

"Vida Lewis. Victor's ex. She hated Kelsey for stealing Victor out from under her. Vida waits tables at the Irish pub."

Then she'd be easy to track down. "Are you moving?" I nodded toward the boxes.

Hannah's flush deepened. "I have to. I thought I could go on here, but seeing Anselm and my sister—" She bit her bottom lip.

"You don't have to see them together anymore." Sal reached for another cookie. That was a little blunt, and I shot her a sharp look.

"No." Hannah swallowed. "I'd give anything..."

"Where are your parents?" I asked.

"They live outside Tahoe City. They're really—" She lowered her head. "They're devastated. I don't think they realized... You know."

An ache opened in my chest. You didn't always appreciate the people you loved until they'd gone. And that was a futile time to try to start appreciating them or trying to make amends. I glanced at Dixie.

"Where's this *Vida* live?" Sal brushed crumbs off her parka.

"In the apartments by the creek," Hannah said. "Why?"

"Just curious," I said and stepped lightly on Sal's foot. We didn't need to have her home address. We knew where she worked. And it was an odd question to ask during what was supposed to be a subtle interrogation.

"Hey, why're you stepping on my foot?" she asked.

Really? Embarrassed, I cleared my throat. "Did the sheriff tell you I found your sister?" I asked.

"No," Hannah said dully.

Sal nudged me. "Ask her where she was yesterday morning."

I glared. How could I ask that question without being obvious now?

"What?" Hannah said.

"It's just that..." I fumbled. "I can't help thinking if the morning had gone differently, if I'd been somewhere else..." Where *was* I going with this? "When, er, disasters strike—"

"I came by yesterday morning, but you weren't in." Dixie brushed back her pink-tipped hair.

"I was in." Hannah's gaze shifted to the piano. "I slept in yesterday. I mustn't have heard when the guard called up. And then the sheriff came... Why'd you come by?"

"I was bored." Dixie shrugged.

Hannah didn't have an alibi. I shifted on the leather couch. "Did the sheriff tell you anything else?"

"She went through Kelsey's apartment but didn't seem to find anything. She wants me to meet her there this afternoon and see if I can spot anything missing or out of place. I don't know how... I'm not sure I can stand it."

"Would you like us to go with you?" I offered.

She looked to Dixie. "Would you?"

"Yeah. Sure. I guess."

Hannah's shoulders sagged. "Thanks. Meet me there at three-thirty?"

"Sure," I said. That would give us just enough time to finish cleaning all the rooms.

We didn't get much more out of Hannah after that. The three of us left, muttering condolences.

"Huh." Sal pressed the button for the elevator. "This Anselm guy sounds shifty. Plus he's got at least one tattoo. I'm not dating any guys with more tattoos than me. Not anymore." The doors glided open, and we stepped inside. "Though Bingo didn't have any ink, and look where that went," she said.

"Bingo? Your ex?" She'd dated a corporate accountant named Bingo?

"Yeah. His real name was Bernard, but I called him Bingo. Don't much like the name Bernie. Reminds me of that dead guy. You know, in that movie? The one where they're carrying his body around a beach house? Creepy if you ask me."

We drove to Anselm's house, a bungalow higher up the mountain in a neighborhood thick with pines. He wasn't home, which was unsurprising since we'd just seen him leaving Hannah's.

It was also a bit of a relief. I wasn't sure if Sal had helped or hurt when we'd met him, but she wasn't the best interrogation partner.

Since the weather was cold, we left his casserole on a lawn chair beside the front door. I scrawled a note on the foil, then we made our way back to my Crosstrek.

"This is getting confusing," Sal said. "How am I going to remember all these suspects? I left my chalk back at the B&B."

"It's easy," Dixie said. "Victor and Vida used to be a couple before Kelsey broke them up. That's V and V."

"Okay," Sal said. "I get the alliteration, but there are other players too."

"Anselm's an artist," Dixie said. "Again, alliteration. And Anselm kinda sorta rhymes with Hannah, and those two used to date before—"

"Kelsey broke 'em up," Sal finished for her. "And who are you?"

An elderly woman wrapped in a thick black coat, scarf, and hat leaned against my Crosstrek. She puffed an e-cigarette. "Investigating another murder, young Susan?" She pulled down her Jackie-Kennedy style sunglasses.

"Sure are." Sal reached for the car door. "You too?"

Mrs. Steinberg straightened off my car, raspberry-scented smoke wreathing her head. Her nostrils flared. "Certainly not."

"You should try it some time," Sal said. "It's loads more interesting than darts at the pub. You've got a pub here in Doyle, don't you?" she asked me.

"And this is...?" Mrs. Steinberg tilted her head, her lipsticked mouth pinching.

"A friend of mine from Nowhere," I said hastily. "Sal, this is Mrs. Steinberg. She was a good friend of my grandmother's."

"Cool, cool, cool." Sal stuck out her hand. Warily, Mrs. Steinberg shook it with her gloved hand. "Nice to meet you."

Mrs. Steinberg adjusted her wooly hat. "I heard you found the body?"

"It was awful," I said. "She was stabbed with a piece of ice. What do you know about Kelsey Delaney?"

The old lady's lips drew into a line. Her chin wobbled. "Not a thing
"

I blinked. "Really?" Mrs. Steinberg worked in town records. She knew everything about everyone. How was it possible she was in the dark?

Mrs. Steinberg looked down at her heavy black boots. "Kelsey was too..."

"What?" I asked.

"Too independent?" Dixie asked. "She wasn't much for leaving a paper trail."

"Too handy with a chainsaw?" Sal said.

"Too young," Mrs. Steinberg burst out and looked up.

Sal nodded. "The new generation doesn't talk to each other like they used to. It's all texting these days. Makes it harder to get in on the gossip, unless you've got class-A vision and can read upside down. Am I right?" She winked.

Mrs. Steinberg nodded. "Ri—" She drew herself up, her nostrils flaring. "I am not a gossip."

"She's more of an intelligence asset," I told Sal. "It's okay, Mrs. Steinberg. I'll let you know what I learn."

"You'll—?" she sputtered. "That's not the way this works."

"No, no, no," I said. "It's the least I can do after all the help you've given me over the years."

"But—"

"Really, say no more. I don't mind one bit. So far we have five suspects. There's Kelsey's sister, Hannah, Kelsey's three boyfriends, and Vida Lewis. Vida was furious when her boyfriend Victor dumped her for Kelsey. So two classic motives—love and jealousy. Or maybe that's one motive? Unless she has other siblings, in which case money could enter into it. Does she, Dixie?"

"Nope."

"And Hannah doesn't seem to have an alibi. Can I drive you anywhere?" I asked Mrs. Steinberg.

She rubbed her temple. "No."

"All right then. I'll keep you posted." We got into my SUV and drove off. I glanced in the rearview mirror. On the side of the road, Mrs. Steinberg stared after us, no doubt relieved she still had sources to tap in Doyle.

Chapter Five

"This casserole gig works like a charm." Beside me, Sal buckled her seatbelt. "You could bring one as cover for a burglary and no one would blink. Who's next?"

I hoped I hadn't given her any ideas. "Enrique," I said and glanced over my shoulder at Dixie and Bailey, seated in the back. "Do you know where he lives?"

"Yeah," my cousin said. "Turn right at that green Victorian."

We drove higher up the hill, where the homes were bigger and spaced farther apart. Even the pines seemed statelier in this neighborhood. "How old is Enrique?" I asked.

"About your age, I think," Dixie said. "So, pretty ancient."

I scowled. I was thirty-four. "Does he, er, come from money?"

She laughed. "No. Why'd you think that?"

"Because you'd have to be loaded to live up here," Sal said. "What is he? Some sort of tech genius?"

"Yeah," my cousin said. "He invented an app and then it got bought out by a bigger company. He's doing okay. The house is here."

We slowed to a stop in front of one of the more modest homes in the neighborhood. It was a modern-looking, two-story, gray shingle-style home with a peaked roof. Its wide front yard was covered in six inches of snow and dotted with evergreens. A Tesla sat in the driveway. Sal growled low in her throat.

Bailey hunched in his harness and gave me a mutinous look. "Fine," I said. "You can stay." I pulled some hand warmers from the glove compartment, stuffed two into my mittens, made a nest for him with a blanket and tucked the mittens inside. He coiled on the blanket and closed his eyes.

The three of us walked down the brick path to the house. "You know," Sal said, "you've confirmed something I've always suspected about kind gestures." She motioned to the casserole in my hands.

"Oh?" I asked. "What?"

"That there's always an agenda. The gestures are never pure."

Heat flamed in my cheeks. "That's not—Okay, it is true in this case. But it's not always true." I made plenty of kind gestures for no reason other than feeling good about it. Or was that an impure motive too?

She looked down at me knowingly. "You sure about that?"

Not anymore I wasn't. Self-reflection could be a real downer.

"Susan does plenty of nice stuff for no good reason." Dixie climbed the two steps to the white-painted porch. She rang the bell. "Look at all those murders she's solved."

"Yeah," Sal said. "But those are fun. Murders are a puzzle, aren't they?"

"They aren't—" Okay, solving murders *was* something of a mental challenge. But that wasn't why I did it. *Mostly.* "People *died.*"

Footsteps sounded from behind the door, and it opened. The living embodiment of my accidental ice sculpture stood inside the doorway. His dark hair curled enticingly. His chiseled face and expressive brown eyes were a study in mournfulness. His wheat-colored sweater stretched tight across his chest, leaving nothing to the imagination. I swallowed.

"Hey, Enrique," Dixie said. "Sorry about Kelsey."

"Thank you." His gaze raked me. "Is that… a casserole?" he asked in a faint Latin American accent.

I nodded, because I wasn't sure I could speak. I glanced at Sal. Her gaze traveled from his bare feet, up the jeans that strained against his thighs, to the top of his head and back again. Even Dixie looked a little dewy eyed.

"That is so thoughtful of you," Enrique said. "Please, come inside." He stepped away from the door, and we filtered into the neat hallway. A wooden clock ticked on the narrow table. Beside the clock, a geometrically patterned basket held a set of keys.

He ushered us into a living room decorated with African art. Masks lined one wall. Two crossed spears hung above the brick fireplace. A near-black, carved wooden figure stood in one corner. More baskets hung on another wall, and the third was taken up with bookshelves. "Have a seat." He motioned to a comfortable looking couch.

I handed him the casserole. "The instructions are on the card." I nodded to the index card taped to the aluminum foil.

"You thought of everything," he murmured. "Are you all right?"

I shook myself. "I'm sorry. You just seem so, ah, familiar."

"He looks like that actor," Sal said. "You know. The guy with the eyes."

And Victor had smashed the sculpture that had looked like him. Out of jealous rage?

"How kind of you to say." Enrique sat in the navy wing chair opposite the matching couch. He set the casserole on the nearby end table. "I have heard about your casseroles," he said to me.

I cringed a little inside and sat. After Sal's comment... *Was I overusing the casserole ploy?*

"Everyone talks about the breakfasts at Wits' End," he continued. "I've even considered booking a room just to enjoy one."

"You totally should," Dixie said. Sal and I nodded.

"Have you traveled to Africa?" I asked, glancing at a framed photo on the end table. Enrique and Kelsey, wearing grass skirts, laughed in a hula lesson on a Hawaiian beach. I squinted at it. Over her bikini top, she wore the same coral necklace she wore in the picture with her sister.

"Yes," he said. "My charity has a program to give solar-powered computer tablets to rural schools in sub-Saharan Africa. We're trying to expand it."

"I didn't realize you had a charity," I said. "That sounds wonderful."

He shrugged. "The field of international aid can be fraught. Sometimes we think we're helping when we're really hurting. Free goods can undermine the local economy. My next project is to start a factory in Ethiopia so we can build the tablets there. But there are so many bureaucratic hurdles. I believe the difficulty in legally starting businesses is one of the main challenges to development. Chaotic legal systems, or the failure to follow a legal system in practice, can kill an economy. And now there's the recent civil conflict." He shook his head. "Sometimes it all seems futile. But I believe we must keep trying. Perhaps in the end, the effort is more for our own souls, but we must keep trying."

Silence fell as we pondered that. The world of international aid was as far beyond me as Arsen's old world in the Navy SEALs.

I shifted on the couch and cleared my throat. "We're very sorry for your loss." And I might have said that already. But I was feeling oddly flustered. It felt wrong that I'd seen so much of him, even if it had been an ice replica.

He braced one elbow on the arm of his chair and rested his face in his hand. "Kelsey. Such a fiery soul. I still can't quite believe she's gone, or that someone would have done this."

"Who wanted to get rid of her?" Sal asked.

His full lips pursed. "That is a question I have been pondering since I learned of her death yesterday." He fell silent. In the hallway, the clock ticked. Then he sighed and shifted position in the chair. "Kelsey inspired deep passions."

"Was there anyone in particular who she, er, inspired?" I asked.

"I could not say. It would not be right."

"Is that what you told the sheriff?" I asked.

"Yes. She came to see me yesterday. She was the one who told me..." He trailed off and swallowed, his Adam's apple bobbing above his sweater's V-neck collar.

"I suppose she asked where you were yesterday morning," I said.

Enrique nodded. "And I told her I was here, working. You see, I work from home. I am fortunate in that regard. And I suppose you are too." He smiled.

"How'd you feel about Kelsey playing the field?" Sal asked, and my stomach clenched. She was about as subtle as a jackhammer.

"Kelsey was a free spirit. I would not presume to tell her how to live her life or with whom to live it with. And I like fierce, independent women." He smiled at Dixie, and her face turned as pink as the tips of her hair.

"Hmph." Sal folded her arms. "You must have some idea who wanted her dead."

He shook his head. "I cannot say."

Sal squinted at him. "Can't? Or won't?"

"Won't. I will not be responsible for causing suspicion to fall on an innocent person."

We made more attempts to get him to talk. But Enrique wouldn't budge. He was irritatingly principled. We left a few minutes later.

Sal stomped down the brick path to my Crosstrek. "That guy's a little too good to be true, don't you think? Anselm's off my list. Enrique did it. He's got to be the killer."

Dixie sighed. "I hate to say it, but Enrique's the real deal, charity and all."

And so was Arsen. So what if Arsen didn't have the sensual accent or smoldering eyes? Or if he'd had this whole other adventurous life I didn't know much about? He was taking me out for a romantic evening tonight. I couldn't wait.

"The real deal?" Sal opened the passenger door. "That's what I thought about—" She snapped her jaws shut, but it wasn't hard to guess where she'd been going. She'd thought Bingo was the real deal too.

But Arsen was no Bingo. "Enrique doesn't have an alibi," I said, changing the subject. "At least we learned that."

"And not much else," Sal grumbled.

We stopped for lunch at an elegant corner restaurant and dined beneath heat lamps on the patio. Bailey was a well-behaved beagle, unless there were squirrels or deputies in uniform around. But dogs were only allowed patio access.

When we returned to Wits' End, Carl and Clara from the Bigfoot group were descending the green carpeted stairs to the foyer.

"Hello, Sal," Mr. Carter said cheerfully. "Want to join us on another hunt?"

"May as well." She shrugged. "Looks like our murder investigation has hit a dead end."

The older man's gray brows rocketed upward. "Murder?"

"I'm assisting," she said. "It's no big deal. You remember. I've helped Susan out before, when we met in—"

"Nowhere," I interrupted before she could utter the J-word. "Nowhere, Nevada. Have you been there?"

He turned to his rosy-cheeked wife. "Can't say as I have. Have you?"

She shook her gray curls. "We were too busy babbling about Bigfoot and your outdoor-wear company. I'm afraid we're terrible listeners." She turned to Sal. "We didn't ask a thing about you."

My stomach wobbled between a hopeful lurch and dropping dread.

"Eh, there's not much to tell about me," Sal said. I relaxed. Sal might be a little unconventional, but not even she would blab about her criminal record.

"What do you do?" Clara asked.

"Sal's—" I wrinkled my brow. What *did* Sal do?

"Gig work," Sal said.

That was suspiciously vague. I just hoped the Carters didn't notice.

"Ah." Clara glanced at her husband, and they shared a knowing smile. "I did some ride share driving myself. Writer's research. The gig economy's not for the faint of heart." She slipped her hand into his.

I bit back a sigh. It was lovely to see an older couple who still shared that spark. And these two obviously did. Romance was *not* dead. They might not have come to Wits' End for my Valentine's special, but it hadn't been a waste. "How did you two meet?" I asked, trying to divert them from the topic of Sal.

"Divorce court," Carl said.

"My husband divorced me for a younger woman and left me with nothing," Clara said.

Her husband scowled. "Same here. But my wife—ex-wife now—did it to me. She got everything."

Clara's mouth stretched into a pained smile. "Not that we're bitter."

"No, no," Carl said a little too heartily. "Everything worked out for the best. Wouldn't change it for the world."

"I hear ya," Sal said. "My ex..." She huffed a breath. "Never mind what he did. Let's just say it was enough for me to put laxatives in his favorite booze."

"Oh." Clara's expression grew thoughtful. "Do you think... do you think he would have noticed it had been tampered with right away?"

"That stuff was expensive," Sal said. "Even if he did notice before drinking much, he was out a bottle. I figure it was a win-win."

"...always do this." Brooke stomped down the stairs.

"I always do this?" Finley snarled from behind her. "You always point out that I always do this, so who's the fool?"

Clara rolled her eyes. "Is everyone ready for our Sasquatch search?"

Finley and Brooke grumbled assent. Clara looked a question at Sal.

"Why not?" Sal said. "Let's find us a Bigfoot."

They trooped outside, the screen doors banging behind them. Bailey shook himself.

"Oh. Sorry." I unclipped the beagle from his leash, and he trotted to his dog bed beside the desk.

"Now what?" Dixie said.

"Cleaning the bedrooms."

My cousin groaned. Shoulders slumped, she hauled herself upstairs. I followed, and we started on the bedrooms.

A *Do Not Disturb* sign hung from Sal's door. I tried not to think about what I might not be disturbing.

Chapter Six

The vacuum fell silent in the room next door, and I looked up from the bathtub I was scrubbing. Since the vacuum had only started up a minute or so ago, why was Dixie stopping?

I wandered from the guest bathroom and peeled off my rubber gloves. Watery Saturday afternoon sunlight filtered through the guest room's pale blue curtains.

I stuck my head into the B&B's hallway. A photo of the famous pie-plate UFOs hung directly across from the door. Low, feminine voices flowed from the open door to Room Five. Had one of the guests returned early?

I stepped into the hallway. The door to Room Five closed with a bang, and I started.

That was... weird. Spray bottle in hand, I crept to the closed door. But Victorian-era builders hadn't fooled around when it came to their homes. I couldn't hear a thing through the thick door. I wavered. Should I knock?

Oh, this was ridiculous. It was *my* B&B. I knocked.

Dixie opened the door. "Yeah?"

I crossed my arms. "Everything all right?" What was she doing in room five? She'd been vacuuming room six.

"Yeah." She began to shut the door.

I stuck my foot in it. "Has one of the guests returned?"

Dixie shook her head. "No."

"Then who—?"

The door opened further. Behind Dixie stood a slender, honey-skinned woman, her brown hair in a thick ponytail. She blinked at me through reddened eyes. "Is this your cousin?" She rubbed her nose, twisting her nose piercing—a slim silver ring.

Dixie grimaced and stepped away from the door. "Yeah. Susan, this is Vida."

Vida Lewis? Victor's ex? "It's nice to meet you, though I'm sorry about the circumstances," I said. "Were you a friend of Kelsey's?"

She sniffed. "Not after what she did."

"What did she—"

"Kelsey manipulated my boyfriend into leaving me," she burst out. "*And* she already had two boyfriends of her own. Victor was none of her business. She deserved to die."

Dixie rolled her eyes. "Or maybe not."

Vida rubbed her nose, and I frowned. How did people wear nose rings without bad things happening when they sneezed? Allergy season had to be trouble.

"Sorry." Vida lowered her head and looked up at me from the corners of her reddened eyes. "That was an awful thing to say. I didn't mean it. It's just that... Now Victor seems to blame *me* for what happened."

"You mean, for Kelsey's death?" I slid my hands into the pockets of my slacks. "That doesn't seem fair." Why blame Vida? Did Victor know something the police should know?

"It's not fair," Vida spat, "but he's upset, and..." She blew out her breath. "He's upset. He hasn't been himself since Kelsey got her claws into him. And she wasn't even that into him."

"Then why do you think she pursued him?" I asked.

Dixie snorted. "Don't be naïve."

"It was this free love business." Vida's angular face tightened. "She believed everyone should be free. No chains. No attachments. I mean, it sounds great in principle, but people *get* attached. That's the whole point of having a partner, isn't it? That you know they've got your back?"

It was certainly one of the benefits. A space in my chest warmed and expanded. I was lucky with Arsen.

"It does seem to be asking for trouble," I said.

"It's no surprise someone killed her." Vida's mouth pinched.

"I suppose the sheriff asked where you were on Friday?" I asked, cagey.

Subtle, Dixie mouthed behind her.

"Yeah," Vida said. "Some deputies talked to me. I was working at the new Irish Pub."

"That place looks fun," I said casually. "What are your hours?"

"We open at eleven."

So she probably got to work a bit before that time. Unless she was one of the cooks. "What do you do there?"

"I'm just a waitress."

"Nothing *just* about it," I said stoutly. "Waiting tables is hard work."

Vida's shoulders collapsed. "You have no idea. Or maybe you do. Sorry, I'm interrupting everyone's work, aren't I?"

"No, no, no," I said. I loved it when suspects came to me, even if they weren't in my schedule. It was much more convenient.

"No," she said, edging from the room. "I am interfering. Dix, I'll see you later. Antoine's tonight?"

"I'll be there," my cousin said.

We trailed after her into the green-carpeted hallway and watched Vida descend the stairs. Downstairs, the front door closed quietly behind her.

"I know," Dixie said. "She doesn't have an alibi."

"She might. Victor saw Kelsey alive at eleven-thirty. But she does have a motive." My gaze flitted around the guest room. It looked like Dixie had already finished in here.

Vertical lines appeared between my cousin's eyebrows. "Nah. Vida's trying to be a wild child because she thinks that's what her ex, Victor wants. Or what he wanted. Vida didn't get the nose ring until after he dumped her for Kelsey. But she never had a chance competing like that with Kelsey. It's not who Vida is. Kelsey was a believer, an anarchist, a risk taker. I mean, she bought Bitcoin when it was just starting out. By trying to be who she wasn't, Vida made things worse." She shook her head. "Love. It makes people crazy."

I studied her. Dixie and I never talked about guys. Maybe we should. I angled my head. "Are you, er, seeing anyone right now?"

She shrugged. "It's a long-distance thing."

"Really?" I grinned, heat radiating from my chest. This was amazing. I hated seeing Dixie alone. With Arsen in my life, I wanted everyone else to have someone special in theirs. "Who is he?"

Dixie arched a brow, crossed the hall to room six, and slammed the door. The vacuum cleaner roared.

Okay then. With a sigh, I returned to my work. As I'd predicted, we finished up at three. It gave us plenty of time to get to Kelsey's apartment to help Hannah with the sheriff.

I was unsurprised to learn Kelsey had lived above the barn where she'd carved her sculptures. I also wasn't surprised the sheriff, after some token objections, let me inside with Hannah and Dixie. After all, we were on the same team.

But I *was* surprised to see how luxurious the barn apartment was. Ferns hung from the beams crisscrossing the slanted roof of the open apartment. Kelsey had done it up in a sort of bohemian urban modern. Throw rugs covered the wood floors. Colorful scarves made curtains over the circular window beside a gas fireplace.

I sniffed. The apartment smelled faintly of patchouli.

I wandered to the kitchen and admired the copper cookware hanging from a ceiling rack. The countertops were sleek metal. A wine fridge stood in one corner.

I studied the photos on the high-end fridge. Most were of Anselm and Kelsey. They were dressed casually in them all. The two on a boat on a lake. The two smiling on a hiking trail. And in all the photos, she wore that round, flat piece of gray coral on its silver chain. I wondered what the simple piece had meant to her.

Hannah stood in the middle of the apartment. She turned, an uncertain expression on her face. "It all looks... normal."

"Check the closets," the sheriff said.

Sheriff McCourt watched Hannah walk to the closet. Hannah glanced over her shoulder at us and pawed a hand through her hair. "This feels so wrong, going through Kelsey's private things."

"But you're doing it for your sister," I said, "to help catch whoever did this to her. It's okay." I smiled encouragingly and came to stand by her side. Dixie wandered to the gas fireplace.

Hannah opened the louvered doors on a chaos of clothing and random junk. A tennis ball bounced from the closet and across the wood floor. A table lamp shifted against a colorful spirit board. "This looks normal," she said.

"You're kidding," the sheriff said. "I was ready to give my deputies hell for leaving a mess."

Hannah's smile was wry. "It was Kelsey's cleaning method—just shove everything in a closet." She turned from the closet. "Where's her laptop?"

"We have it," the sheriff said.

"And there's a floor safe," Hannah said.

The sheriff straightened. "Where?"

She winced. "Somewhere in the floor? I don't know exactly."

I stared, aghast. The barn's wooden floor was huge. How were we supposed to tackle this expanse?

Dixie stepped experimentally on a floorboard. "Nothing here."

"All right," I said. "Let's get organized. Dixie you take the southwest quadrant. I'll take the southeast. Hannah, you take the northwest, and—"

"I'll take the northeast." The sheriff tossed her broad-brimmed hat onto the sofa. "Got it."

We walked our quadrants and tested the floor for squeaks or uneven rectangles of wood. A floorboard beneath me seemed to give a little. I got on my knees and studied it. There seemed to be a bigger gap between this floorboard and the ones around it.

I pressed the board. Nothing happened. I pressed the other end. A squarish section of wood popped up. Pulse quickening, I lifted it, exposing a charcoal-colored safe with a keypad. "I've found it."

"Hallelujah." Hannah hurried to me.

"Hold it," the sheriff said. She pulled on a pair of latex gloves and knelt beside me. "Do you know the combo?"

"Yeah, though I wish she would have told me where exactly the safe was." Hannah rattled off a string of numbers.

The sheriff's fingers skimmed across the keypad. The safe clicked open.

Sheriff McCourt pulled the door wider. She retrieved a bundle of documents and a red file folder with a label reading *Kelsey Delaney Trust*. The sheriff flipped through the document. "Looks like you're the beneficiary," she said to Hannah. "Everything goes to you. Unless there are some... No," the sheriff said. "There aren't."

Hannah peered over the sheriff's shoulder. "Is that everything?" Her voice dropped on the last word. She tapped the ends of her too-long nails on her palms.

"Were you expecting something else?" the sheriff asked.

Hannah shrugged one shoulder and stepped away. "I wouldn't have been surprised if my sister had buried a box of cash in the yard. I never knew what to expect with Kelsey."

"But you had her safe combo?" the sheriff said.

"She gave it to me in case something happened. Because of the documents and stuff. There should be passwords and other useful things in there. Not that she believed anything would happen to her," Hannah finished quickly. She ventured another glance into the open safe and shook her head. She nodded toward the legal documents in the sheriff's hand. "May I have those?"

"I'll make you a photocopy," the sheriff said.

Hannah glanced toward the closet. "Do you mind if I stay here and look around some more? Just in case?"

"Knock yourself out," the sheriff said.

"You didn't find anything that—that might have indicated who killed her?" Hannah asked.

"No," Sheriff McCourt said shortly.

"Do you want us to help?" I held my breath. It would give us an excuse to really dig in and look around.

"No," Hannah said. "I feel silly now asking you to come. You've got things to do."

"Okay, see ya." Dixie strolled to the door and down the stairs to the barn's exterior.

I hesitated. It didn't feel right to leave her alone here. I wasn't worried about anything bad happening. But the barn had to be filled with memories. "I noticed Kelsey had a favorite necklace, made of gray coral. Is there a story behind it?"

"No," Hannah said. "It just went with everything. Honestly, you can go. I'm fine."

Darn it. "If you're sure..." I trailed off.

"I'm sure," she said, curt.

Sheriff McCourt held the door for me. I followed Dixie outside and down the barn's exterior stairs. "That was a waste of time," my cousin said.

The sheriff tucked the documents under the arm of her jacket. "Not for me." She strode to her black-and-white SUV and got inside.

"I don't know why Hannah asked us to come," Dixie complained. "I could have been in a UFO chat room with—" She shoved her hands into the pockets of her khakis. "With everyone."

"She probably knew she'd have trouble finding that floor safe," I said.

"Whatever." Dixie rubbed her arms. The sun had lowered behind the western mountains, and the temperature was dropping. "Can we go?"

"I guess so." I drove her to her Airstream trailer, and then I drove home.

I'm ashamed to say it was a little too easy to put aside worries about the people Kelsey had left behind. But Arsen and I hadn't had a special night out in weeks.

I collected the mail and discarded it on the kitchen table. I added a note to my planner, then went to my bedroom closet and studied the clothing inside.

Heart light, I shifted dresses on their hangers. What I needed was a dress to mark the occasion that would also work in the cold. Or maybe not a dress. I smiled, remembering. Arsen's romantic evenings could tend toward outdoor adventures.

Reluctantly, I discarded the beaded dress I'd worn to a murder mystery theater last year. I pulled out a low-necked red top. It was more Valentine's appropriate, even if the big day wouldn't be until Monday.

The cellphone rang on my bed, and I checked the number. *Arsen.* I answered, smiling. "Hey." My stomach fluttered. Why did it feel like I was prepping for our first date? We saw each other nearly every day. Tonight wasn't any more special than our last. We were a couple. Every date was lovely.

"Uh," he said, "I've got some bad news."

I dropped the top on my bed. "What's wrong?"

"I'm still in Sacramento."

I checked my watch. It was only four-thirty. He had plenty of time. "I can wait. My night's all yours." I'd blocked it off in my planner.

"Uh, the thing is, it looks like I'm going to be here for a few more hours, at least."

"Oh." My breath hitched, my heart shrinking.

"Can we try this again tomorrow?"

"Sure," I said, forcing cheer into my voice. "It's no biggie."

"Susan?" Sal called from the kitchen.

"I'm really sorry about this," he said.

"It's fine," I said hurriedly. Really, it was no big deal. What was one cancelled date? Things came up, and I could be understanding. "We'll do it tomorrow. Sorry, but Sal's in the kitchen. I'd better go see what she wants."

"I'll talk to you tomorrow."

"Bye." Limbs heavy, I hung up and walked into the kitchen. Bailey snoozed in his dog bed beneath the small round table. Sal stood beside it wearing a tight, red knit top and plaid skirt.

She looked up from my open planner. I tensed. I hadn't left it open like that. She'd been going through my private planner. My *life* was in there.

"Oh, there you are," she said. "Those Bigfoot seekers sure can walk. They invited me to dinner, but I thought you and I might paint the town. What do you say?"

I stretched my mouth into a smile. "Sure. Why not?" My romantic plans for the evening had gone down the tubes anyway.

She pointed at my open planner. "But it looks like you've got a date."

I shoved my hands into the pockets of my blue slacks. "No, Arsen's stuck in Sacramento. I'm free."

"Arsen's loss is my gain." She stood, jostling the table, and the stack of mail slid to the linoleum floor. Bailey looked up. "Whoops." She bent to pick up the mail. "I reckon your Arsen kept up his end after all." She handed me a thick red envelope. "Looks like a Valentine to me. Go ahead and open it. I won't mind."

There was no name on the front of the envelope. Arsen must have left it on the table before his trip today—a romantic gesture to start our evening—and it had gotten jumbled with the mail.

My heart softened. After all, he hadn't *meant* to get stuck in Sacramento. "Thanks." I took a table knife from a kitchen drawer and slit it open, pulled out a card with roses on it.

"Fancy," Sal said.

I opened the card. One word was written in it in block letters: DIE.

Chapter Seven

"Heh. *That's* a funny Valentine." Sal peered over my shoulder. Her hip knocked one of the kitchen chairs. It screeched across the linoleum floor, setting my teeth on edge.

"I don't think it was meant to be funny," I said shakily.

The three letters were in a cheery Valentine's Day red. In the homey warmth of the Wits' End kitchen, they were an offense, an intrusion. I'd like to say I shrugged the threat off. I was a seasoned detective, after all. There were people who'd not only wanted me dead but had actively tried to make that happen.

Last Christmas, one such person had come to Wits' End. I'd raced across the snowy yard, stumbled in the dark, known at any moment the blow could come. Now an echo of that winter fear pinged through my chest.

You never got used to that sort of thing. And you never forgot.

My jaw hardened. I dialed Arsen. And my call went to voice mail.

"Who're you calling?" Sal asked.

"Arsen," I said shortly.

"Good idea. He's in security."

But this wasn't the sort of thing one left a voice mail about. I didn't want to panic him. I hung up and dialed the sheriff.

"Who're you calling now?" Sal asked.

"Sheriff McCourt." I stared at the envelope and forced the wheels in my brain to start turning. The paper was rough, as if it had been handmade, though the card itself was fairly cheap. There was no postmark. Someone must have just put it in my box.

She shook her head. "Bad idea. You can't trust the cops."

That was just silly. Of course I could trust the sheriff. "We're friends. It's fine." I pressed the phone tighter to my ear.

"What?" the sheriff said in my ear. A siren sounded in the background.

"Someone just sent me a..." I gave a short, disbelieving laugh. "Well, a poisoned pen letter. A Valentine."

"You're calling me about a nasty letter? Susan, I'm really busy."

"It says *die*." I would never waste her time, and she knew it. This had to be connected to Kelsey's murder. No doubt word had gotten out I was investigating. It was a small town. It was bound to happen. The murderer knew I was on his trail and was panicking. As he or she should.

She sighed. "All right. I've got my hands full right now. There's been an accident heading east on Highway Four. It's a real mess."

My heart seized. Arsen was driving up that highway. "Was anyone hurt?"

"Not seriously, and no one you know."

I relaxed, which was terrible. Arsen might be safe, but it was still awful for whomever was in the accident. But I couldn't help myself. I *did* care more about Arsen and Dixie than other people. "What should I do with the card?"

"Stop handling it for starters," she said.

I dropped the Valentine on the table.

"I'll come over later if I can," she continued.

"Thank you," I said. But she'd already hung up. The sheriff really must be busy, poor thing. It was fortunate she had me to take some of the investigative load off her. Murder investigations could be a handful.

"Well?" Sal asked.

"She's coming over later, maybe."

Sal raised a skeptical brow. "Huh."

Annoyed, (because it was easier than being scared), I grabbed salad tongs from the drawer and moved the letter and envelope to a counter.

"I've got steaks marinating in the fridge," I said, keeping my voice light. Whoever had sent me that letter wanted me to freak out. I wasn't going to give him or her the satisfaction. "Want me to make dinner?" It wasn't that I was nervous about going out. But those steaks *were* ready for cooking.

"I won't say *no* to a steak." Her eyes narrowed. "How are you going to cook 'em?"

"I thought I'd use a cast-iron pan."

Beneath her red top, Sal's shoulders relaxed. "That'll work. Not everyone knows how to handle a good steak. No offense."

"None taken." It had taken me ages to figure it out.

I baked potatoes and cooked the steaks and made a salad. The activity kept me busy. But when we sat down at the kitchen table, the red envelope on the counter kept pulling my gaze.

Sal finished chewing a bite of steak and moaned. "This marinade is amazing." She pointed her empty fork at me. "You're not just a one-trick pony, I'll give you that. You've got breakfast *and* dinner down."

"Thanks," I said absently.

She sliced off another piece of steak. "So what happened to your date with Arsen tonight?"

I dragged my gaze back to her. "He got stuck on a job in Sacramento. And now with this accident on the highway, I'm not sure when he'll get home." But uneasiness wriggled in my gut. What could have happened in Sacramento that would keep him there hours late?

She eyed me. "You sure that's all it is?"

"Of course," I said sharply. "He's not lying to me."

"No, no, I didn't mean that. I mean, you just seem a little—I dunno, unsettled. And not because of the poisoned pen note. You seemed unsettled when I first laid eyes on you."

It was true. And maybe it was the glass of Zinfandel I'd drunk, but suddenly I had an urge to confide in Sal. Maybe an outside perspective would help. And I certainly couldn't confide in Dixie. "It's embarrassing to admit, but I guess I... Arsen and I have known each other since we were kids."

"A friends-to-lovers scenario." Sal nodded, chewing. "Those are my favorite."

"I just haven't seen much of him lately. He's been busy with his security firm, and I've been busy with Wits' End. I think a part of me... I know it's ridiculous, but Valentine's Day is Monday. I spent so much time on this Valentine's special, that I guess... I was hoping for more romance between us."

She aimed her steak knife at me and swallowed. "Valentine's Day hasn't happened yet."

"No, but now there's this murder." Usually Arsen and I solved murders together. I ran my hand jerkily through my hair. He'd acted concerned when he'd learned of it, but since then... Why wasn't he more interested in solving it?

I glanced at my phone on the table. I hadn't left a message earlier, but Arsen would have seen that I'd called. And he hadn't called me back. But he was driving. The road was narrow and winding, and he could be sitting there for hours.

"Don't worry," Sal said. "I get it. Murder takes precedence over love. And I'll help you like I did last time."

Terrific. "Thanks." My gaze traveled again to the red envelope on the counter.

"Did you know there's an interesting history behind poisoned pen letters?"

"Really?"

She nodded. "Oh, yeah. It started in 1909 in Elizabeth, New Jersey. The city's most prominent people received typewritten letters accusing them of all sorts of things. Prostitution. Corruption. Bad fashion sense. That sort of thing."

"Fashion—?"

"Some were just catty." She smeared butter on her potato. "Anyway, the cops finally caught the woman. She was something of an upstanding citizen herself. She was even a member of the DAR, like me." She added a dollop of sour cream.

My fork froze above my green beans. "You're in the Daughters of the American Revolution?"

Sal doused the potato with salt and pepper. "It's no big deal. It's not like I fought in the war myself. Anyway, typewriters are each unique, as you probably know. They were able to prove her typewriter had been used. But the jury either didn't get it or just couldn't believe someone like her would do it, so they acquitted. She went right back to her nasty letters. Except this time, she used that old letters-pasted-from-the-newspaper trick."

"And then what happened?" I asked, fascinated despite myself.

She picked a cherry tomato out of the salad and set it aside. "They arrested her again. This time, she confessed. She'd done it all out of jealousy. Well, really out of insecurity. She was fined two hundred dollars and expelled by the DAR. Those Daughters of the American Revolution don't mess around, let me tell you."

Which led me to wonder how Sal, with her police record, was still a member. Maybe their standards had relaxed?

"This is a quality meal, Susan. Not many people cook for me." She patted her stomach. "Bingo did though. He'd taken a class."

I smiled. "It sounds like you miss him."

"Bingo?" She sniffed. "Hardly. Not after what he did."

I couldn't help myself. "What happened?" I'd just unburdened myself about my romantic life. Asking about hers only seemed polite.

"After I got out of jail with you, everything was great. At least I thought it was." Her hand clenched on her steak knife. "Until I found out he'd thrown out my special gummies. The ones with CBD in them for my back pain."

"Why'd he throw them out?" Arsen and I would never throw out each other's things without asking. Of course, his things were all new and top-quality and mine were mostly junk. But still.

Her gingersnap eyes turned flinty. "He *said* it was because they'd expired."

"But you didn't believe him?"

"I did, at first. And then I saw him with *her*."

"Her who?"

"Exactly. They had their heads together like..." Flushing, she set down her knife and fork with a clatter and pushed away from the table. Bailey looked up hopefully. "Well, you get the picture. Scrawny little thing. He told me he liked a woman with some curves, but I guess he was just saying what I wanted to hear."

"And you thought he threw out the gummies, because—"

"Well, I'm not exactly tiny, am I?" She screwed up her face in a scowl. "I'm not fat though."

"No, of course not," I said hastily. I believed in bold truth in relationships. But only a jerk or a fool would criticize a woman's weight. It's just not done.

"I can't help it if I'm big boned." She slapped her bicep. "This is real muscle here. And that weighs more than fat. I work out, you know."

"I've always thought I should have more muscle tone myself." These days, the only exercise I got was housekeeping.

"Yeah, you really should think about lifting. I can give you tips if you want. Got a weight set?"

"Ah, no."

"I guess it's back to your cast iron pans then." She returned her attention to the steak. "You won't regret the investment in a real set of weights. You'd be surprised how fast lifting pays off. And you don't have to get worried about getting too bulky. You have to work pretty hard and undergo a strict diet to become one of those muscle-bound women you see in the competitions. Looks like that Arsen of yours knows his way around a gym though, if you know what I mean." She winked.

"He *is* active." Suddenly, I found it hard to swallow. We finished dinner. I brought out the apple crumble I'd baked for Arsen for dessert. Beneath the table, Bailey growled.

Sal peered beneath the cloth. "Sorry, buddy. I'm tapped out."

"Bailey," I scolded. "Sorry. He usually only gets grumpy around—"

Sheriff McCourt strolled through the swinging door into the kitchen. *Uniforms*, I finished silently.

Sal glanced over her shoulder and faced front. Bailey growled.

"Where's the letter?" the sheriff asked.

Sal coughed. It sounded suspiciously like *bacon*. "Sorry," she said. "I'd better get my cough drops. Upstairs." She hurried from the kitchen. Tail low, Bailey followed.

The sheriff frowned. "Who was that?"

"Just a guest."

"You don't usually let guests into your kitchen."

"No, she's sort of an acquaintance too."

She stared at the slowing arcs of the kitchen door. "She looks familiar."

"It's unlikely you've seen her before." *Unless Sal's face was on a wanted poster.* My stomach went queasy. "She's from Nowhere. The town. In Nevada. With the big things? Should I get a plastic bag for the card?" I pointed to the counter. "I'm afraid all sorts of people have already touched it. Me. Sal..." *Oh, no.* Sal's fingerprints had to be in the system.

The sheriff strode to the counter and stared down at the card and envelope. "Hm. The envelope might be tough to get prints off of anyway with those rough fibers. But we'll try. And I've got my own evidence bag." She drew a bag from the pocket of her bulky, near-black jacket and pulled on a pair of latex gloves.

I rubbed my arms. I needed to tell the sheriff about Sal. She might waste her time considering her a suspect otherwise.

I opened my mouth. Closed it.

I couldn't do it. It felt like a betrayal, or like I was labeling Sal unfairly. I'd been in jail right there beside her. And I'd prefer it if people didn't define me by that single mistake. Though I got the feeling this hadn't been Sal's first.

Besides, Sal was checking out tomorrow. I didn't want the sheriff to delay her departure. So what if Sal's room would be empty the rest of the week? The other rooms were occupied.

Sheriff McCourt dropped the envelope into the bag. She opened the card and grunted. "Any idea who wants you dead? Aside from all the people you've been foisting casseroles on?"

"Everyone likes my casseroles," I said, offended. "All the Wits' End reviews are four and five stars. My breakfasts have been a big part of that."

"And there's no chance one of your lucky casserole winners might think you've been snooping? Again?"

"Ah..." Maybe I *was* becoming too predictable?

"Stay out of my investigation, Susan," she said wearily.

She didn't mean it, obviously. But I nodded anyway and smiled.

Chapter Eight

Dixie ambled into the B&B kitchen and looked around. "Where's Arsen? Did I miss him? He's usually here for breakfast."

I slid the last breakfast plate into the dishwasher and closed its brushed-nickel door. "He texted. He's busy this morning."

And Sal was checking out today. Maybe now I could investigate in peace. Though I'd rather investigate with Arsen. And I still hadn't had a chance to tell him about the creepy Valentine I'd received yesterday.

"Doing what?" my cousin asked.

"Work, I'm sure." I turned and leaned against the butcher-block counter.

She snorted. "At this hour?"

"You know he's a one-man operation. He works all sorts of hours." But a quiver of anxiety touched my heart.

Nonsense. Arsen and I are solid. He was just busy, and that was fine. Even if it was after ten o'clock, and he normally stopped in for breakfast by seven.

Her absinthe eyes narrowed. "Yeah, but it's Arsen. What'd you do to him?"

"I didn't do—" I whipped the damp dishtowel off the counter and hung it on the stove handle. "He cares about his work."

"Huh." She grabbed a cold pancake off a plate and strode onto the porch.

A few minutes later, Sal wandered into the kitchen and patted her broad stomach. "Another killer breakfast, Susan." She dropped into a chair by the kitchen table and scratched Bailey behind his ears. "It's not going to be easy to leave such luxury."

The kitchen door opened behind her, and Sheriff McCourt strode inside. "Sal Bumpfiss?" A ridge of fur rose on the beagle's back.

Sal swiveled in the chair. Her eyes narrowed. "Yeah?"

The sheriff swept the broad-brimmed hat off her head and tucked it beneath one arm. "Why were your fingerprints on the envelope for that death threat Susan received?"

"I told you," I said, "Sal handed it to me. I brought the mail in, and it got knocked off the table. She picked it up."

The sheriff's jaw tightened. "How'd it get knocked off the table?"

"Don't remember," Sal said. "I talked to one of the neighbors this morning." She jerked her head toward the house next door. "She said she saw a hiker walk past yesterday, early afternoon. Maybe he stuck that card in the box." She examined her nails. "I noticed there was no postmark."

I stiffened. I should have talked to the neighbors. They were *my* neighbors. I blew a slow and calming breath through my mouth. *Sal's leaving today. It doesn't matter.*

The tips of the sheriff's nostrils whitened. "Susan, may I have a word?" She shot Sal a hard look. "In private."

"Ah, sure." To Sal, I said, "We'll be right back."

She shook her head. "You shouldn't talk to the cops without a lawyer. You want me to call you mine? I've got her on speed dial."

The tips of my ears heated. "No, it's fine. Thanks." I opened the parlor door. Sheriff McCourt walked inside the black-and-white room, and I followed. It was the one modern room in the house. Sort of. My gran had decorated it in contemporary Victorian, with black velvet furniture and a fluffy white rug. Bookshelves lined the walls.

"Your guest has a police record," she said.

"Oh, you mean that thing about punching someone? He totally deserved it."

She ruffled her blond hair. "You knew?"

"We sort of, ah, met in jail when I was in Nowhere."

She goggled at me, her curls quivering. "So you invited her to stay? And what do you mean, he deserved it?"

"He called her fat. What was she supposed to do?" And why was I defending Sal? I sounded like Dixie.

"She could have not assaulted him, for starters."

"The point is, she didn't send me that Valentine's card," I said. "And she didn't kill Kelsey with an icicle." Bailey barked in the kitchen.

"Starburst," the sheriff said, rubbing the back of her neck. "It was a piece of the starburst from that cupid sculpture." Bailey kept barking, rhythmic and insistent.

I glanced uneasily at the door to the kitchen. "Were there any other fingerprints?" I asked.

"Just yours," she said. "What's wrong with that dog?"

A clash of musical notes sounded outside. "What the devil?" The sheriff strode to the black velvet couch. Bracing one knee on it, she thrust the curtains aside. "What's he doing?"

I hurried to the window. Arsen, in a blue fleece jacket and matching cap, stood in the yard. He held a boom box in one hand and wore a panicked look. *"I'm roaming in my car with my friend, on a steep winding trail, running to the end..."* he sang.

A squirrel raced along the picket fence behind the roses. It hopped onto the top of my Gran's spirit house from Thailand and stared.

"Warriors taking me to the place I was waiting for..."

Another squirrel appeared beside the first. They chittered to each other. In the kitchen, Bailey howled.

"What on earth is your boyfriend doing?" the sheriff said. "I mean, Arsen's got a great voice. But what's he going on about?"

More squirrels appeared on the lawn and between the rose bushes.

"I... He's... I don't know," I stammered. The song was familiar, from our childhood. We'd thought it was hysterical back then—a one-hit-wonder that I hadn't heard in years. "I should probably..." I pointed to the door.

"Please do."

Embarrassed, I hurried through the kitchen. I didn't know what Arsen was up to, but he surely hadn't meant to do it in front of the sheriff.

Sal stood in the doorway to the side porch letting the cold air in. "Your boyfriend's got a nice baritone."

Bailey carefully made his way down the porch steps.

"I know." But the song was awful. Even the squirrels knew it. I'd swear they were nudging each other on the fence rail and laughing.

Bailey trotted toward Arsen. The squirrels hastily vanished into my neighbor's yard. The beagle leaned against Arsen's leg, threw back his head, and howled.

"Funny sort of serenade though," Sal said.

She'd get no argument there. Hugging my arms against the chill, I hurried past her and down the porch steps. "Arsen?"

He turned off the boom box. "Um. Hi." His hazel eyes were slightly wild.

"What's going on?" I asked carefully.

"I mixed up the CDs. I mean, I had the right CD, but it was at the wrong spot. I couldn't find a digital version. So. CD."

"Oh. Okay. And you...?" *Never mind.* There were bigger issues. Like deadly Valentines. "Arsen, there's something I need to tell you."

His face reddened. "Yeah. Me too."

"Oh. You go first."

"Uh... I was just... You know, Susan, we..."

"Spit it out," Sal shouted from the porch. "I can't hear you from here."

"I was just goofing around. Gotta go." He kissed my cheek and raced across the lawn. Arsen vanished around the corner of the Victorian.

"But—"

Bailey howled. Sal turned and went inside.

Mystified, I returned to the kitchen with Bailey. Sal leaned against the butcher-block counter. She blew into a cup of coffee she'd helped herself to. Beside my refrigerator, the sheriff studied her from beneath lowered brows.

"So," I said, baffled. "I guess all's well." Even if I hadn't had a chance to tell him about the Valentine. But the sheriff knew, and maybe a police report was more important. Still, it seemed the sort of thing he'd want to know about.

"All's well aside from a death threat and a murdered woman," the sheriff said, caustic. She jammed her hat on her head. "I'll see you around." She strode out the swinging door. In the foyer, the front door slammed.

"Not if I see you first," Sal said darkly. "Trouble's brewing in all sorts of places. It's not a good sign when the sheriff pays a visit."

She and Bailey really needed to get over their prejudice against law enforcement. But I'd been lucky. Jail hadn't scarred me like it had Sal. "No, no. We're friends, really. She was just coming to tell me about the fingerprints."

She scowled. "About *my* fingerprints."

"Yours and mine were the only prints on that envelope and card."

"So the guy—or gal—who left the card wore gloves. Figures. They must know we're onto him. Or her."

"Yes," I said, uneasy. "That's a real possibility."

"I'm getting a bad feeling about this. Your boyfriend's acting squirrely. You got a poisoned pen letter. There's a murdered woman and a suspicious sheriff on your tail. It's a darn good thing I've been here."

"Oh," I said weakly. "Yes. It sure is." *And now you can go. Please.*

"That's all right then." She straightened off the counter and clapped my shoulder. I staggered. "I've got nowhere to be. I'll stick around a few more days and help you fix everything."

I gulped. "I wouldn't want you to go to any trouble."

She grinned. "No trouble. No trouble at all."

Chapter Nine

As much as I wanted to, I couldn't kick Sal out of the B&B. My radical honesty policy meant admitting that her room would be open the rest of the week. Besides, she seemed so pleased by the prospect someone might try to kill me. I just didn't have the heart to tell her I'd be fine on my own.

True, someone had sent me a death threat in a Valentine's card. But the sheriff and I had dealt with these things before. *And Arsen.* My heart plunged. Where *was* Arsen?

As someone who occasionally suffered from anxiety attacks, I knew that letting my mind spin through all the disastrous possibilities never helped. What helped was action. And Arsen and I were fine.

I sat at the B&B's kitchen table and pulled my planner to me. "All right." I opened it to the *suspects* pages and scanned the neat grid. "We still don't—"

"Do you keep murder notes in your planner?" Sal leaned back in her wooden chair. It groaned beneath her weight. In his dog bed beneath the table, Bailey rolled onto his back.

"Yes. It's specially designed for my B&B and for murder investigations." I paused, thinking. "And sometimes Bigfoot and UFO investigations. My planner gives me more control over the process." When everything was falling apart, having a plan was a godsend.

"Planning only gives people an *illusion* of control." Her legs sprawled beneath the round table.

My jaw tightened. It was no illusion. Planning worked. "It's about more than control. Planning helps me stay organized." I motioned to the pages. "We need to have a real talk with Anselm Holmes."

She sniffed. "*That* guy. Tattoos," she muttered.

"A neck tattoo doesn't make him guilty. He may have an alibi for Kelsey's death."

She checked her watch. "I don't suppose he goes to church on Sundays."

"Even if he does, church is over by now." It was nearly eleven. "And after we talk to Anselm, why don't we grab lunch?"

"I won't say no to some grub."

"Have you tried the Burger Barn?" There was also the Irish pub, where Vida worked. But I wanted to inflict Sal on as few suspects as possible.

She brightened. "Nope. Not yet. And I'm always up for new experiences. But won't it be a little weird if we just show up at Anselm's door? We already dropped off a casserole. What's our excuse this time?"

"We were going for a walk and just passing by, and we stopped in to make sure he got the casserole. Also, I want my dish back."

"You really do cover all the angles," she said admiringly. Sal slapped her hands on the kitchen table and pushed herself away.

Bailey rolled onto his stomach. His tail gave a tentative wag.

"I'll get my coat," she said.

The "just going for a walk" excuse was more believable with a dog, so we brought Bailey. Dixie told us we didn't need her to talk to Anselm, and she'd stay at Wits' End. Since many of the Bigfoot Seekers were still milling about upstairs, that seemed like a good idea. At Wits' End, we prided ourselves on good customer service. Or at least I prided myself.

We drove to Anselm's neighborhood, higher up in the hills. I parked three blocks away. The snow was thicker on the ground here, in one of those upscale neighborhoods that didn't have sidewalks.

We walked up the path to the artist's bungalow, climbed the porch steps, and knocked on the door. I studied the stained glass piece in its center.

Sal adjusted her grip on Bailey's leash. The beagle lay down beside her red boot and stared up at her adoringly.

After a few moments, the door opened. Anselm looked at us, his brown eyes impassive. "Yes?"

"You may not remember us," I said. "We met at Hannah's?"

A flush darkened his Hollywood face. He scraped a hand through his thick, auburn hair. "Oh. Yeah." He wore jeans and an emerald sweater that set off his brown eyes.

"I'm Susan Witsend, and this is my friend Sal." At my feet, the beagle whuffed. "And Bailey."

"We were just going for a walk," Sal said. "Wondered if you were finished with that casserole."

Color crept up his tattooed neck. "Oh. You were the ones who left the casserole on my porch. I haven't, uh…"

"We didn't expect you to eat it right away," I said. "We just thought… since we were in the neighborhood…" Darn. He obviously wanted us gone. How could I stretch this out and subtly work my way into an interrogation?

"Can I use your bathroom?" Sal asked, and my shoulders loosened with relief. He'd have to let us in now, and that would give us a chance to chat.

"Um, yeah. Sure." He backed from the door.

Bailey shook his collar.

"May I bring Bailey inside?" I asked.

"Yeah," he said. "Sure."

We walked inside a wood-floored hallway with pale brown walls and white trim.

"Thanks," Sal said. "Shouldn't have had all that coffee, but a girl's gotta do what a girl's gotta do."

"It's down the hall and to the left." He pointed, and she ambled down the hallway.

I looked around. "Is this a Craftsman?"

"Yeah. How'd you know?"

"The stained glass was a giveaway." I nodded toward a set of sliding doors on the right made of stained glass framed with wood.

Anselm seemed to remember himself. "Come on in." He pulled the doors open and ushered Bailey and me into a dining area. A simple rectangular wooden table and matching chairs were centered in the narrow room. A modern brushed nickel set of lights hung above the table. Windows looked into a side yard filled with pines. A stone fireplace stood opposite.

"What a lovely home." I walked to a set of framed images, black and white sketches of the woods the size of a square business card. They were set in nine-by-twelve frames with over-sized white matting. "Did you do these?"

"Yes." He rubbed the geometric tattoo on the back of his neck. "Most of my work is commercial. I'm not sure if you can call it art."

"Of course you can. No wonder you and Kelsey had so much in common."

His smile was bitter. "Yes, but the art was only a superficial connection. What we had..." He swallowed. "Is it strange to say she swept me off my feet?"

Not from what I'd heard. I smiled. "She seemed to have that effect on people."

"She was a force. I still can't believe she's gone. My only regret is—" He clamped his jaw shut.

"Hannah?" I suggested quietly.

Anselm shook his head. "I handled things badly with her. We weren't right for each other. Kelsey made me see that. But I shouldn't have ended things with Hannah the way I did. She's a good person. Hannah's got just as much talent as Kelsey did, maybe more. But their parents discouraged her. It wasn't fair," he said hotly.

My chest squeezed. His feelings for Hannah were all over his face. I hoped they could work things out. "Hannah is old enough to make her own choices," I said, but I winced. I knew something about parental pressure. Even when you thought you'd grown out of it, the old lessons about who to be and how to be kept a tight hold. Sometimes those lessons were useful. Other times, not so much.

"You don't understand." He lowered his head. "She spent so much time just doing what she was told, and now... I'd like to think now her parents will see her for who she is, will accept her for who she is. But I don't know." He stopped in front of the picture window.

"Are her parents really that terrible?" I glanced toward the open doorway. Sal was taking her time in the bathroom. My stomach quivered with unease. What was she up to?

He laughed, a harsh croak. "They cut her off when they found out we were serious. I wasn't good enough for Hannah."

I glanced around the room. Doyle wasn't the most expensive part of California. But it was still affected by California real estate prices. And this was a lovely, if small, home in a nice part of Doyle. "Why not?"

"They thought my work was unserious," he said shortly. "Never mind that I do just fine. They're traditional."

I'd like to say his parents' attitude seemed unfair. But my parents had their own terrifying little quirks. I shuddered, remembering one awful prom.

They'd bugged my date's car *and* his boutonnière. Everything had been fine until we'd danced too close to the speakers. The feedback had been so loud it had caused a stampede. Which of course, my parents, parked in a nearby van, had leapt into action to retrieve me from. Talk about humiliating.

Sal sauntered into the dining room. "Nice digs you got here."

"Thanks," Anselm said.

"So who do you think killed Kelsey?" she asked, and I smothered a groan. You just couldn't be that direct in an interrogation.

He exhaled. "I can't imagine anyone wanting to hurt Kelsey. She was a remarkable woman."

At least he hadn't gotten defensive. "Not even one of her other, er, friends?" I asked.

Anselm's smile was taut. "You mean Enrique or Victor? No. They understood the situation when they went into it, and they didn't mind." His brow creased. "Or at least they said they didn't. I don't know."

I thought of Victor, smashing that ice sculpture. He'd minded Enrique, at least. "It's so strange," I said in a low voice. "If Victor hadn't delivered the wrong ice sculpture, I wouldn't have gone to her barn at all. And if he'd delivered it sooner, I'd have returned it sooner. I might have seen something, been able to stop it. But I suppose there's no use wondering what could have been."

"I keep thinking the same thing," he said. "I was here, working on a project, and I had no idea what was—" His full lips formed a line.

The doorbell rang, and Anselm frowned. "Excuse me." He turned and strode through the open sliding doors and into the hall.

"Good job with the diversion," Sal whispered. "No drugs in his medicine cabinet. Nothing weird in the bedroom either."

I glared. She'd gone into his bedroom? I wanted to go through his bedroom.

Sheriff McCourt strode into the dining room. "Out." She swept her broad-brimmed hat off her head and motioned with it toward the sliding stained glass doors.

I looked around. Who was she talking to?

Head down, Sal scuttled past her.

Wait. She was talking to us? "We were just—"

"Casserole delivery," she said. "Got it. Now go."

"Potential pick up, actually," I said slowly. What was the sheriff doing here? Kelsey had been killed on Friday and today was Sunday. She'd doubtless already interviewed Anselm. Why had she returned? "If there's anything I can—"

Anselm walked into the room. The sheriff glared at me.

Fine. I could take a hint. She couldn't interview him with me around. It would let him in on the secret that I was assisting her investigation.

Reluctantly, I walked Bailey into the hallway. The front door was closed. Sal was nowhere to be seen. I dawdled, digging through my purse as if for keys and cocked my head toward the dining room.

The sheriff gave me a pointed look. She slid shut the stained glass doors.

It was a clever ruse. Sliding doors never had the soundproofing that normal doors did. Unfortunately, these were stained glass. I could hardly press my ear against them without Anselm noticing.

I flattened myself against the wall and held my head as close to the doors as I dared. Low voices, too soft for me to hear distinctly, murmured within the dining room.

I huffed an annoyed breath. The sheriff wasn't thinking clearly. How was I supposed to overhear if they were practically whispering? No doubt she'd tell me what she learned later though.

I strode to the front door and stepped onto the porch. Sal, leaning against the white-painted railing, looked up. "No offense, Sue, but I'm not sure a sheriff makes such a great friend."

"It's been useful in the past." I walked down the porch steps. Bailey sat on the porch and shot me an indignant look.

Sal picked up the beagle. He hated going down stairs. It was rather sweet that she'd noticed. They followed me to my Crosstrek.

"I wonder if there's hope for Anselm and Hannah?" I said. "It's awful, now that her sister's gone, but still..."

Sal opened the car door. "No use trying to revive old flames. What's dead is dead, and good riddance." She loaded Bailey into his harness and scowled. "There's a reason those two broke up. And if it was another woman, that just shows the relationship wasn't worth much to begin with."

"But love can take all sorts of strange turns." It certainly had with me and Arsen. We'd been friends since childhood. I'd never dreamed it would turn into something more. Now I couldn't imagine life without him.

"What most people call love is a sham," she said gruffly. "People get all caught up in romance, but it never lasts. That's not love." Sal nodded toward the Craftsman-style house. "If that idiot inside had any brains, he would have known it from the start and never left Hannah once the flames died down." She got inside and slammed the door.

Chilled, I walked to my side of the car. Those giddy feelings between Arsen and me *had* been coming less and less frequently. But we had more than fleeting passion. What we had was solid. Lasting. Meaningful.

I gripped the door handle. I just hoped Arsen thought so too.

Chapter Ten

"I'm hungry enough to eat my own hand." Sal braced her elbow on the edge of the car window. Her expression turned speculative. "Why don't we try that, er, Irish pub for lunch instead? It's closer. I checked the website. It's dog friendly."

"Murphy's?" I turned down a winding residential street and glanced her way. She avoided my gaze, and I bit back my annoyance. She had an ulterior motive—of course she did. Sal wanted to interrogate Vida. The worst part was, it was *my* ulterior motive. It felt like she'd stolen it.

I wavered, torn. If I didn't take her to Murphy's, she might tackle Vida on her own, like she had my neighbors. It was better if I tried to contain this. "Okay," I said. "Why not?"

I drove to Main Street and found a parking spot a block away. We strolled down the street, passing clumps of piled snow, and into the Irish Pub. People at the square tables near the door shot us annoyed looks. Hurriedly, I shut the door.

A fire crackled in the wood stove at the other end of the room, and Bailey strained toward it. Old pots, lanterns, and beer mugs hung from the ceiling beams. We hesitated on the slate floor beside the hostess stand.

A man in a black apron, his white sleeves rolled to his elbows, appeared. "Bar or table?" He angled his head toward the long, wooden bar.

"I have a dog," I said.

He shrugged. "Bar or table?"

Table," I said, and he showed us to a small, square table beside a faux-stone wall.

I sat, and Bailey curled by my feet. "By the way, a friend of mine was thinking of applying for a job here. If a waitress starts work at eleven, what time is she expected to get in?"

"Ten-thirty," he said. "We've got table set-ups. But there aren't any openings right now."

"Is Vida working today?" Sal asked casually, and the spot between my shoulder blades tightened.

"Yeah, she is," the waiter said. "Are you friends of hers?"

"She's friends with my cousin, Dixie," I said.

His face lit. "I know Dixie. She's awesome. I'll tell Vida you're here." He handed us paper menus and strode away. The group at a table behind me cheered.

Sal peeled off her crimson gloves. "It's been a dog's age since I've been in a good Irish pub."

Bailey's ears perked.

"I can't vouch for how good it is," I said, unbuttoning my coat. I usually went to Antoine's, the western bar on the other side of the street.

"That's the thing about Irish pubs." Sal shrugged out of her parka and draped it over the back of her chair. "It doesn't really matter. It's all about the people." She scanned her menu. "Bread pudding for dessert? Count me in."

I cleared my throat. "I actually spoke to Vida yesterday. She stopped by Wits' End to see Dixie." And I didn't want Sal going over ground we'd already covered.

"Why?" Her parka slipped to the floor. She stooped to retrieve it.

"They're friends. I think she was looking for a sympathetic ear."

"From your cousin?" Sal snorted and returned the parka to its place. "Not sure she was looking in the best direction. No offense."

That wasn't fair. I straightened in my chair. "Dixie's..." I frowned. Sal wasn't entirely wrong. Could Vida have had another reason to drop by Wits' End?

"I'm not so sure about your investigative technique either." Sal squinted at me.

I folded my arms. "What's wrong with my technique?"

"You're not exactly action oriented, are you? All you do is wander around and talk to people."

"To suspects! To witnesses!" What did she expect me to do? Hack into my suspects' computers? Ransack their homes for clues?

"What's to stop them from lying to you?"

"Nothing, but..." I picked up my menu and pretended to study it. "Well, some people are lying, obviously. Or at least not telling us everything. But it's like a puzzle. You need to tease the truth from the lies."

"And how are we going to do that?"

I glanced at her over the paper menu. "By talking to more people. There are alibis to be broken, and such. It takes time," I said, flustered.

She shook her head. "I can't stick around here helping forever. All I can give you is a few more days. Then the training wheels will have to come off."

Training wheels? I was a seasoned investigator! The sheriff's secret weapon! What the heck did Sal know about the law aside from how to get arrested? I set the menu on the table and forced a smile. "I'm sure we'll figure out something."

"I know what you're thinking."

I shrank back a little. "You do?" Had I been that obvious? She might be annoying, but I didn't want to hurt her feelings. Sal wasn't a bad person, even if she *had* been in jail once.

At least, I hoped it was only once. What if she was a repeat offender?

"You're thinking you're going to need to rush the investigation. If it goes long, it'll mess up your big Valentine's plans with Arsen."

"That's not..." I *didn't* want to mess up Valentine's evening with Arsen. We'd had so little time together lately. And sure, murder was more important than romance, but Arsen was important too. "I'm sure I'll be able to manage it," I said, voice taut.

I pulled my planner from my oversized purse and opened it to the suspects pages. "Do you mind if I make some notes about our interview with Anselm?"

She waved airily at the open planner on the table. "You do you. But I'm telling you, it's all an illusion."

Vida appeared beside our table, her hair tight in its long ponytail. "Hello, ladies. I'm Vida, and I'll be taking care of you today." She set a water bowl beside Bailey. The beagle eyed it suspiciously.

Sal squinted at her. "I thought you were at Wits' End yesterday. Don't you know Susan?"

The waitress pinked and rubbed the end of her pencil against her nose ring. "Oh. Sorry. I'm so used to my spiel that I didn't even... Hi, Susan."

I closed the planner. "Hi. It's fine."

"Have you had a chance to look over the menu?" Vida asked.

"I'll need more time," Sal said. "But let's get started with those scotch eggs and a Guinness."

Vida smiled. "And for you?" she asked me.

"Oh," I said. "I'll just have water. I'm driving."

"Sure thing." The waitress bustled away.

I opened my planner again and wrote down my impressions and notes on Anselm. "No alibi," I muttered.

"None of our suspects have one," Sal said. "Do they?"

I shook my head. "Kelsey died some time before I found her at a quarter to two. I don't know where Vida was before that time the day Kelsey died. She started work here at eleven Friday."

"Let's nail her down then. What else have you got in that book of yours?" She reached across the table and grabbed my planner.

I sucked in a breath and tried to relax. It was only a planner, not a personal journal. And it wasn't as if she was going to damage the leather-bound book.

Roughly, Sal flipped the pages forward and back and frowned. "Everyone's got a motive, huh?"

"Every one of our suspects," I said. "Which is why they're suspects."

Vida strode to our table carrying a tray of drinks. Somewhere in the pub, a tray clattered on the wooden floor.

"What's this about free love?" Sal mashed her finger on a page. The crowd at the nearby table roared.

Vida paled. "Free love?"

"A silly Valentine's Day promotion I saw online," I said hastily. "It seemed in poor taste."

"Yep," Sal said, "nothing to do with you at all. That my beer?"

"Guinness," Vida corrected, setting it on the table before her. "And here's your water, Susan."

"I heard you were friends with the deceased," Sal said, somber. "I'm sorry for your loss."

"Oh." She lowered the tray and ran her hand down her black apron. "We weren't really. I mean—" A glass crashed at the rowdy table, and there were shouts of laughter. "Oh, that's my table. I'd better... Excuse me, please." She hurried to the other table.

Darn it. Between Sal and the other patrons, the odds that I'd learn anything useful from Vida were low.

Sal scowled. "Some people. It's a little early for a party. Now what's this *really* about free love?"

"Vida said Kelsey was a believer in it."

"Isn't that some nineteenth-century BS?"

"Not just the eighteen hundreds, but yes."

Sal shook her head. "I don't know how some women do it. I couldn't stand to be juggling all those men. It seems so shallow."

"I know, right? I'd much rather have one relationship that mattered." I bit my bottom lip. Why hadn't Arsen and I been able to make much time for us lately? Had we gotten so busy we were losing each other?

And why had he sung that weird song? It was as if he'd been trying to drive off my guests. He'd said it was a mistake, but why sing at all? And why *that* song?

"What's wrong?" Sal asked.

I shook myself. "Just thinking over the case. The sheriff said if I hadn't gotten there when I did, the murder weapon would have melted away. But it doesn't sound like she got any fingerprints off it in any case."

"Killer probably wore gloves. No one would have given gloves a second glance in this weather." Her round face creased. "I wonder if the gloves left any fibers on the ice?"

"That's a good question," I said. When ice got really cold, it *could* be sticky. Sal might be irritating, but she wasn't stupid.

She shrugged. "I saw it on TV."

Vida returned to our table. "Sorry about that." She bent and handed Bailey a dog treat. "Who's a good boy?" she cooed and straightened. "Now what can I get you?"

"I'll have the corned beef and cabbage," Sal said.

"And I'll try the bangers and mash." I closed my menu and handed it to Vida.

"But what I really want," Sal said, "is to know if you saw anyone shifty around Kelsey's barn Friday morning."

I smothered a groan. *This. This* is what came from working with amateurs. This was not the way to go about an interrogation. You didn't just blurt out your questions. You had to work your way into them—gain the subject's trust.

"What?" Vida's hazel eyes widened. "But I didn't see anyone. I mean, I was home all morning until I came to work. I wasn't anywhere near that barn." Her tanned brow creased. "Although—"

"Oi! Waitress!" One of the men at the loud table stood up and waved to her.

"Excuse me," she said. "I'll get your orders into the kitchen."

"Although *what*?" Sal called after her departing back. She gulped her drink and banged the mug on the table. "Those guys are getting on my last nerve."

"I know the feeling," I muttered.

"*Oi, waitress*," Sal mimicked. "That's just rude. You ever wait tables?"

"One horrible summer." It had been awful. The tips often had nothing to do with the quality of service and everything to do with the clients' habits. I couldn't control the quality or timing of the food coming from the kitchen. The bar was always slow... I shuddered.

"It ain't for the faint-hearted, that's for sure. And Vida was going to tell us something before we were interrupted."

"I think so too," I admitted.

"At least she's got to come back to deliver our food. Unless she sends someone else," she said darkly.

Fortunately, Vida did not send someone else. Twenty minutes later, she returned to our table with our steaming plates. "Here you go."

"Mine looks great," Sal said. "But I can't stop thinking about what you said. What *were* you going to say?"

"About what?"

"The barn the morning Kelsey was killed," I said.

"I didn't see anyone at the barn," Vida said. "Like I said, I was nowhere near there."

"But you thought of something?" I prompted.

She pressed the empty tray to her chest. "It's only... A few weeks ago Hannah was here, at the pub. She knew what happened to me with Victor, and I knew what happened to her with Anselm. And she said... Well, she said neither of us would be too sad if something happened to Kelsey. And then—"

"Waitress!" The same man stood up at the table again and waved to her. "Waitress!"

Sal threw her napkin on the table, and Bailey jerked to standing. "That does it." She stormed to the other table. "What's wrong with you? Didn't you learn any manners? That's not how you talk to your server."

"Aw, lighten up." The man smiled lazily.

"I'll lighten you up." She grabbed his ear and twisted. He yelped. The other men at the table laughed.

My hands spasmed on the table. "Oh, no," I said.

Vida hurried to their table. "It's fine. Really."

The burly man who'd seated us hurried from behind the counter. "I'm the owner. What's going on here?"

"A lesson in manners." Sal snarled. "This one was being a pest to the waitstaff."

The owner drew back his shoulders. "I'm afraid you'll have to leave."

She released the customer's ear. Rubbing the side of his head, he dropped to his chair.

"Ha." She sneered. "See?"

"I meant you need to go," the pub owner told her. "We don't need any trouble."

I groaned and buried my head in my hands. My first time in Murphy's, and my guest was getting thrown out? This was a nightmare.

"What'd we do?" Sal said.

"You assaulted a customer." He pointed a meaty finger at me. "Out. Both of you."

My face burned. *Both?* I was being thrown out of a bar? This was almost as humiliating as getting arrested.

Sal's mouth pursed. She nodded. She bent and said something to the man whose ear she'd pulled, and he glared.

"All right." She snatched her parka off the back of the chair. "Cabbage is no good for me anyway, and you served your Guinness too cold." She grabbed her gloves off the table. "Come on, Susan. We've got better fine dining establishments to patronize."

Shooting Vida an apologetic look, Bailey and I trailed after Sal and onto the sidewalk.

She nudged me. "Heh. Did you see that? We didn't even have to pay for our drinks."

I jerked the zipper higher on my jacket and did not point out that my water had been free.

But I really wanted to.

Chapter Eleven

"I think that went well." Sal rubbed her red-gloved hands together. On Main Street, a Porsche with ski racks on its roof drove past. Its wheels tossed up slush and water in their wake.

"It did? We were thrown out of a bar," I fumed. I'd never been thrown out of a bar before, and shame heated my chest. I *lived* here. This would be all over town before dark. What would Mrs. Steinberg say? Even worse, what would Dixie say?

"Sure," she said. "Vida will remember us and think we're on her side. She'll spill the beans next time we meet for sure."

Or avoid us like bubonic plague. Public humiliation had *not* been part of the investigation plan. Bailey whined at my feet.

"So where next?" she asked.

My stomach rumbled. And I hadn't even gotten to eat. "The Burger Barn." I knew I should have stuck to my original plan. Things always went south when I freewheeled it.

"Then what?"

My mind raced. I needed something to keep Sal busy that wouldn't do any more damage. "And then we're going to the barn where Kelsey was killed."

She snapped her fingers. "The scene of the crime. Huh. But won't the sheriff have already cleaned the place out?"

"You never know. It might give us some inspiration."

"Sounds like you're reaching, but this is your show. Let's do this."

The speed she'd agreed with the idea left me worrying it hadn't been a good one. But we drove to The Burger Barn. It had been decorated with paper hearts and pink balloons.

The balloons had begun to sag, and I hoped it wasn't a metaphor for my love life. But Valentine's Day was tomorrow. I wasn't going to take it or Arsen for granted.

We ordered and migrated to the patio and huddled beneath a heat lamp. The Burger Barn liked dogs, but only outside.

Sal had ordered all the Valentine's Day specials—Valentine's Strawberry shake, the Double Lover Cheeseburger, and Cupid Curly Fries. We "It's not that I'm a romantic," she said, brandishing a fry. "Not after Bingo's betrayal. Trust me, my eyes are open. I just like specials."

After lunch, we dropped Bailey at Wits' End. Then Sal and I drove to Kelsey's barn studio and parked beneath oak. We stepped from my Crosstrek.

Sal pursed her lips and studied the yellow police tape over the barn door. "How would your sheriff friend feel if we, er..." She motioned toward the tape.

"Not good," I said. Besides, I'd already been inside the barn and the apartment above it.

"Gotcha." She turned in place in the driveway. "So she was killed inside?"

"Yes," I said, terse.

"Lots of trees around here." She motioned up the thickly wooded hillside behind the barn. "Someone could have come through there and not have been seen."

That was another a good point, and I scowled. One minute she was helpful, the next causing chaos. It was giving me whiplash. I drew a deep breath and forced a smile. "If they did, they may have left a trail."

"Broken branches, bits of clothing snagged on bushes, footprints, I'm on it." She strode to the oaks at the base of the hill.

I stood by the barn, uncertain.

THUNK.

I turned, frowning. That had sounded a lot like someone using a shovel. I circled around the front of the barn to its opposite side.

Hannah, one foot braced on a shovel, levered it out of the ground. She grunted, her long, brown braid swinging.

"Hannah?" I asked.

Kelsey's sister started and dropped the shovel to the uneven earth. She examined her hands. "Damn, I broke a nail."

Only one? I'd tried long nails once, when I'd been a bridesmaid in a wedding. They'd lasted until the first time I'd tried to open the dishwasher. "What are you doing?"

Twin spots of color appeared in her cheeks. "Looking for clues."

"In the ground?" I raised an eyebrow. Small holes dotted the earth. Clumps of dried grass lay on their side, bare roots exposed.

Sal appeared from behind the barn. "Hey, did you know there's a trail back here?" She jerked her thumb over her shoulder.

"Yes," Hannah said testily.

"Where does it lead?" Sal asked.

"To the houses in the neighborhood up on the hill." Hannah pointed.

"Hannah, why are you digging?" I asked, impatient.

"The sheriff asked me to let her know if I thought of anything. I thought I might find some clues outside, since I'm not allowed inside without her."

"Why would the killer bury a clue in the yard?" Sal's broad face creased.

She tossed her head, her braid swinging. "Why were you looking for a trail?"

"It's a public trail." Sal raised her chin. "Ain't it?"

"Hardly anyone uses it anymore," Hannah said.

I gritted my teeth. "Why are you digging up your sister's yard?"

She blew out a breath and picked up the shovel. Sal took a hasty step backward. "I'm looking for my sister's cash box," Hannah blurted.

I frowned. "Cash box?"

Hannah shook her head. "Kelsey... She wasn't a prepper or anything, but she didn't entirely trust banks. She kept a cash box for emergencies."

"And she buried it in her yard?" I asked, incredulous.

"For safety."

But Kelsey'd had a floor safe. We'd all seen it. Wasn't that safe enough? "Why? Burying something in her yard doesn't make sense."

"It did if you knew my sister. She was always doing stuff like that. Diversifying, I mean. Cash. Bitcoin. Gold."

"Where'd she keep the gold?" Sal asked.

She leaned on her shovel. "That was in the cashbox too."

"How much was in it?" I asked.

"Not much." Hannah shrugged. "Just twenty thousand in cash. I'm not sure about the gold."

Sal's eyes goggled. "That's not much? I could buy a getaway car with that."

"It's enough that it's worth a little digging," Hannah said. "Want to help look?"

I *had* offered to help Hannah if she needed anything. At least, I thought I had. It was the sort of thing one usually says to a grieving relative. But I really didn't want to, and she only seemed to have the one shovel. "Er—"

"No," Sal said flatly. "I'm not hunting for someone else's treasure."

"We're just going to check out that trail," I said. "Sal loves hiking. But good luck with the cash box."

I followed Sal around the barn and pulled out my cellphone. "I'm calling the sheriff."

"Why?" she asked.

"To tell her about Hannah."

Her expression turned baleful. "No one likes a tattle-tail."

"This is a murder investigation. We can't withhold evidence."

"I guess." She scratched her head. "But it doesn't feel right."

"If we do find the killer, we're not going to arrest him or her ourselves. We'll need the sheriff."

Sal grunted. "There." She pointed to a tangle of bushes.

"That's the trailhead?" It sure didn't look like one.

"Yeah, see?" She turned sideways and sidled through a break in the low bushes. "You can squeeze right through. And come here. Look."

I edged between the bushes to join her. Why did I think I was going to regret this?

She picked up a dangling branch. "This branch is green inside," she said. "This is a fresh break. Someone came through here recently." She clapped my shoulder, and I staggered at the impact. "I got to give it to you. I doubted when you suggested the barn. But we found the trail the killer came down *and* some suspicious digging. This was a good call."

Had we stumbled on an actual clue? "Thanks," I said uncertainly.

She plunged deeper into the bushes. Reluctantly, I followed. It was most likely a wild goose chase, but at least it was a harmless one.

To my surprise, the break in the bushes *did* turn into a real trail. It was a narrow trail, with branches that whipped back on me when Sal passed. But it was definitely a trail.

The path steepened, and Sal fell silent, huffing. "This is good," she gasped. "I was missing my aerobic exercise."

I was in better shape for the climb, thanks to Arsen. My thoughts returned to tomorrow night, and my heart bubbled. He'd told me he had something special planned. Another night hike? A picnic in the gazebo? It didn't matter, as long as we were—

Sal stopped short, and I bumped into her broad back. "Do you hear that?" she whispered.

"Hear what?" I whispered back. Bushes and oaks crowded around us. A branch snapped.

"That," Sal said in a low voice.

I stopped, listened, and heard nothing. But the back of my neck gave a disconcerted prickle. "It's probably another hiker."

"Off trail?"

I shivered. She had a point. There was no way I'd tackle this hillside off trail. It was barely worth it *on* the trail. Another branch cracked, and I whirled, staring into the underbrush. If it was an animal, it was a big one. There were bears in the hills. And the occasional mountain lion.

"What if it's the killer?" she whispered.

My insides quivered. *Nonsense.* "Why would he still be here?"

"Maybe he dropped something incriminating, and now he's coming back for it."

"Off trail?"

Leaves rustled, and we stilled. She shot me a worried look.

"Let's keep going," I said.

"Right. Right. Keep going." She turned.

The bushes trembled. A fall of dried leaves showered us, and a dark shape burst onto the trail.

Chapter Twelve

I flinched and gasped, my heart jumping in my chest. I'd had some experience with people leaping out at me, and that sort of thing never ended well. But I'd also learned a few defensive techniques. Fists clenching, I dropped my weight.

"Whoa!" Sal's hand shot out and struck me in the upper arm.

I staggered sideways and into the thick brush. My feet skidded from beneath me. I tumbled, branches cracking. Something sharp speared my rib, and I yelped.

They'd be on me any minute. I flailed helplessly, something keeping me in place. I had to get up. I had to—

"Susan?" A pair of binoculars stared down at me.

"Oof." I tried to roll from the manzanita bush. Its spiny branches plucked at my clothes, pinning me. "Wha—?"

The binoculars lowered, and Mrs. Carter peered at me. "Oh, dear. Are you all right?" She wore camo. Leaves and branches stuck from the shoulders of her thick jacket and tangled in her gray hair.

Honestly. Did it look like I was all right? And what were they doing jumping out at innocent innkeepers?

Sal thrust her head through the bushes. "There you are. What are you doing in that bush?" She reached a hand through, grabbed me by the collar, and hauled me to standing. Branches snapped and tore at my jacket, and I was on the trail again. She brushed me off. "See? Right as rain."

Finley hurried toward me. "Sorry I startled you. You okay?" He wore a bulky, dark-colored parka like a cape, to accommodate his sling.

"Of course she's not okay," his ex-wife, Brooke, snapped. She clawed a hand through her frosted hair. "I told you that you looked like the Phantom of the Opera in that jacket."

The Carters forced their way through the underbrush to the trail. "We didn't expect to see you two here," Mr. Carter said. "I presume you heard the news?"

"What news?" I asked, tensing. *Not another murder.*

"That there was a Bigfoot sighting on this trail just last Friday," the older man said.

Oh brother. Although... Kelsey had been killed on Friday not far from here. Could there be a connection? It wouldn't be the first time Bigfoot had made his way into one of my cases. "What time on Friday?" I asked.

"Late morning," the older man said. "Around eleven o'clock."

My pulse sped. That was around Kelsey's time of death. "That's—"

"I don't think that was Bigfoot." Sal shook her head.

"Why not?" Brooke asked her.

"Because we're here tracking a killer," Sal said. "He may have been right on this very trail late Friday morning. Yup. I'm willing to bet your Bigfoot is our killer."

"It's possible," I said, grudging. Just because Sal had been quicker to voice her deduction was no reason to get defensive. "Tell me more about this sighting. Who was the witness?"

"A woman named Francine Sokolnicki." Mr. Carter nodded up the trail. "She lives in the neighborhood at the top of the hill. She said she saw him disappearing into the bushes at the top of the trail."

I smothered a groan. Francine Sokolnicki saw Bigfoot *everywhere*. She thought she had some special spiritual relationship with the beast. For Francine, every deer, every shadow in the forest was Bigfoot.

"We should talk to her," Sal said. "I mean, Bigfoot. That's big."

Glum, I nodded. Sal had no idea what she was letting us in for.

"The problem with Bigfoot," Finley said, "is that he keeps moving around. You find a track in one place, and it's too late, he's somewhere else."

"Too bad you can't tranq him," Brooke said dryly. "That would slow him down."

Her ex-husband glared. "No, the problem is we can't get near him. How's a dart gun supposed to help with that?"

"Not that we would ever shoot Bigfoot," Mrs. Carter said hastily. "Not even with a tranquilizer gun."

"I'm pretty sure those are illegal," Mr. Carter said.

Sal snorted. "Isn't everything illegal in California?"

"Anyway," I said before Sal could elaborate on any crimes she might like to commit. "We'd better be going."

Finley typed into his phone and grunted. "See you later."

Sal and I continued up the trail. "You're trying to find a tranq gun online, aren't you?" Brooke's voice floated after us.

"No," Finley said. "I'm—" We rounded a bend and his voice faded, too low to hear.

We huffed up the overgrown trail. At the top, we emerged in a cul-de-sac surrounded by ranch houses in natural browns and greens. Sal shaded her eyes with one hand. "You know where this Francine woman lives?"

My shoulders slumped. I sighed and pointed at a yard filled with whirligigs. A dusty white Toyota Corolla sat in the cracked driveway. "There."

"Looks like she's home." Sal strode down the driveway. I trailed after her onto the concrete stoop, and she rang the bell. It trilled loudly.

I checked my watch. Forty minutes had passed. We'd wasted five or so talking to the Bigfoot seekers. The hike down would likely take even less time, but I made a mental note to clock it on our return.

The door opened. A gnomish, gray haired woman in glasses, a lumpy gray sweater, and sweatpants beamed. "Susan! You heard about my latest sighting and want to include it in your lectures. I knew you would. Come in, come in."

We followed the plump woman inside. The hallway was papered with topographical maps. Colorful pushpins marked Bigfoot sighting locations. A ceramic cast of a giant foot sat on an end table. A dozen cats trotted down the hall toward us, meowing. The house smelled like cat, and I sneezed.

"And who's your friend?" Francine asked, toddling into the living room. A frayed, lumpy gray sofa sat against one wall. Two matching chairs and a coffee table stood opposite. Magazines about the paranormal lay thick on the table.

"This is Sal, a, uh—"

"Bigfoot seeker." Sal grasped the little woman's hand and pumped it vigorously. "Can't get enough of the big guy."

Francine beamed. "Of course you can't. Once you've encountered him, you can't forget it. It's a spiritual experience. Sit down, sit down."

We sat on the couch. Francine waddled to a bookshelf stuffed with binders and folders and paperbacks. She drew a blue binder from the shelf, dropped into a chair, and opened the binder in her lap. "I have some notes for your presentation right here."

"I don't actually give Bigfoot presentations," I admitted, and Sal glared at me. But I don't like to lie, even in the course of an investigation. Truth and reality were hard enough to distinguish sometimes without muddying the waters myself. "Wits' End focuses on UFOs."

"But I want to hear everything you've got," Sal said.

I extracted my planner from my big bag and opened it. Pulling out a pen, I flipped to my note pages.

Francine cleared her throat. "It was Friday at eleven-oh-seven AM. It's important to be precise when recording a sighting. There was a thick cloud cover, but the lighting was still quite good. It was forty-seven degrees Fahrenheit. My gout was acting up, but I was otherwise uninhibited physically."

Sal frowned. "Don't you mean unimpaired?"

"That too," she said. "I was wearing my glasses, because I'd been doing some online research. Now, I'd recently had corrective surgery. The doctors gave me the choice of being nearsighted or farsighted. Naturally, I chose to have good far vision. If I was a crafty sort of person, I might have chosen good near vision. But I'm not much of a reader or knitter, so I chose far. Much better for driving and Bigfoot sightings."

Save me. I shook my head. "Don't the glasses blur your far vision?" I asked.

"They do. That's why I whipped them off as soon as I saw Bigfoot. I just caught the bushes closing magically behind him. I was standing right in that window." She pointed to the front window, which looked over the court. "As you can see, it has a good view of the trailhead. The sighting lasted approximately five seconds."

But for most of the time, her vision would have been blurred. Not that I believed she'd really seen a Bigfoot. "Can you, er, describe the Bigfoot?"

"He was quite tall. I'd say at least eight feet. He was here for the chocolate."

"Chocolate?" I asked.

"Oh, yes, he loves chocolate. Didn't you know?" She laughed. "He's *famous* for his love of chocolate. I can't believe you weren't aware."

My mouth pinched. I'm not saying Bigfoot would turn down chocolate, but nearly everybody likes chocolate. It didn't seem like such a revelation.

"I might have a weakness for the stuff myself," Sal said. "Especially milk chocolate." She sighed. "My Bingo used to bring me the fanciest chocolates."

"I told your guests from Wits' End that milk chocolate is Bigfoot's favorite too," Francine said. "I leave some out every night, and they're usually gone by morning. He's a clever one though. He always waits until I'm asleep to take them. But that's okay. I'm not trying to trap him. The chocolates are gifts, offerings. It would be wrong to expect something in return. If he wants me to see him, he'll show me, like he did on Friday."

"What did he look like?" I asked.

"Like Bigfoot." Francine beamed. She reached beneath the coffee table and retrieved a white box of chocolates. "Help yourself." She handed the box to Sal.

Sal opened it and took three. "Don't mind if I do." She pocketed two and popped one in her mouth. "Thanks."

Francine leaned forward. "Now, about your Bigfoot lecture—"

"I don't do a Bigfoot lecture," I said repressively. As a civic-minded person, I was trying to get into the Bigfoot spirit. Really, I was. But weren't UFOs *enough* for Doyle?

"Yes," Francine said, "of course. Naturally, I think you should talk about my experiences. Bigfoot is a *transcendent* creature. He knows things. He understands the world in a deep way that we as humans no longer can. We're too disconnected from nature. We can learn so much from him." She fisted her tiny hands at her heart. "Late at night, he sometimes draws me from the house. Mentally, you understand. And we *commune*."

"You mean, like, telepathically?" Sal furrowed her freckled brow.

"Oh, yes. We're all spirit. That's how we can communicate. But if you want to speak with Bigfoot, it's important to be pure."

"Then I've got no chance." Sal nudged me and winked.

Francine clasped her hands. "Oh, but he *knows*. He goes beyond pure human ideas of rules and right and wrong. He sees inside."

"Maybe this Bigfoot fellow isn't so bad," Sal said thoughtfully.

"Yes," I said, "well, thank you, Francine. You've been very helpful."

She pulled a sheet of paper from her binder and handed it to me. "I have copies."

I stared at it. It looked a lot like the Bigfoot investigation form I handed out at Wits' End. A *lot*. "Thank you," I said tightly.

We said our goodbyes and left. "Eight foot tall, huh?" Sal said. "We got any eight-foot suspects?"

"No," I said. "But I don't think Francine is the most reliable witness."

She pulled a chocolate from her pocket and stuck it in her mouth. "Maybe not, but she's got good taste in candy. This stuff's almost as good as Bingo's."

We returned down the trail. At the bottom, I checked my watch. It had taken us twenty-five minutes. *If* she'd spotted the killer at 10:07, he would have made it to the barn around 10:30. On the opposite side of the barn, a shovel thunked into the ground.

"What next?" Sal asked.

"Next... I call the sheriff."

Chapter Thirteen

My cousin shoveled in another mouthful of strawberry pancakes. "What did McCourt say?" she mumbled.

Bailey whined beneath the kitchen table, and I bent to ruffle his tawny fur. The B&B's kitchen smelled of bacon. The scent was enough to drive any dog crazy, even if the beagle had already been fed.

Silverware clinked faintly from the breakfast room on the opposite side of the foyer. I'd gone all out for the big day with pancakes, bacon-rose quiche, scones, potatoes, and pomegranate mimosas.

"The sheriff didn't say anything," I said. "I couldn't get through to her yesterday. There was an accident on Highway Four, and she was busy." Otherwise, she definitely would have taken my call.

The phone rang at my elbow, and I glanced at its screen. *Sheriff McCourt.* I smiled. She was always prompt in returning my calls. That's what came from having a professional relationship. "It's her now." I answered. "Hello, Sheriff."

"Witsend. You called and left a message yesterday."

"I did. Do you know what time Kelsey was killed?"

"Yes."

I waited. When she didn't continue, I said, "Francine Sokolnicki spotted someone on the trail at the top of her court. That was Friday around ten AM. The trail leads down to another trailhead behind Kelsey's barn. It's a bit overgrown, but there are signs someone was on it recently. Someone aside from my guests, I mean. They're the ones who told me about the sighting." I hesitated. "Francine thought the person might have been Bigfoot."

The sheriff groaned. The kitchen porch door opened, and Arsen walked in carrying an armful of red roses. He stopped short at the sight of my cousin. Dixie eyed him.

"It's the sheriff," I mouthed, and he nodded, frowning at Dixie.

"Also," I continued, "we saw Kelsey's sister, Hannah, digging around the barn yesterday. She said—"

"We? You and Arsen?"

He shifted his weight, then put the roses on the butcher-block counter. Dixie threw an arm over the back of her kitchen chair and raised an eyebrow. He mouthed something at her. She shrugged.

"Er, no," I said. "Sal and I."

A pregnant silence fell. "You and Sal Bumpfiss. The ex-con," she said flatly.

Arsen kissed the top of my head. "I'll come for you for dinner tonight," he whispered. "You're busy."

Frantically, I shook my head for him not to leave. "No. I mean, yes, she is," I told the sheriff. "But the point is, Hannah told us Kelsey might have buried some cash in her yard."

"Despite the fact she kept a hidden floor safe, she buried cash in her yard? Why?"

Arsen sidled to the porch door. I pointed to the covered plate waiting for him on the counter. He shook his head and backed from the kitchen. Bailey whoofed.

Disappointment weighted my chest. I'd wanted to treat Arsen this morning. I'd even saved a bottle of champagne and pomegranate juice for the two of us. I sighed. At least we'd see each other tonight.

"I thought it sounded odd too," I told her. "And yet, Hannah was digging."

"What were *you* doing there anyway?"

My gaze flicked toward the white-painted ceiling. She knew exactly what I'd been doing there. But now she was going to go through this big pretense of telling me off. Suddenly, I wasn't in the mood.

"Just passing by," I said with false breeziness. "And then Sal found the trail and we ran into my guests on it. I decided to ask Francine about her so-called Bigfoot sighting. You know how it is."

The line went dead. We must have been cut off. Shrugging, I returned the cellphone to its place beside my plate.

"What did he say to you?" I asked Dixie.

"He didn't say anything."

"He mouthed something."

"Oh. He asked why I was here so early." Dixie grabbed her plate and went to the sink. She pulled aside the blue-checked curtain and frowned. "What's she doing?"

"What's who doing?" I rose and went to stand beside her. On the snow-dotted lawn, Sal, in a pink sweat suit, slowly raised her arms. Carefully, she lifted one leg. "Is that tai chi?" I asked.

"I don't think so. She keeps doing the same movements over and over." She nodded toward the roses on the counter. "What are you going to do with all those?"

"Put them in a vase."

"Have you got one big enough?"

My heart warmed. She was right. There had to be... A hundred long-stemmed roses. Arsen had brought me flowers before, but nothing this elaborate. What had he planned for tonight? My stomach fluttered at the thought.

I'd snipped off the ends of half the roses when Sal trooped into the kitchen. "Chi gung sure works up an appetite." She thumped her chest with her fist.

"Is that what you were doing?" I set a half-dozen roses in a slender, clear-glass vase. Other vases filled with roses lined the counter. Dixie strolled into the kitchen carrying plates from the breakfast room.

"Gotta get my corners in for healthy aging—strength, balance, aerobic and anaerobic. Hey, hey. Someone's having a good day." Sal winked "That's a lot of roses."

"Arsen's got a guilty conscience," my cousin said.

I sucked in my cheeks. "He does not."

"I dunno." Sal rubbed her double chin. "Could go either way. Big romantic gesture or big trouble. My ex only sent me flowers when he'd messed up. The bigger the mess, the bigger the bouquet. But not all men are like Bingo, lucky for you."

"It's Valentine's Day," I said. "I think we can assume it's a romantic gesture."

"What did you two do last Valentine's Day?" Sal asked.

"We went on a hike," I said. The two women stared at me. "And then we had a romantic picnic," I finished.

"In February?" Sal asked, incredulous. "It's freezing."

"It was..." It really *had* been cold. "He brought a lantern for heat. He's very outdoorsy. And I was happy to do something he loved. Valentine's Day isn't all about the woman."

"It sort of is," Sal said.

"It totally is," Dixie agreed.

"Those are quality roses though." Sal stuck her nose into one of the vases I'd filled. "Dating the richest guy in town has its perks, eh?"

"He's not the richest—" Actually, Arsen kind of was. "Where'd you hear that?" I asked, flustered.

"At the Burger Barn yesterday. You were in the bathroom, and I got to talking with one of the waitresses. She said you'd taken the hottest bachelor in Doyle off the market." She chuckled. "I'd think twice about eating anything she brings you from the kitchen."

I barely *knew* that waitress. How did she know so much about me and Arsen? "I don't think our relationship is anyone's business."

"Honestly, Sue." Dixie opened the dishwasher and jammed the unrinsed plates inside. "This is a small town. It's everyone's business."

"Must make Valentine's Day extra rough," Sal said. "Not only does he have to meet V-Day standards, but the whole town's watching what he'll do."

"They're not watching," I said grumpily.

"Yeah?" Sal asked. "So I guess it's not true that you two were dining at a place called Antoine's two weeks ago?"

"We go there all the time." I shifted uneasily. The last time *had* been about two weeks ago. "How did you know that?"

She shrugged. "That waitress told me. Anyway, I'm going to change my clothes. Let me know who we're shaking down today." She stomped from the kitchen.

"We're not shaking anybody..." I said to the door swinging shut in her wake.

"Now you know why I prefer a *long-distance* romance," Dixie said. "What you've got is too much drama."

"How far away is this guy you're seeing?"

"I dunno. We never met in person. Never talked about it."

"Never... How'd you meet him?"

"In a UFO chat room. Duh." Dixie strode from the kitchen.

I finished with the roses and set vases about the B&B. The final vase went on the table in the octagonal breakfast room. Near-empty chafing dishes lined the serving table. Shifting a tall-backed wooden chair an inch into place, I looked around the room. The blue toile wallpaper was a cheerful counterpoint to the red roses. I retrieved a gum wrapper from the wooden floor, then shuttled used plates and chafing dishes into the kitchen.

When I finished washing up, I opened my planner on the table. I scanned my investigation pages. Who *were* we shaking down today?

Something thumped upstairs, and I looked up at the ceiling. The kitchen's overhead lamp swayed.

I frowned. Sal's room was directly above the kitchen. Was she doing aerobics up there?

There was another loud thump. The lamp danced a quick jig. Bailey shot me a worried look.

Uneasy, I closed my planner, pocketed my phone, and hurried through the foyer. Dixie sat behind the computer and scowled at the screen.

"What's wrong?" I asked.

"They changed the name of the Area 51 UFO Convention to the Area 51 UAP Convention. I'm fed up with our evolving language."

I shook my head and jogged upstairs, knocked on the door of Sal's room. No one answered.

"Sal?" I knocked again, an unpleasant tingling spreading through my chest. "Are you okay?" An unearthly gargling sound emanated from behind the closed door. "Sal?" I knocked again. "Sal?" I tried the knob. It was locked. I drew my master key from the pocket of my slacks and opened the door.

Sal, eyes closed, lay unmoving on the throw rug between the unmade bed and the dresser. An open heart-shaped box and empty dark-brown paper candy cups lay scattered around her. A thin stream of drool trickled from her half-open mouth.

Heart banging against my ribs, I knelt beside her. "Sal?" I grasped her wrist. She had a pulse. She was alive. I rocked back on my heels unsteadily.

Sal snorted and jerked upright. Her hand flew upward and smacked my cheek.

I tumbled backward. "Sal! I thought—"

She collapsed backward. "Chocolate. Desk. On the desk," she muttered. "Been poisoned. Pois— Fish. Crackerjack," she mumbled, into the rug.

I rubbed my cheek. "It's all right. You'll be fine." Shakily, I pulled out my phone and called nine-one-one. The dispatcher promised to send paramedics.

"And the sheriff," I said, my voice thin. "Don't forget the sheriff."

Chapter Fourteen

"This is your emergency?" Staring down at Sal, the sheriff scowled and adjusted her broad-brimmed hat.

Two paramedics—Brayden and a man I didn't know—knelt on the throw rug around Sal. She mumbled incoherently and slapped the dark-haired paramedic's hand away. Brayden turned to look at me and arched his dark brows.

Sorry, I mouthed from the doorway. I wanted to help out inside, but the guest room just wasn't made for so many people. I also wanted to tackle the chalk markings Sal had left all over one wall. She seemed to have created her own murder board, and I was torn between photographing it and cleaning up the mess.

"We're going to need to take her to the hospital," Brayden said. "Until we know what was in these chocolates, we're running blind."

"But she'll be okay?" I asked anxiously.

"It helps that you found her so fast," he said and glanced at his partner. "Get the stretcher."

"On it." The other paramedic leapt to his feet and hurried from the room.

The sheriff nudged Sal's foot. "What did you take?" she asked.

"Poison. Chocolah... Mmph."

The sheriff shook her head, her blond ringlets swinging. "She looks stoned to me. Where'd she get the chocolates? And why are the names of all my murder suspects on that wall?"

"I don't know. It could have been—"

"Desk," Sal slurred. "Front desk. Thought for everyone." Her eyes rolled up in her head.

"Was there a card?" I asked her. Sal didn't respond. "If there was a card," I said, "it should be somewhere in here or at the front desk." Chest tight, I hurried to the waste basket beside the room's small, antique desk. There were a few gum wrappers in it, but it was otherwise empty.

"Check downstairs," the sheriff said. "I'll keep an eye on things up here."

"Right." I jogged from the room and down the B&B's green-carpeted steps to the foyer. Dixie had abandoned the computer at the reception desk and was nowhere to be seen.

The other paramedic bumped through the front door carrying a stretcher. "Temperature's dropping out there. Looks like it's going to snow."

"We need the water," I said automatically to his departing back. It had become something of a mantra in California. I strode around the desk and peered inside the waste bin there. There were a few scraps of paper, but no cards.

I sat behind my desk and called Arsen. It went to voicemail. "Arsen, something's happened. It looks like Sal's been... poisoned. And... Just call me when you can. Please." Biting my lip, I set down the phone. He'd call back.

I booted up the computer. Arsen had installed security cameras on the exterior doors. Maybe they'd caught something. I opened the program and studied the morning's video files. The Bigfoot group had gone in and out through the front door. Dixie had come and gone through the porch door to the kitchen. But no stranger had come inside Wits' End.

The door opened, and Finley walked in carrying Brooke. His sling had been discarded. His sunburnt cheeks were redder than usual with the effort.

Quickly, I rose. "What happened?"

Brooke winced, her ankle wrapped in a bandage. "I slipped on some ice in town. I didn't know who to call—"

"So she called me," he said. "It's just a mild sprain."

"You're not a doctor," she said tartly. "And I'm not one of your alpacas."

"Which is why I took her to that little clinic," Finley said. "They said she'll be all right but needs to stay off her foot for a couple weeks."

"Oh, no." I pressed my hand to my chest. How was he carrying her after his injury? His sling was nowhere in sight. "Your Bigfoot hunt. Search, I mean."

"What's with the ambulance?" he asked, jerking his head in the direction of the driveway.

"A guest ate some chocolate and got sick."

His brown eyes widened. "What? What chocolate?"

"That's what we're trying to find out. Apparently she got it from my desk. I don't suppose you saw anyone deliver a box of chocolate this morning?"

Finley paled. "No. No, I didn't. Is she going to be all right?"

Carrying Sal on a stretcher, the two paramedics maneuvered down the stairs. "No good," she muttered. "Bingo."

The sheriff followed behind them. "Find anything?" She held a plastic evidence bag pinched between two fingers. The chocolate box was inside it.

"No," I said, guilt twisting inside me. Finley stared after the departing paramedics.

"We'll get this analyzed," Sheriff McCourt said. "But I'll bet the hospital will get the results before we do."

Brooke coughed in Finley's arms. "Uh, do you mind—?"

He started. "Oh. Right. Sorry. I'll just..." He carried her up the stairs, and the sheriff shot me a questioning look.

"Slip and fall," I said.

The sheriff nodded and moved toward the front door.

"What if there's more than twenty thousand dollars in Kelsey's missing lock box?" I blurted.

Sheriff McCourt turned, one hand on the doorknob. "Then it belongs to Hannah."

"I heard Hannah and her parents were on the outs, they'd disinherited her. If she's in Kelsey's will or trust or whatever, then—"

"She had an incentive to murder her sister. Yes. I figured that out," she said dryly. "Any other brilliant deductions that weren't chalked on your B&B's wall?"

"Ah, no." But it had been lucky for the sheriff we'd caught Hannah digging in her sister's yard. Of course, she didn't need to say anything about it. We both knew.

The sheriff grunted and left. I stood there for a long moment behind the reception desk. Then I hurried into the kitchen.

Dixie sat at the table studying her phone. "What happened?" One of Arsen's bouquets sat centered on the round table. The kitchen smelled of roses.

"Sal ate some poisoned or drugged chocolates. I think someone left them on the reception desk."

"The old poisoned-Valentine's-chocolates gag? How trite."

"Trite or not, it worked," I snapped, then clawed my fingers through my hair. "Sorry. But Sal could have been seriously sick. Can you hold things down here? I want to ask if the neighbors noticed any delivery people on the court this morning."

Dixie shrugged, which I took for assent. I got a coat and scarf from my bedroom and went outside. The temperature *had* dropped, the sky darkening to iron gray. I almost returned inside for a pair of gloves, but I was on a schedule.

Hands jammed in my coat pockets, I hurried down the gravel driveway and around the picket fence. I jogged into my neighbors' yard, cluttered with toys. Trotting up the porch steps of the Victorian cottage, I knocked. A child wailed inside the house. I blew into my cold hands.

After a few moments, the door opened. My neighbor, Sarah, looked out. She held a child on one hip and what looked like a flyer advertising chickens for sale in her free hand. "Hi, Susan. What's up?" She shifted the toddler.

"Did you see anyone on the court this morning? A delivery van or a hiker, or just someone who doesn't live here?"

She shook her head. "No. Why? Has something happened?"

"I'm just trying to figure out who delivered some chocolates to the B&B." There was no sense worrying her.

She sighed. "A secret admirer? It must be Arsen, don't you think?"

"I don't think so. And it's really bothering me."

"There *was* a woman... I saw her wandering around. She looked kind of suspicious to me."

"Woman?" I asked sharply. "What did she look like?"

"Red hair. Tall. Big boned. She came to my house Saturday asking if I'd seen anyone around the court. She had a red parka."

A low sound escaped my throat. *Sal.* "I think you're describing one of my guests."

"Oh. Sorry. Have you ever raised chickens?"

"No. Are you thinking of buying some?" I nodded at the brochure in her hand.

"Eggs are getting so expensive. And I thought raising chickens would be educational for the kids." Something crashed inside the house, and she winced. "I'd better go." She shut the door.

A few flakes of wet snow dampened my cheeks as I jogged across the street and through an overgrown yard. The scent of marijuana oozed from the brown ranch house. A group of young men shared it. They generally kept to themselves, but they'd always been pleasant.

I eased past a dead bush and rang the bell. A brown bird gave a single, weak chirp from a nearby pine, gave up, and fluttered away. I rang the bell again.

Heavy footsteps sounded inside the house. A twenty-something man in a stained t-shirt and bare feet opened the door. He peered from beneath his shaggy brown hair. "Yeah?"

"Hi. I was wondering if you saw any strangers or delivery people on the court this morning?"

He stared blankly at me. Or at least I think he did. I couldn't see much of his eyes behind his shaggy bangs. "Why?" he asked.

"Someone delivered some... well, drugged chocolates to Wits' End."

His head bobbed. "What kind?"

"Of chocolates? I'm not sure."

"No, what kind of drugs?"

My gaze flicked toward the gray sky. It figured that part would pique his interest. "No idea. But one of my guests went to the hospital." And I needed to go there soon to see how she was doing.

His tanned face creased. "Bummer."

No kidding. "So, did you see anyone?"

"Nope."

I tried a different tact. "Did any of your roommates see anyone?"

"Nope."

"Okay," I said uncertainly. "Thanks."

I returned to Wits' End. The Carters stood beside the brochure rack in the foyer. Mrs. Carter studied the Doyle map.

Mr. Carter slid his brochure back into the rack. "We saw an ambulance. Is everything all right?"

"One of my guests ate some chocolate she found on my desk. Apparently, some, er, prankster had drugged it." I tugged guiltily at my collar. Obviously it had been connected to the murder we'd been investigating. It was a classic murder ploy—take out the cunning investigator. Unfortunately, Sal had gotten in the way. But it *could* have been a prankster.

"Good heavens." Mrs. Carter clapped a hand to her mouth. "I hope she'll be okay?"

"So do I." I glanced at my phone on the desk. Why hadn't Arsen returned my call? Reception could be iffy in the mountains though. "I'm going to the hospital shortly to check on her. I don't suppose you saw any strangers around Wits' End this morning, did you?"

They looked at each other and shook their heads. "Not me," Mr. Carter said. "Although I hate to say it, but Sal does seem like the type who might think that was a funny joke. Didn't she put laxatives in someone's bourbon?"

"It wasn't Sal," I said. "She was the one who got sick."

"Oh." He grimaced. "I'm sorry to hear that."

"If you think of anything," I said, turning, "please let me know."

"Oh, Susan," Mrs. Carter trilled. "We noticed a very interesting young man with you here earlier. Brownish hair? Broad shouldered? I wanted to introduce myself, but Carl thought we might be interrupting."

"That was probably Arsen," I said.

"He looked quite fit," she said. "Has he ever done any modeling?"

"Ah, no," I said.

"He would be perfect," her husband said. "Can we get his number from you?"

"Sure. Why not?" I scribbled his number on a brochure and handed it to them.

They muttered assurances that they would stay alert. I collected my purse, extracted a promise from Dixie to start cleaning the rooms, and drove to the hospital.

Doyle was too small for its own hospital, so we shared one with the county. It was a tall, modern building covered in blue glass. I walked through its sliding glass doors and into a high-ceilinged entry. On the right was a waiting area with a small library and an atrium with tropical plants. I ignored both and strode to the help desk.

From behind the narrow, high desk, a gray-haired volunteer in yellow smiled at me. "How can I help you?" she asked.

"A friend of mine was admitted this morning. Her name is Sal Bumpfiss."

"Of course." She pecked at the computer keyboard. "Bumpfiss?" She frowned. "How do you spell that?"

I spelled it for her, and she typed some more. Her head tipped. Her face creased. "I'm so sorry. She's gone."

Chapter Fifteen

Gone? I swayed and grasped the high desk, feeling the blood drain from my face. People walked past holding flowers. Low voices echoed off the hospital's pale tiled floor.

Sal was dead? Someone had sent poisoned chocolates to my B&B, a guest had eaten them. And Sal had been a good guest, even if she *had* spent time in jail.

And who was I to judge? *I'd* spent time in jail. Not for long, and the charges had been dropped, but still.

Sal had only been trying to help, and now she was dead. And this had happened at my B&B, my home. I was partly responsible. "When?" I whispered. "When did she pass?"

The elderly volunteer blinked. "Pass? She's not dead. She just left the hospital."

My knees weakened, and I gasped. "You're sure?"

"That's what it says here." She swiveled the computer monitor to face me. "It says she left twenty minutes ago."

"That's—" My mouth puckered with annoyance. Why hadn't she called me? I checked my watch. It was just after two o'clock. "Thank you."

I hurried back to Wits' End. Sal leaned against the reception desk and chatted with Dixie. Her parka lay pooled on the carpet at her feet.

"Hey," Dixie said from behind the desk. "Sal's here."

"Yes," I said tartly, "I can see that. How are you feeling?" It would have been nice if I'd known she'd walked out of the hospital before I'd trekked down there.

Sal tapped the head of an alien bobblehead with one finger. "A little shaky but okay. I didn't want to stick around in the hospital. The food's the pits. When I told them I didn't have insurance, they agreed I could go."

I shifted my weight. "Oh. That's—but—Do you need to lie down?" If the hospital wasn't going to take care of her, I owed it to her to do the job.

She set the bobblehead back on its shelf. "Nah. I'm ready to get back to work and find out who tried to poison me."

"Did the hospital tell you what you were drugged with?" I asked.

Sal shrugged one shoulder. "Some sort of heavy-duty tranquilizer. I'm okay, but what if a little thing like you had eaten it? You could have really been hurt."

"Tell me more about the candy," I said. "Where exactly did you find it?"

"Right here on the desk," Dixie said. "That's what Sal told me."

"There was no card," Sal said. "I figured it was part of your Valentine's Day special. Let me tell you though, it's not the kind of special I was expecting."

"No," I said absently. Arsen still hadn't called. "I don't suppose it would have been."

Sal inclined her head toward Dixie. "We were just talking about your murder victim."

"She's not my— Did you know anything about Kelsey's lock box?" I asked my cousin.

Dixie twined a lock of pink-tipped hair around one finger. "Nope, but it doesn't surprise me. Kelsey was an anarcho-capitalist. She didn't trust the system."

"Who does?" Sal asked, and the two women bumped fists.

"If she kept cash or gold it wouldn't surprise me," Dixie said.

"But Kelsey had a floor safe," I said. "Why bury something in her yard?"

"Maybe she liked to diversify," Dixie said.

Sal's round face contorted. She shook her head. "Ugh. Maybe I *will* lie down for a little bit. I'll see you two later." She climbed the stairs. Her footsteps sounded above us, and a door closed.

"What else were you two talking about?" I asked.

"Who could have put horse tranquilizers in those chocolates," Dixie said. "None of your suspects work with horses. But you can get it on the street. Or maybe online."

"They were actual horse tranquilizers?" I asked.

"That's what the hospital told Sal."

"It's like that Valentine's card." I smoothed the front of my blouse. "Nasty but not deadly." Though Sal was right. Who knew what the effect would have been on a smaller person?

"What Valentine's card?" Dixie asked.

I told her about the poisoned pen card. "It must be the same person," I concluded.

"Sounds like something Hannah would do. Not the drugged chocolates, but the card. She can be spiteful."

My belly raveled into a tight knot. And Hannah had been aware that I was snooping around. *And* we'd been the ones to catch her digging in her sister's yard. It was possible she'd done it. Or it could have been someone else. How much did I know about any of them? It was time to do some research online.

I returned to my kitchen and booted up the laptop on the table. Bailey rolled over in his dog bed by my feet and yawned.

I typed in Enrique Aguilar's name. The computer screen remained blank. I clicked the refresh button.

Nothing.

Impatient, I checked the wi-fi connection. I was connected, but the internet was moving at the pace of a jetlagged snail. After a moment, several articles popped up, all in various local business pages.

I clicked on one and drummed my fingers on the table. After another interminable wait, it opened.

Enrique had created and sold an augmented reality app. It was listed in the top five in the online store. That must have been the app Dixie had mentioned.

My eyes bugged. The app had sold for millions. Unless he was an incompetent money manager, it was unlikely Enrique was hurting for cash. Bailey sighed and leaned against my leg beneath the table.

I watched the second hand on the wall clock tick forward. Enrique's social media page opened. It was filled with nature photos, and they were good. Did this guy have *any* flaws?

Anselm Holmes had a single web page. It included a portfolio of his tiny art pieces and a contact form. I tried to scroll down to see more of his art, but all I got were white boxes with x's in them. I cursed. "What is *wrong* with the internet today?"

I returned to the search page and found an article about a showing Anselm had held in a local gallery. But when I clicked the headline, that webpage wouldn't open either.

Jiggling my foot, I checked my planner and jotted down the name of the gallery to visit tomorrow. At this rate, going in person would be quicker than searching online.

I opened the page of an online bookstore. That opened right away. I typed in Mrs. Carter's name. Nothing came up. She must use a pseudonym. Or the web page had frozen.

The kitchen door opened, and Sal ambled in carrying a laptop. "Your internet's slow as molasses in an Alaskan winter."

My neck tightened. "I know. I don't know what's going on today. I don't usually have these problems."

"It's frustrating. I'm trying to stream this new video game, and the play's lagging."

I stared. "Video game?" That was... She'd... Who came to Wits' End to play video games? I didn't have the bandwidth for that. No wonder the internet was slow. And I thought she'd gone to lie down.

"Yeah, I'm kind of a champion," she said modestly. "What are you doing?"

I exhaled through my nose. *Patience.* "I'm trying to search for information on my—our—suspects."

"Cool." She closed her laptop. A flurry of articles I'd clicked and given up on popped onto my screen. "What'd you find?" she asked.

I typed in Vida's name. All I found was a social media page with pictures of her and her friends.

Sal snorted. "Everyone's showing off online. Makes you wonder if they're really having fun offline. Hey, is this cyber stalking?"

"Of course not. That would be criminal." Next, I cyber stalked Victor. He had a page with a Sacramento talent agency. He worked as a male model.

Sal ogled his bare-chested photos. "Wasn't he delivering ice for Kelsey?" She snapped a photo of the page with her phone. "He must not get that much modeling work. I'll bet he's the killer."

Annoyed, I typed Hannah Delaney's name into the search engine. She had an interior design company. At least, that's what it seemed like. The website was a little unclear. It was definitely interior design—I thought. There were photos of sleek kitchens and bedrooms. But I didn't see anything about consultations.

Maybe she got paid for the products she promoted? The company's headquarters was listed as Doyle, but there was no address.

"Interior design is a con," Sal said. "You don't need a college degree to make your house pretty. Everyone says my apartment could have been designed by a pro, but that was all me."

"Uh, huh." I unearthed an article about Hannah in an online home magazine.

Doyle-based interior designer Hannah Delaney is the moto-moto mind behind some of the chillest spaces you'll ever experience.

We toured her modern, mission-based home studio, dedicated to integrated, environmentally responsive design, and asked Hannah about her design philosophy.

What inspires you?

"I get my groove on biophilia and biomimicry. I want my designs to restore and regenerate the soul. In the end, it's less about colors and textures and more about people's well-being. It's all about the concepting."

How can our readers shake up their own interiors?

"It helps to think about how to thread the juxtapositions together. That's the key to creating balance."

"Biophilia?" Sal said. "What kind of a pervert is she?"

"I don't think it's, ah... It's a love of nature." At least I thought it was. But what the heck was *moto-moto*? Some sort of design trend? Why was language today so confusing?

I searched some more. Hannah also had an Instagram page filled with more interior design images. But there were no personal pictures, and nothing that implicated her in a murder.

Sal read over my shoulder. "How does she get paid?"

"That's... I... I'm sure it all makes sense when you understand it." I drew down my brows. My circular reasoning hadn't made sense even to me.

"She's probably laundering money," Sal said. "Happens all the time."

"She's not laundering money," I said sourly.

"How else is she making money?"

I had no idea, and it was very frustrating. "I don't know."

I retyped her name in the search bar and added *Doyle*. The local crime blotter appeared, and I clicked the link.

Blotter: Sisters Flee Bar Fight on Tuesday Night

A twenty-six-year-old woman and a twenty-eight-year-old woman were found hiding behind an abandoned barn after fleeing the scene of a fight at Antoine's Bar Tuesday night. Sheriff's deputies determined the twenty-eight-year-old had begun the fight by swinging at her sister, Kelsey Delaney, after an argument at the country-western bar. Both women were determined to have been drinking.

"Antoine's," Sal mused. "That's the place on Main Street, right? We should go there."

"Yes," I said absently, "we should." The crime blotter report wasn't very detailed. But the article was dated three months ago. A waitress or Antoine himself would likely remember.

A physical fight, only three months before Kelsey's murder. The sheriff had to know. One of her deputies had arrested the two sisters.

I ran my finger between my watch and my wrist. What had been bad enough to cause Hannah and Kelsey to come to blows? Had they been fighting about Anselm, the man who'd dumped one sister for the other? Or something darker?

Chapter Sixteen

Sal stopped in front of Antoine's batwing doors. Heat and country music flowed from the bar and onto the raised, wood-plank sidewalk. Her mouth pursed. "Is this a western bar?"

I shivered. The afternoon was darkening, clouds blotting out the sun, and the temperature was dropping. "Yes, didn't I mention it?"

She stood unmoving. "No. You didn't." The batwing doors swung open, bumping her hip. A man in a three-piece suit sidled through them and from the bar. Her jaw worked silently, but that was the only part of her that moved. She seemed planted to the plank sidewalk.

"Is there a problem?" I finally asked.

"I'll say." Her shoulders twitched. "Nothing good ever happens to me in western bars. They're a jinx."

I shifted my weight. "That can't be true. It's only a bar."

She scratched the back of her head. "I dunno. Maybe it's a past life thing. Maybe there's something haunted about western bars. The weight of history…" She shook herself. "Oh well. Detecting ain't for the faint of heart, right?" She raised one hand and pushed open the swinging doors, striding inside.

I followed. Red paper hearts dangled from the brass chandeliers. Sawdust muffled our footsteps on the wooden floor. Patsy Cline played on the jukebox. Cowboys and men in suits lined up at the long bar. Only a few of the booths and tables had been taken.

I frowned. With the light crowd, there'd be fewer waitstaff this afternoon. We might not find someone who'd witnessed the fight.

But we were here, and it was still early. Maybe more customers and staff would arrive.

"That guy I punched was in a western bar." Sal shot a dark look at the men at the bar. "He was wearing a business suit too."

We made our way to an empty four-top and divested ourselves of our coats and scarves, draping them over the empty chairs. A waitress in boots and a skirt dotted with blue hearts bustled to our table. "Hi there. What can I get you?"

"Just coffee for me," I said.

"I'll have a Sierra Nevada pale ale," Sal said.

The waitress nodded and strode away, her skirt swinging.

"Coming here might not have been such a hot idea for me." Sal glanced uneasily at the jukebox. "We shouldn't stay long."

I checked my watch. "We won't. Arsen and I have plans for the evening." And the night was going to be perfect. I had no idea what he had in mind, but we'd be together, and that was all I needed.

She scowled at the paper heart dangling above our table. "Right. The big day."

"It's just another day, but it does make a good excuse for romance." I smiled at the thought. Arsen was *very* good at romance when he put his mind to it.

Her wide brow furrowed. "You two need an excuse?"

"No, I mean—that wasn't what I meant." I brushed back my hair. "It's just a nice reminder to put some extra effort into a relationship."

She heaved a sigh. "That's what happened to Bingo and me. At first, everything was easy. It just worked, you know? And then *we* had to work. That's when it all fell apart."

"Are you, er, sure it's over? It's just that you talk about him an awful lot," I added quickly. "And there's nothing wrong with that."

Her eyes flashed. "I can't be with a man who's embarrassed by me and doesn't accept me for who I am."

I wilted in my chair. I hadn't meant to suggest that. "No, of course not." If Arsen didn't accept me... But he did. He knew I wasn't perfect, and neither was he. But who was?

The waitress returned carrying our drinks on a tray. She set them on the table, then laid a red foil-wrapped heart beside each. "Happy Valentine's Day from Antoine's."

"Thanks," I said. "Say, were you working here three months—?"

"I'm not in the mood." Sal glowered at her chocolate.

I bit back a sigh. *Really?* I got why she might be off chocolate after being poisoned, even if she had bounced back remarkably quickly. But she didn't need to make a fuss right now.

The waitress's smile faded. "I hear you. My boyfriend broke up with me two days ago." She blinked rapidly. "I think... I think he just didn't want to deal with Valentine's Day."

Sal banged her fist on the table, and our drinks jumped. "I don't care if Valentine's Day is high pressure. If a guy can't take it, he ain't worth the trouble. It just shows weakness."

"I know," the waitress said. "And it's not like I was expecting a diamond ring."

"And how hard is a rose or a box of chocolates?" Sal asked.

The waitress shuddered, the tray dropping to her side. "My boyfriend—ex-boyfriend—gave me roses right before he dropped me."

"The creep," Sal snarled.

I shifted on the hard wooden chair. My thoughts flitted to the roses filling my kitchen.

"I think he thought they were some sort of consolation prize," the waitress continued. "But it just meant I was blindsided when he—" She hiccupped a sob and hurried away, one hand to her face.

My hands fisted on the table. All I'd wanted was a little information. Just a little. Was that so much to ask? Did Sal *have* to drive off the waitress at a key moment?

"Whoops," Sal said. "Guess we can't ask her about that bar fight now."

"No," I ground out. "We can't."

"But don't worry. Arsen's not going to break up with you just because he brought you all those flowers. That's a different situation." She laughed unconvincingly and sipped her beer.

"Of course it is." But something cold wriggled in my gut. He *had* been acting oddly. I hadn't seen much of him at all lately, and this went beyond him being busy. He'd been busy before but always had time to drop by for breakfast.

He'd been avoiding me.

But I hadn't been putting pressure on him over the day. Arsen was at his best when he was spontaneous. You can't put pressure on someone to be spontaneous.

I stood, my thigh knocking into the table. Sal's beer slopped. "I'm going to talk to Antoine about that fight. You can stay here if you want. I'll let you know what he says."

She eyed the bar. "Yeah. You go. I'll stay put."

Relieved, I nodded and crossed the floor to the bar. I squeezed between a cowboy and a man in a navy suit.

Antoine ambled down the length of the wooden bar toward me. "Hi, Susan. Can I get you something else?"

"Not right now, thanks. But have you got a minute?"

The bar owner nodded.

"I wanted to ask you about a fight that took place here about three months ago," I said. "It happened between Hannah and Kelsey Delaney."

He rolled his eyes. "Not much I can tell you. One minute they were sitting at that table where your friend is. The next, they were grabbing each other's hair and screaming."

"Do you have any idea what started it?"

He shook his head. "I was behind the bar. You might try asking your waitress. She was waiting their table. But you'd better hurry.

She just knocked off work." A cowboy hailed him, and Antoine moved off.

The man in the suit turned to grin at me. His face was attractive but florid, I presumed from too much drink. "It's always the women, eh?"

"In my experience," I said tartly. "It's rarely the women." Not that women were innocents. We could be plenty mean. We just didn't tend to punch each other. We used other, more subtle, weapons.

"Not in my experience," he said. "A woman socked me in a bar once."

"Did you deserve it?"

He laughed. "Hardly. She was crazy. I mean, *really* crazy."

I turned to go, and he grasped my arm. "Can I buy you a drink?"

I jerked my arm free. *Definitely too much to drink.* "No. I'm with a friend."

"I'll buy her a drink too." He swiveled in his chair to face our table. Sal met his gaze, and her eyes narrowed. His handsome face paled. "Oh, hell."

Sal stood up so fast she knocked her chair to the floor. "You!" She stormed to the bar.

He slithered from his barstool and backed away, hands raised. "Stay away from me." He met the gaze of a tall cowboy. "She's crazy. Keep her away from me."

"It's fine," I said, "it's okay. We were just leaving."

"I'm not leaving," Sal said. "I haven't done anything wrong."

"You assaulted me," he said loudly. "You went to jail."

"You said I was fat," she said.

"Whoa." The tall cowboy looked at him askance and edged away. "That's just asking for it, fella."

"Fighting words," his companion agreed and adjusted his fawn-colored hat.

Our waitress strode to the bar and handed Antoine her order pad. "He's been giving me trouble all night." She nodded to the guy in the suit.

"I have not," he said. "I was just being friendly. None of you women know how to take a compliment anymore. Plus, look at her. She's not exactly skinny."

Sal moved so fast I almost didn't see the punch. But I heard the *crack*. I gasped and pressed my hands to my face in sympathy.

The man staggered backward, one hand clapped to his eye. He bumped into the cowboy behind him.

"Hey!"

The man in the suit threw up his hands and whirled, elbowing the shorter cowboy in the jaw. I winced.

Barstools clattered to the floor. A chair flew through the air followed by a male body. Men jostled me. A basket of curly fries zoomed past my head.

On the street, a siren wailed. Strong arms grabbed me, and I was stumbling backward between Sal and the waitress.

"Move, move, move," Sal shouted.

The two women dragged me down the hallway toward the bathrooms. The waitress opened a side door. Sal thrust me, blinking, into the parking lot.

"He's got a restraining order against me." Sal panted. "I can't get arrested."

"My car," the waitress said.

And then I was jammed, pulse thumping, into the back of a beige Toyota that smelled of wet dog. The Corolla rocketed from Antoine's rear parking lot. We drove past two sheriff's SUVs going in the opposite direction.

Sal punched the ceiling. "Woot! I think we're clear."

I glared at the back of her red hair. Clear? Someone could have been hurt. I could have been hurt. Hand trembling, I pulled a curly fry from my hair and looked for a place to put it.

"Where to?" the waitress asked.

Sal twisted in her seat. "Maybe it's not such a good idea to go back for your car just now, Sue."

"No," I agreed shakily. I tried to steady my breathing. At least I was getting some time with the waitress. It would just be silly to waste the opportunity. I cleared my throat. "Speaking of fights—"

The waitress groaned. "Do we have to?"

"Were you there when Hannah and Kelsey Delaney got into a fight at Antoine's?" I asked.

"Yeah. You want to go to Hannah's?"

"Why not?" I sighed. At this point, I didn't have any better ideas. I ate the fry. "What happened? Do you know what started the fight?"

"A guy. What else?"

"That Anselm dude?" Sal asked.

"Yeah." She shook her head. "You ask me, he's trouble. Hannah's better off."

"But the heart wants what the heart wants." Sal sniffed and stared out the passenger window.

"But haven't Anselm and Hannah been broken up for a while now?" I asked. "Why fight over him now? I mean three months ago." I realized my seatbelt wasn't fastened and tugged it across my chest.

"I didn't catch the *whole* conversation," the waitress said.

"But you caught part of it?" I jammed the seatbelt into the latch. It popped out. I tried again. No luck. Annoyed, I jammed the belt in the latch again and wiggled it.

The waitress glanced in the rearview mirror. "I think Hannah said Anselm was just after Kelsey's money. But like I said, I only got bits and pieces."

"But I thought Kelsey was on the outs with their parents too." The latch clicked, and I relaxed against my seat. "Didn't they have all the money?"

"Yeah," the waitress said. "But she always said she didn't need her parents. And she sounded like she meant it."

"Ice sculptresses can't make that much," I reasoned. "Why drop one disinherited sister for another disinherited sister if he was after money?"

The waitress shrugged. "No idea."

"Sounds like sour grapes to me," Sal said.

"Probably," the waitress agreed. "But I definitely heard *you can't trust him*, something something, *after your money*, something. And then Kelsey laughed, and Hannah got mad, and they were fighting." She turned into the parking lot for Hannah's luxury condo complex.

"You think she still lives here?" Sal asked. "Hannah was moving last time we saw."

Rats. Hannah probably had already moved. Clearly, the fracas in the bar had rattled my thinking. But I wanted out of the car. The wet-dog smell was getting to me. "We can try."

"You two need a lift back?" the waitress asked.

"No thanks," I said. "We'll get a ride share."

She dropped us in front of the sheltered paving stone walkway. Sal and I walked into the foyer. The beefy guard looked up from behind the curved security desk.

"Hey, Frankie." Sal strolled up to him and they did a complicated hand greeting.

I jammed my hands into my jacket pockets. When had they gotten to know each other well enough to do that?

"We're just going up to see Hannah," Sal said.

The guard frowned. "Does she know you're coming? She's moving out, you know."

"Oh, yeah," she said. "Just buzz us up, will ya?"

"Cool, cool," he said.

I followed Sal to the elevator. "When did you get to know Frankie?" I asked in an undertone.

"You know how it is. I saw him around town. We got to talking. He's okay."

We rode up in the elevator and walked down the hall, our shoes tapping on the shiny wood floor.

"All right," I said. "When we talk to Hannah, I think we should—"

Sal banged on the elegant door. Silently, it swung open. My stomach dropped. "Oh, no," I whispered.

"Looks like we're in luck," Sal said and strode inside.

"No," I hissed. "Wait." I hurried after her. What was she doing? *Everyone* knew it was never a good thing when the door just opened like that.

"Uh, oh." Sal stopped short, and I bumped into her broad back.

I edged around her. The furniture was gone. Behind the picture windows, the sun glittered low over the mountains.

Hannah lay on the bare floor beneath them. Chocolates and gold foil wrappers lay scattered on the wood floor beside an open heart-shaped box.

"What's with these drugged chocolates?" Sal said. "Is someone trying to K.O. all of Doyle?"

A chill traveled up my spine. "She's not knocked out," I whispered.

"She looks pretty out of it to me." Sal moved toward the fallen woman, and I grasped her arm.

I shook my head, acid climbing my throat. "She's dead."

Chapter Seventeen

We waited in the complex's lobby for Sheriff McCourt. I didn't trust Sal not to accidentally touch something inside the apartment. And as awful as it was, there was nothing we could do for Hannah.

Besides, if we stayed with the body I thought I might cry. The sense that this should have been preventable, that I could have stopped it, clung to me like a sticky film.

Magazines lay artfully arranged on the lobby's low coffee table. Not a single fleck of dust marred its polished surface. The floor gleamed perfection. And upstairs, a body waited.

A knot tightened in my throat. You never got used to murder. I didn't think I wanted to be the kind of person who could.

Frankie watched us from behind the tall guard desk. "She wasn't home?"

"She—" I exhaled raggedly. "Was there a delivery for her earlier today?"

He nodded. "Oh, yeah. A box of chocolates."

"Who delivered it?" I forced myself to ask. Telling myself that I'd failed, that I should have seen this coming, that I should have done something, wouldn't help Hannah now.

"I dunno," Frankie said. "Someone left it lying against the door this morning." He nodded toward the glass door to the foyer.

The sun had slid behind the mountains. I couldn't make out much beyond the windows in the darkening gloom.

"Delivery people do that sometimes," he continued. "I called Hannah, and she came and got it."

"Did you see who the delivery person was?" I asked. "A man? A woman?"

He shook his head. "Nah."

"Maybe there's a camera outside." Sal rose from her chair and strode to the door.

"Something wrong?" the guard asked.

I wasn't sure what to say. But he'd learn soon enough though. "I'm sorry. There's no easy way to say this. Hannah's dead."

His broad face whitened. "But she was fine this morning. I saw her." He strode from around his curving desk and toward the elevators. "I gotta get up there."

"I've called the sheriff," I said. "She should be here any minute. She'll want you to escort her upstairs," I lied. She'd want no such thing. But she wouldn't want him accidentally tampering with the crime scene either.

"But... the delivery," he said. "What does that have to do with anything?"

"Maybe nothing," I said. "There was an open box of chocolates near her body. I just thought—"

"Poison," he croaked, and I nodded.

Sal returned inside. "There are cameras out here. They're a little hidden, but they're there."

"Yeah," Frankie said. "Yeah. Hold on." He hurried behind his desk and tapped at his computer keyboard. "Okay, okay. Yeah. Got him. Look."

We came to the high desk, and he turned the monitor to face us. "Look. It's a guy."

A male figure, his jacket collar up, a baseball hat hiding his face, walked down the covered walkway. With gloved hands, he set a slim box beside the door, turned, and exited the screen.

Sal grunted. "He knew that camera was there. Look. You can't see his face. Or his hands. Or even his ears. Ears are very distinctive."

"It's definitely a man though," I said. "That's helpful."

Sal shook her head. "With all the guys in Kelsey's life? We've talked to three, but she could have had dozens on the string. I told you, if a small person had eaten that chocolate, it could have done worse."

"But it wasn't the same chocolate as you ate," I said. "Yours came in dark brown paper cups. Hers was in gold foil."

"Chocolate you ate?" Frankie asked. "Were you poisoned too?"

"Someone left drugged chocolates at Wits' End," Sal said.

His eyes widened. "Are you saying there's someone dropping off boxes of poisoned chocolate around town? For just anyone?" he yelped.

"No," I said. "I'm saying..." What was I saying? They had definitely been two different boxes of chocolate. But there was no law saying a killer had to use the same brand.

The glass door slid open. Sheriff McCourt strode into the foyer with two deputies. "Witsend. Where is she?" She whipped off her broad-brimmed hat and ruffled her curly blond hair. "I got held up by a fight at Antoine's, and—" Her cornflower gaze narrowed. "What's Bumpfiss doing here?" She jabbed a finger at Sal.

"We, ah, discovered the body," I said. "Together."

"Yeah," Sal said. "We were nowhere near Antoine's."

The sheriff's brows slashed downward. "You—"

"Hannah's upstairs," I said before we could go any farther down that road.

"I know the way." The sheriff tucked her hat beneath one arm and walked to the elevator. "Denton, secure any security video and get the guard's statement. Witsend, Bumpfiss, you two stay where you are."

We dropped into two soft leather chairs in the corner of the foyer. The deputy, a fair-haired, blue-eyed young man, spoke in low tones to Frankie. Sal picked up a magazine and leafed through it. Time passed.

I fidgeted and checked the clock on my phone. You couldn't rush a murder investigation, and murder took precedence over romance. But—and yes, I know this was inappropriate—I hoped to have time to change before my date. Normally, I wouldn't give it a thought. Not after discovering a body. But Arsen had been acting so distant. We were fine of course, but... were we?

Sal eyed me. "You got a date or some—" Her mouth puckered. "You do have a date. It's the big day. Are you gonna be late?"

"I might be. I'd better give Arsen a call." Murder trumped a Valentine's evening. And my romantic issues didn't mean a whole lot in the face of a life taken. But it wasn't like him not to return my call. I phoned Arsen.

"Susan," he answered a little breathless. "Hey, I got a weird call from one of your guests about some modeling?"

"Oh, yeah," I said, impatient. I swept a lock of hair from my forehead. "Mrs. Carter."

"She said you gave her my number," he said slowly.

"I didn't think you'd mind." My chest hardened. Modeling? He got a message about modeling but no mention of my call about Sal being poisoned?

"No, but... You're on board with this?"

"Why not?" I said tartly. I bet they'd give him all sorts of sportswear. Not that he needed a discount or anything.

"Is something wrong? You sound funny."

"Did you get my message? About Sal?"

"No, what happened to Sal?"

"She was poisoned." And that was old news at this point. Why was I harping on it? "She's okay. But Arsen... I'm at Hannah's. She's... Well, she's dead. It looks like someone killed her."

"My God." His voice dropped. "I'm sorry. Are you okay?"

"Yes." My throat tightened with guilt. "I'm just waiting for the sheriff. I mean, she's here, but you know how these things can drag on. She wants me to stay and make a statement, I think."

"Of course you have to stay."

"The thing is, I'm not sure how long I'll be here. And I know you had plans, or maybe a reservation or—"

"It's fine," he said, brisk. "We can do it another night."

"Are you sure? It's Valentine's Day, and—"

"I'm sure," he said firmly. "We don't need a special day on the calendar to act like a couple. We'll reschedule. You're sure you're okay? You're somewhere safe? The sheriff's there?"

"Yes, I'm fine. Sal's with me and Denton and—"

"Um—Sorry, I have to go. I'll talk to you later."

"I love—"

But he'd hung up. I bit my lip and stared at the phone. Surely I'd imagined the sense of relief in his voice? I straightened. Yes, I'd definitely imagined it.

Hadn't I?

"He said no problem, right?" Sal nudged my arm with her elbow, the magazine in her hands rustling.

"Ah, yes." I looked down, fumbling my phone into my big purse. I swallowed down the hard lump in my throat. "No problem."

She closed the magazine. "So why don't you look like there's no problem? What gives?"

"Nothing. I just... I don't know. He seemed almost relieved." And he'd sounded a bit odd about the modeling for the Carters. I didn't care if he modeled or not. It was his choice. But had I done wrong giving her his number?

Sal shrugged. "He probably is. Valentine's Day puts pressure on people. There are all sorts of unrealistic expectations." She drummed her fingers on the leather arm of her chair. "But back to business. Why kill Hannah? Did she know too much? Or was killing her part of the plan all along? Maybe Hannah was the real target, and Kelsey had to die so the plan could go on?"

"Please don't talk to each other," the deputy said from beside the guard desk.

I flushed. Of course. The sheriff didn't want us to contaminate each other's stories. I should have known better.

"So what do you think?" Sal whispered. "About this murder?"

"I think we should be quiet," I whispered back.

"I said, no talking, please," the blond deputy said.

We fell silent. Sal shifted in her seat. She picked up a magazine, put it down. "We're key witnesses," she hissed. "We found the body. You'd think we'd be important enough to interview first."

"Ms. Witsend," the deputy said sharply, and I twitched. "Please, go stand over there." He pointed to the other end of the foyer, where a potted Ficus tree stood.

"Well, that's just dumb," Sal said.

"Ms. Witsend." The deputy scowled.

I froze in my chair, as if stillness would make me invisible. Getting told off by him was more than a little embarrassing. We knew each other, and I knew I'd been in the wrong.

"Do you want her to face the wall too?" Sal asked.

The deputy's face reddened. "Susan!"

My face grew hotter. Like a school child being sent to stand in the corner, I rose and trudged to the spot.

Chapter Eighteen

It's a funny thing about expectations. No matter how well you plan, they can be dashed. But until yesterday, I hadn't believed I'd *had* any Valentine's expectations. Had I been putting pressure on Arsen and hadn't realized it? But that was all just background noise to my sick sense of responsibility for Hannah's death.

"I don't see why you're blaming yourself." Sal plucked a piece of bacon from the plate in the kitchen.

Standing at the stove, I turned to glare. I really needed to start enforcing my no-guests-in-the-kitchen rule. Grabbing bacon off the plate was a little unsanitary.

Though stealing bacon *was* the sort of thing Arsen would do, if he were here. So by criticizing Sal, I was a hypocrite on top of everything else. And why *wasn't* Arsen here, cadging bacon and pancakes as usual? He couldn't really be upset I'd given Mr. and Mrs. Carter his number. Could he?

"I'm not blaming myself," I said.

"Huh." Sal cocked her head, strode to the blue-painted cupboards, and scrounged up a plate and fork.

I had to give Sal one thing—she was an early riser. It was still dark outside the curtained window above the sink.

She came to the stove and speared two pancakes from the skillet. From his dog bed beneath the table, Bailey raised his head, interested.

"Now we know two things," she said. "One, Hannah was an integral piece of our murder investigation. Two, one of those guys did it. Or some other guy we don't know about. But it was a guy for sure."

"How fortunate, since we can't go back to the Irish pub to question Vida," I said bitingly. I wasn't sure if I'd ever be able to show my face there again. If I was persona non grata in Antoine's too now, I didn't know what I'd do. I *liked* Antoine. And I never had this problem in bars until Sal had arrived.

Oblivious to my tone, she brandished her fork. "Exactly."

The porch door opened, and Arsen stuck his head in. My heart loosened with relief. He wasn't avoiding me.

"Happy belated Valentine's Day." He strode into the kitchen and presented a heart-shaped chocolate box with a flourish.

Sal and I recoiled. "You've got to be kidding me," Sal said.

He stopped short. "What? What's wrong? You love chocolate."

"Someone left a drugged box of chocolates on the reception desk yesterday," I said. "Sal ate them." Which he would have known sooner if he'd returned my call.

"Whoa." His tanned brow furrowed. "That's how you were poisoned? Susan mentioned it, but it didn't sound like a big deal. I figured it was food poisoning. I'm sorry, Sal. I should have asked about you first."

She shrugged. "It was no biggie. I've got a tough metabolism."

"Susan, why didn't you tell me?" He pulled me into a hug.

I *tried*. "And it looks like that's how someone killed Hannah," I mumbled into his chest. But despite my annoyance, I relaxed slightly.

Arsen stepped backward and studied me. His jaw set, and he gave a curt nod. "All right. Let's bring it back to Wits' End. What about the B&B's security cameras?"

"I checked them," I said. "No one came in and out through the doors Monday morning who didn't belong." Which meant someone who *had* belonged had left the chocolates. And that was a little disturbing. None of my friends or guests could be involved in the murders. Could they?

"What about the windows?" Sal asked through a mouthful of pancake.

"The cameras cover the windows too." Arsen raked his hand through his whiskey-colored hair. "I'll run background checks on your guests."

I shook my head. "I don't think—"

"Good idea," Sal said. "You can't trust people are who they say they are."

My jaw tightened. "Yes, I do. There's nothing wrong with my guests."

"This is serious, Susan," Arsen said. "You're sure the candy was left Monday morning?"

"It wasn't there Sunday night when I locked up," I said.

"Then it had to have been from someone inside the B&B," he said.

My stomach churned bitterly. "Is it possible one of my guests is connected to Kelsey and Hannah? But they all seem so... normal."

He took me into his arms again, and all my doubts evaporated. Of course he cared. He'd just been a little distracted. And once he got undistracted, he'd explain.

"We'll figure this out," he said. "Don't worry. I'm good at this."

We. We were a team again. "I know you are," I said, "but—"

He glanced at Sal and kissed my forehead. "I'll get right on it." He strode outside.

Wait. What? What had happened to we? Teamwork? The two of us solving the murder together?

"A real man of action, ain't he?" Sal said.

"Yes, but..." I hurried to the porch door and walked outside. Arsen was already vanishing around the corner of the Victorian. I rocked on the edge of the top porch step. It was almost as if he'd been... eager for an excuse to escape.

No. I was overthinking things. Arsen was one of those people who said what they thought and meant what they said. He said we'd figure this out, and we would. Together. Later.

Pensive, I returned inside. Sal helped me put the breakfast things out for the guests. In the octagonal breakfast room, I lit tea lights beneath the warming trays. I blew out my match and adjusted the toaster on the sideboard.

Sal poured herself a glass of orange juice from a carafe. "Here's what I'm thinking. I'll stick around here for breakfast and keep an eye on those Bigfoot hunters."

If only I could get her to stay at the B&B all day so I could get some investigating in. Though maybe...

"You know..." I turned and leaned against the windowsill. A chill seeped from behind the closed glass. "You've got an inside track with that group. You've already gone on one Bigfoot hunt."

Her round face brightened. "You're thinking I should hang out with them today too and keep my ears open? That's a great idea." She clapped my shoulder, and I staggered sideways. "We'll split our resources. What are you going to do?"

"Anselm Holmes had a showing at a local gallery. I thought I'd go there this morning and see what the gallery owner has to say about him."

Her forehead creased. "Sounds like a longshot if you ask me."

"Most likely," I agreed. "You'll probably get much better intel with the Bigfoot seekers."

"Well, you know your business. I'll take Bigfoot, you take the gallery."

Yawning, Finley wandered into the breakfast room. He rubbed his injured arm. "Hello, Susan. Hi, Sal."

"Hi," I said. "How's Brooke?"

"Hobbling," he said. "Would it be okay if I brought breakfast up to her?"

I grimaced. I should have thought of that myself. "Of course. I'll get you a tray." I walked to the kitchen.

Sal trailed behind me. "This could be a problem," she said in an undertone. "The group is splitting up, and I can't be in two places at once. What if Brooke stays at Wits' End?"

The porch door opened, and Dixie ambled in. "Yo." She bent and scratched her ankle, rucking up the hem of her cargo pants. "Did Arsen pop the question yesterday?"

My stomach dove all the way to my tennis shoes. "No. Why would you think—? No."

She shrugged. "With all those flowers, I figured he was either working up to a proposal or an apology."

"Our Valentine's was canceled," I said. "Not that it matters. Valentine's Day is so overrated. We don't need it to prove our love." I frowned. Had that sounded defensive? Because it had felt a little defensive. But between the murders and the poisoned chocolates, I was starting to go a little *off* the holiday.

"Hannah Delaney was killed," Sal said. "Poisoned."

Augh. I should have been the one to tell Dixie. What was wrong with me? Who cared about my love life? Another woman was dead.

Dixie's backpack dropped to the linoleum floor. My cousin's face paled. "What? She's dead?"

"I'm sorry," I said. "I know you two were friends."

"Not really," my cousin said distantly. "But..." She pulled out a wooden chair and sat at the small, round table. "I can't believe it."

Sal patted her shoulder. "It's a cold, brutal world. Sorry, kid. The question is, are you going to help us catch who did it?"

Dixie looked up. "What happened?"

"I'm not sure," I said, "but it looked like she was poisoned. A man hiding his face delivered a box of chocolates to her condominium complex."

"That's..." Dixie pursed her lips. "But the chocolates you ate didn't kill you," she said to Sal accusingly.

Sal wandered to the butcher-block counter and shrugged. "Go figure."

"They looked like different chocolates," I said. "But two boxes of tampered chocolates is a strange coincidence."

Sal grabbed another pancake off the plate. "So we need you to stick around Wits' End today. I'm going to keep tabs on the Bigfoot group. But Brooke might decide she can't go out on that ankle. You'll need to watch her."

"I thought you said a man delivered the poisoned chocolates," Dixie said. "That would mean Mr. Carter or Finley. I checked your security videos from yesterday after Sal's little problem," she added. "No one came in or out of Wits' End who wasn't a guest Monday morning."

"I know," I said, worried. I'd thought our number of murder suspects was narrowing. But now we had two more. And they were both staying in my house.

I pushed open the art gallery's glass door. A bell above it jangled.

The gallery was one of those wide-open spaces. Its burnished, light-colored wood floors and walls glowed. Large, square windows faced Main Street and displayed abstract paintings. Though I prefer the classics, I had to admit their bold colors lifted my spirits.

It was also one of the only businesses on Main Street without paper hearts in its windows. So there was that. *Stupid holiday.* Everyone knew it had been invented to sell cards and candy.

A woman in a black dress wafted toward me. "Good morning." She touched the elegant streak of silver in her long, near-black hair

"Oh," I said. "Hi."

She motioned toward the paintings. "If there's anything you'd like to know about the art, please ask. All of our artists are locals."

"So I've heard. I'm Susan Witsend."

She waited, a bland expression on her face, her head cocked.

"I run Wits' End. The B&B."

Her face cleared. "Ah, that funny little B&B with the UFO in the roof. Yes, I've heard of it. Are you looking for something for your inn?"

"Ah. No. The paintings here are lovely, but we've pretty much committed to the UFO theme."

Her smile grew pained. "I see."

"I was wondering about an exhibit you had last year, with Anselm Holmes."

"A talented designer."

"Designer? Not artist?"

She motioned toward an abstract painting in autumnal colors. "Art has a certain fire to it. There is technical competence, and then there's soul, when the artist brings something of himself or herself to the work. I'm afraid Anselm has the former, but not the latter."

"But you hosted his work."

"Yes, we do make an effort to support local talent. His didn't sell as well as we'd hoped, however."

"I see. You're saying he's not very successful."

"Did I?" She lifted a dark brow.

"Then he *is* successful."

"I suppose it depends on how one defines success."

I gritted my teeth. I don't think of myself as an unsophisticated person. Not that sophistication matters. But here, in this gallery, I was starting to feel out of my depth. "I'm defining it with sales."

"In that case, no." She smiled ruefully. "I'm sure he'd be happy to sell you a piece, though I don't think he's broken into the UFO genre."

"Is there a UFO genre?"

"Yes. It's mostly terrible. But it would be fine for your little B&B, I'm sure."

My mouth tightened. I was fairly certain I'd just been insulted. But this was murder, and I was bigger than petty offenses. *Mostly.* "What else can you tell me about Anselm Holmes?"

"What else?"

"About him. As a person. Or anything."

Her brown eyes widened. "Why? You're not a journalist, so I know you're not writing an article on the local arts scene."

"It's for my blog. I mean, for the Wits' End blog," I said, talking too fast. Coming up with things to write about was always a challenge. I might as well write a post about art in Doyle, then it wouldn't be a lie. "Was Anselm in any way... unusual? For an artist?"

She barked a laugh. "Hardly. He's thin skinned and convinced of his own greatness. Of course, not every artist shares those traits, but they're hardly unusual."

He hadn't seemed that way to me. I'd found his humility charming. Maybe it had been knocked into him after the disastrous showing. "Did anything odd happen during his showing?"

"No."

Defeated, I gathered up brochures about the gallery's showings and trudged to my Crosstrek. Sal had been right. This had been a longshot, and it hadn't panned out. Aside from the blog article I'd gotten out of the adventure.

Something thumped the raised sidewalk behind me. "Well, well," Mrs. Steinberg said. "Sticking your nose into another murder, I see."

Chapter Nineteen

On the elevated sidewalk, I leaned against my SUV. Mrs. Steinberg had already encountered me investigating the first murder. She could hardly be surprised I was looking into the second. But pointing that out would be churlish.

Bundled in a thick black coat, she took a puff of an e-cigarette. "Well? Cupid got your tongue?" Raspberry-scented smoke curled around her head.

My face spasmed, the movement reflected in her Jackie-O sunglasses. "Cupid can stuff it," I said.

"What happened? Did Arsen drag you on a romantic ten-mile death march up the mountain?"

I forced a smile. It wasn't Arsen's fault Valentine's Day had been a bust. And it was a silly day anyway. "I had to cancel. I got stuck at the crime scene." Well, it was *partly* true.

"I heard about Hannah." She bent her head and studied the ground. "What happened? Word is it was poison." She leaned against a wooden post. Ivy trailed from a basket hanging from it.

I nodded. "That's what it looked like. Poisoned chocolates. What else have you heard?"

"Nothing," she said bitterly. "My sources have dried up. You?"

I sympathized. There was nothing worse than feeling out of the loop. "Kelsey was involved in a romantic tri—quadrangle." *Square?* "And one of her partners was her sister's ex-boyfriend."

"Which would give her sister a motive for murder, except now she's dead too."

"Exactly. There's a waitress at the Irish pub who also lost a boyfriend to Kelsey, but she has an alibi."

"Who? Not Vida."

"Yes, Vida," I said, surprised. "You know her?"

"No." She took a long draw from her e-cigarette. A car roared past on the street behind me leaving a trail of exhaust.

I adjusted my scarf. "Well, she had to be at work before eleven, and Kelsey was last seen alive at eleven-thirty. I don't see how she could have snuck away."

"Alibis can be broken," Mrs. Steinberg growled.

"Vida's seems pretty solid. I think the killer is one of the men Kelsey was involved with. These open relationships never work. Someone always gets their feelings hurt."

"Cupid's arrow gone awry, eh?" She puffed a raspberry-scented smoke ring. "It wouldn't be the first time. Love gone wrong is one of the prime motives for murder."

My stomach burned. Had *my* love gone wrong? Had I been taking Arsen for granted? Had he gotten bored? He was an action-oriented type of man, and I, well, wasn't. Not if I didn't have to be. I'd much rather putter in the Wits' End kitchen, dreaming up new breakfast casseroles. I should never have given the Carters his number without asking him first.

"Where's Arsen in all this?" Mrs. Steinberg asked. "He's usually up to his neck in these investigations too."

A thread broke inside my chest. "Oh. He's been really, ah, busy. With work."

She arched a snowy brow. "When has he ever cared about work?"

"He takes his security company very seriously."

Beneath her dark glasses, her expression turned dubious. "Arsen Holiday? Taking work seriously? What's going *on* in this town?" she burst out. "Everything's changing. I don't like it. Two people are killed, and I'm reduced to—" Her mouth pinched.

"Asking me what's going on? Don't feel bad. I don't know what's going on either. And Arsen *has* been acting odd," I blurted. "It's almost like he's been... avoiding me."

Saying it out loud didn't make me feel any better. Especially when Mrs. Steinberg didn't tell me I was being ridiculous and Arsen loved me. Instead, she threw me a contemplative look.

"If that's true," she said, "you need to find out why. Best to tackle these things head on."

My heart numbed. Was that why I'd confided in her? Because I'd known she'd give me the hard facts, even if I didn't want to hear them? "But how?"

"Have you asked him what's going on?"

"No." Though it was the obvious solution. "I suppose I should."

"Ha. Do you go around asking suspects if they're the murderer?" Her lips curled.

"Well. No."

"No, you investigate. So? Investigate."

"Investigate Arsen? That doesn't seem right."

She blew another smoke ring. "It's your funeral. Who are your suspects?"

"For investigating Arsen?"

"For the murders."

"Oh." I rattled off the names. "What's weird is I saw Hannah digging in her sister's yard the other day. She said she was looking for a cash box Kelsey may have buried. But Kelsey had a safe. We found it beneath a floorboard in her barn."

"Was the safe empty?"

"There was a trust and such, but no valuables." I straightened off my Crosstrek. A clump of snow slithered from a nearby pine and thumped to the ground.

"Cleaned out by the killer, no doubt. You don't think it was cash Hannah was looking for?"

"I suppose it could have been. Apparently Kelsey didn't trust the banking system. It just seems odd."

"Love and money." She shook her silvery head. "I knew their parents. The father was a bully, and the mother went along with it. I guess it's no surprise young Kelsey bucked the system. Her sister was always more pliable though. It's a sad story, and one that isn't unique. That said, having some gold and silver is never a bad idea if things go wrong."

"Or Bitcoin," I said.

The old lady pursed her lipsticked mouth. "I won't buy anything I don't understand, and I don't understand cryptocurrency. Anything that's electronic can be deleted. What if a hacker gets to it?"

"You can keep it offline in a digital wallet. A hacker can't get to that."

"Huh!"

"It's not that complicated." Arsen had explained everything to me. "It's just a digital currency that uses a blockchain."

"What's a blockchain?"

"It's ah, you know, for security." It had made sense when Arsen had told me about it. Mostly. But I didn't remember all the details. There had been a *lot* of details.

"But what *is* it?"

"It's a... a... public ledger," I said triumphantly. Ha. I'd remembered that at least.

"But what's a public ledger?"

"It's, ah, distributed?"

She snorted. "Never mind. I'll stick to precious metals." She turned and stomped away.

I coughed. All right. So maybe I didn't know much about Bitcoin. But I knew Arsen. He was a good man. If something was up... He might not tell me about it right away, but he'd do the right thing.

I drove home. In the kitchen, I divested myself of my hat and coat. The vacuum roared upstairs.

Guiltily, I hurried up the steps to help Dixie. Bailey lay in the open doorway to room six. The vacuum cleaner shut off as I stepped inside. Dixie wound the cord around its handle.

"What did I miss?" I asked.

"Cleaning. I'm done." She arched her back, stretching, hands on the hips of her camo pants.

"You got all the rooms?"

"All but room four. It's got a DO NOT DISTURB sign on it." She sneered. "Brooke and Finley have been holed up in there all morning. I thought they were divorced."

"They are."

She huffed a laugh. "Some divorce. When people decide to stay apart, they should just stay apart. *Valentine's* Day."

"Mm." My new anti-Valentine's stance was feeling more and more like sour grapes. Everyone was having a romantic Valentine's but me and Sal. Even *Dixie* had a guy.

My cousin braced a fist on her hip. "No, *I think it's romantic*?"

"Of course it's romantic. I'm very happy for them."

"You don't sound happy."

"I'm thrilled," I snapped. "Come to Wits' End and find romance. That was the whole point of our Valentine's promotion."

"I thought it was to make money."

"That too. Thanks for finishing the rooms." I grabbed the cleaning bucket, turned, and stomped down the stairs. I shouldn't be so grumpy. If Brooke and Finley had repaired their fractured relationship, that was wonderful news.

The front door opened, and the Carters trooped inside smiling and holding mittened hands. "Have you heard?" Mrs. Carter stomped snow off her boots. "Brooke and Finley are getting back together. I can't imagine a more romantic Valentine's."

Mr. Carter smiled down at his wife. "We may not have found Bigfoot, but we found something much more precious."

Her cheeks pinked. "This vacation has brought a spark back into our marriage too. Wits' End is just magical."

"I'm so glad." I forced a smile. It was just silly to feel jealous. I'd put together this promotion for my guests, not for myself.

But if I were being honest, a small part of me had hoped the air of romance would rub off on Arsen and me. Was that manipulative? Maybe I *had* been putting too much pressure on Arsen.

"Is something wrong, dear?" Mrs. Carter asked me.

"What? No. It's wonderful to hear."

"Do assure Arsen that you're okay with his modeling, will you?" Mrs. Carter said. "He told me he'd have to ask you about it."

"I did. I just need to... Put this away." I raised the bucket in my hand.

"Of course," Mr. Carter said. "We won't keep you."

I hurried into the kitchen, remembered the bucket belonged in the upstairs closet, and set it on the table to deal with later. I pulled my planner from my purse and opened it on the table. I just needed to get organized. That was all.

I stared blankly at the planner. It gave me nothing. No fresh ideas. No inspiration. No plans of action.

I shut the leather-bound book. Grabbing a stick of incense and a matchbook from a drawer, I wandered outside. The roses were blooming despite the snow. Their scent was clean and lovely in the crisp air.

I walked to my Gran's spirit house near the picket fence, lit the incense, and set it in its holder. A few rose petals lay scattered across the peaked and curling roofline of the tiny wooden house.

"I wish I could ask your advice, Gran. Something is wrong. I'm just... afraid to find out what it is." A lump hardened my throat. But I had to find out. One way or another.

I nodded. "Your friend Mrs. Steinberg is right. I can't pretend nothing's going on. It's making me miserable, and it can only get worse." That wasn't entirely true though. Worse would be losing Arsen. And I wasn't sure I could face that.

Smoke rose in coils from the stick of incense to the gray skies. I blinked rapidly. I had to know the truth. "Cupid be damned. I'll just ask him."

There was no warning. No shiver of premonition. Just a whistling in the air, and then a thud. And then rose petals bursting into the air from the force of the arrow, quivering in the spirit house.

Chapter Twenty

Rose petals drifted to the ground. I gaped at the arrow in the side of my Gran's spirit house for too long before ducking. Heart jackhammering, I crawled between a rose bush and the miniature house's wooden post.

I clung to the post with one arm and dug my phone from the back pocket of my khakis with the other. The rose bush clawed at my jacket. I yanked my arm free of its thorns. The cold of the ground seeped through the knees of my slacks. A tremor wracked my body, and I nearly dropped the phone. I called the sheriff.

"What now, Witsend?"

"Someone shot an arrow at me," I whispered.

"What?"

"Someone shot an arrow at me," I said more loudly, and my voice cracked. It just didn't seem fair. What sort of person goes around with a bow and arrow?

"Are you hurt?" Sheriff McCourt asked briskly.

Was I? I squeezed the post more tightly, assuring myself I was okay. "No."

"Where are you?"

My breath came in quick gasps. "I'm trapped in the garden, by the spirit house. I'm hiding. I'm not sure if I should make for the house, or—"

"If no one's tried to shoot you since you've gone into hiding, stay put. Deputies are on their way." She hung up.

I crouched beneath the spirit house and shivered. I'd been cursing Cupid right before the arrow had come flying. Did the universe hate sarcasm? In the distance, a siren sounded.

But the shooter hadn't been the universe. It had been a person, and I lowered my head, listening for footsteps.

The siren grew louder. Another siren joined the chorus.

Okay, think. From the direction the arrow pointed, the archer must be on the hillside. There was plenty of cover there—lots of pines and manzanita bushes. And a hiking trail led along the ridge. Someone could have hiked here and shot the arrow.

I checked my watch. It was eleven thirty-three. The sheriff would want to know the time... She already had the time. She'd have logged my call. But it wasn't easy staying clear-headed when someone was trying to kill you.

A pair of dirty boots edged into my line of vision. "What are you doing?" Sal asked.

My face warmed. "Get down," I hissed. "Someone shot at me."

"Rightey-o." She dropped into a squat and pushed into the roses.

A branch cracked, and I winced. My grandmother had planted these roses. Though she would have approved of them being used for shelter from a mad archer.

"So that arrow in the elf house roof *isn't* normal?" Sal asked.

I glared. Why would she think that was normal? Just because I had a UFO in the roof of my B&B didn't mean I wanted projectiles in all my roofs. "No."

"Hey, I had to make sure. Doyle's not exactly your typical small town, is it?" Sal's mouth turned downward. "Though where I'm from isn't much better. We don't have Bigfoot though. Or UFOs. Well, maybe UFOs. You know, Nevada's kind of famous for them."

"Yes," I said, clutching the post. "I'm aware."

"Right. I'm running on like a leaky faucet, ain't I? The thing is, I've never been shot at with an arrow before. It's a unique experience." She shifted her weight, and another branch snapped.

I frowned. She *still* hadn't been shot at. Hopefully, she wouldn't be. Gravel crunched in the B&B's driveway, and a car door slammed.

"Think the shooter's still up on the hill?" Sal asked. "It's just that nothing much is happening here. All this squatting is hard on my knees."

Arsen ambled around the corner of the house, and my blood froze. "Arsen, look out!" I shouted.

He turned his head toward us, and his tanned brow furrowed. Arsen strode toward the spirit house, seemed to notice the arrow, and blinked.

His expression hardened. He pivoted and charged across the lawn. Arsen raced between the gazebo and the UFO fountain and up the manzanita-covered hillside.

I opened my mouth to shout for him to stop, come back, be safe. Then I closed it, my chest squeezing. Arsen had never been a safety-first kind of guy, and I didn't want to change him. Even if it did terrify me.

"Now there's a man of action," Sal said.

Sirens blared. Sheriff McCourt, gun drawn and aimed low, strode around the corner of the Victorian. Sal tensed.

I pointed. "Arsen's gone up the hill," I shouted. So *please don't shoot him.*

The sheriff nodded. "Stay there." She strode after him and vanished behind the gazebo.

Sal muttered something under her breath. Another branch cracked.

"What?" My shoulder muscles tightened. If we stayed here much longer, she'd destroy that rose bush.

"This is just humiliating. Letting a *cop* save me?" She stood. "I'm done waiting around for the next arrow to drop. I'm going inside."

My heart jumped. "But—"

Sal stomped across the lawn to the porch. She climbed the steps and walked into the kitchen. The door banged shut behind her.

My leg cramped. I rose slightly and peered over the spirit house's peaked roof. The sheriff and Arsen stood talking on the hillside. Arsen motioned up the hill.

"Hi, Susan," Deputy Owen Denton said in my ear.

"Gagh!" I jumped.

The blond deputy nodded. "Sorry I startled you." He edged around me and studied the arrow. The deputy whistled. "Looks like your offering to the spirits paid off." He nodded toward the incense. "Better that little house than you."

A final wisp of smoke melted into the air. The orange spark at the tip of the incense stick faded.

"It's not an offering— It doesn't matter," I said. I never thought of it as making an offering. Lighting the incense had become habit.

The sheriff and Arsen emerged from behind the gazebo. "Denton," she shouted. "We've marked off the crime scene. Get some pictures."

"Sure thing, ma'am." He touched the brim of his broad-brimmed hat. The deputy hurried across the lawn and up the hillside.

I edged from behind the spirit house. "You found something?"

"The spot where the archer shot from," Arsen said. "There's a knee print, but no footprints that I could see. Maybe Owen will turn up more."

"Did you see anyone?" Sheriff McCourt asked.

"No," I said. "No one."

The sheriff took my statement and left. Arsen walked with me to the house, his muscular arm around my shoulders. "You sure you're okay?" He held the porch door open for me, and we walked inside the kitchen.

"I'm not hurt." But I was shaken. True, one doesn't become the sheriff's secret weapon in crime solving without facing down some danger. But it really wasn't fun when it happened.

Sal sat at the small, round table sipping coffee, the aging beagle at her feet. "No one would have taken a pot shot at you with an arrow if I'd been there," she said. "From now on, I'm sticking to you like glue. No rhyme intended."

Oh, great. "What are you doing back here so soon?" I asked Arsen.

He glanced at Sal and flushed. "I, uh, just wanted to let you know the background checks are in the works. I've got a guy on it."

"Outsourcing." Sal slurped her coffee. "Smart."

"This has gone too far," Arsen said. "Whatever's going on, someone's got their sights on you. We've got to stop this. Now."

I sat and opened my laptop on the kitchen table. "Let's see if any of our suspects have an archery connection." I typed a name into the search engine. Arsen pulled out a chair and sat beside me.

Doyle Archery Team Win's Second State Championship
DOYLE, CA
When the points were tallied at the State Championship last month in Sacramento, CA, the Doyle archery team had won their second state championship. Doyle High also lay claim to having the three top archers in the state—Anselm Holmes, Victor Fernheim, and Enrique Aguilar.

Doyle High is now aiming at the Nationals.

I huffed a breath. *All three?* How was I supposed to whittle down the suspects? And why hadn't I found this out before? I should have been uncovering this sort of intel on my suspects much earlier in the game.

Sal whistled. "I told you it was one of those dudes."

"I should have realized they all went to school together," I said, uneasy. Did it mean anything? This was such a small town, everyone was connected somehow.

Dixie wandered into the kitchen. "Why is Owen Denton taking pictures of our hill?"

"You didn't notice the sirens?" Arsen asked.

"I had my headphones in," she said.

"Someone shot an arrow at Susan," Arsen said.

Dixie nodded. "Huh. That's new."

"This is serious," Arsen said sharply.

I shook myself. It was time to get back to basics: means, motive, and opportunity. All our suspects knew how to shoot, so that was means. Motive—they all had motive. All that was left was opportunity.

"We need to find out where everyone was around eleven thirty this morning," I said.

Sal's stomach rumbled loudly. She patted it. "Sorry. I missed my mid-elevenses."

"I don't know where they were this morning," Dixie leaned against the oven. "But they'll be at the Irish pub at one."

"How do you know that?" Arsen asked.

"Because they invited me," Dixie said.

"Why?" I asked.

She glowered at me. "Why wouldn't they? They want to figure out who killed Kelsey and Hannah."

"Great," Arsen said. "We'll go talk to them there."

"I'm not going." Dixie's jaw jutted forward.

"Why not?" I asked. Because that was really inconvenient.

My cousin's expression turned shifty. "I've got a thing with someone online."

I grimaced. "But you need to go." I glanced at Sal. "We've sort of been... banned."

Arsen's hazel eyes narrowed. "How'd you get banned?"

I glanced at Sal. She raised her chin. "It was a misunderstanding," I said.

"Then I'll go talk to them by myself." Arsen scraped back his chair and stood. Beneath the table, Bailey lifted his head.

"Whoa, whoa, whoa," Sal said. "You're not cutting us out of the fun. That arrow could have killed me. I'm in this. We'll just disguise ourselves."

Killed *her*? She hadn't been there.

"Disguised as what?" Dixie asked.

"As other people," she said. "It's easy. You got any wigs?"

"No," I said. "And Arsen can handle this on his own." This was no joke. Wigs. Disguises. Someone had tried to kill me.

"Yes," Dixie said. "I've got wigs. You should totally go."

I glared at my cousin. I'd nearly been killed, and Dixie was enabling this ridiculous idea? "Why do you have wigs?"

My cousin shrugged. "I prefer to go incognito at UFO conventions. The secret is you also have to change your whole persona. A wig isn't enough. You have to get into it, *be* the other person."

Sal nodded. "Yeah, that's right. I saw it on the internet."

It *was* right. Don't ask how I knew, but it wasn't from the internet.

Arsen's eyebrows lifted. "You can try, but this is a small town. People will recognize you."

"I'm going and you can't stop me," Sal said. "Disguise or not."

Dixie smirked. "I'll get you both wigs."

"No," I said to the swinging door. "We don't…" But Dixie was gone.

"I'm on it." Sal slapped my shoulder, rocking me sideways. She strode after Dixie.

"This is a very bad idea," I called after them. So of course, they ignored me.

Unenthusiastic, I studied myself in the black-and-white parlor's mirror. The bulky sweater added ten pounds. The blue-haired wig was not my color. And the wide-brimmed beach hat was completely inappropriate for winter. "I look ridiculous," I mumbled through my thick red scarf.

I'd hoped playing dress-up would be enough of a delay for Sal to rethink her plan. Or at least give our suspects time to leave before we got there. But Dixie'd had us in disguises in a matter of minutes, and Sal was even more determined to invade the pub.

Arsen shook his head. "You still look like you to me. And not ridiculous," he added hastily. "I know you want to take care of this yourself. That arrow was personal. But—"

"I don't *want* to. And of course these disguises won't work. But if I don't play along, Sal will crash your interview. And then where will we be?" Besides, if I stayed home, I'd just keep thinking about that arrow. I *did* need to take action.

"Sal seems fairly savvy."

I rolled my eyes. "She's an amateur. I need to be there to make sure things run smoothly."

Arsen, Sal and I loaded into his Jeep Commander. Dixie opted to stay at Wits' End and supervise the removal of the arrow from the spirit house.

The three of us drove into town. Arsen pulled into a spot a block from the pub, and we walked there, my stomach churning. We were going to get caught. This was such a bad idea.

"This is gonna be great," Sal said. "No one will catch us in these outfits."

The woman who owned the local coffee shop, Ground, walked past. "Hi, Sue," she chirped.

I shrank deeper into the scarf. People I knew were seeing me in this getup. This was just humiliating.

"It's for a good cause." Sal grinned. "Buck up."

We walked through the courtyard. Arsen opened the pub door and walked inside. Sal and I glanced at each other. I nodded and followed him into the gloomy interior.

A beefy doorman rose from his stool and held out a hand. "Stop right there."

Chapter Twenty-One

My insides tensed. I was going to be thrown out of the same bar *twice*? And dressed like this? I'd *known* this wouldn't work.

The doorman folded his muscular arms. "IDs."

"What?" I squeaked.

"Let me see your IDs. You need to be twenty-one to drink here."

"Oh." I scrambled in my purse and pulled my driver's license from my wallet.

Belatedly, I realized once he saw my license, I'd no longer be incognito. But maybe it was for the best. If we both got tossed out now, Arsen could do his thing without Sal's interference.

The doorman squinted at the license then studied me. He frowned. "Okay."

Okay? Seriously? He glanced at Sal's license as well and let her in too.

We hurried to Arsen, waiting behind the doorman. "See them?" he asked.

"There." I pointed out a big, circular table in the gloom.

Victor, Anselm and Enrique sat, each with an empty chair between them. Victor glowered. He crossed his arms over his chest, his brawny shoulders bunching beneath his fisherman's sweater. Anselm glared right back and tapped a paint-stained finger on the table. Enrique relaxed in his chair and smiled.

Arsen strode to the table and pulled out a chair for me. "Mind if we join you?" he asked.

I sat before they could respond. "Thank you." I smiled up at Arsen. How could I have had any doubts about him? Seeing him leap into action after the arrow attack...

Actually, he would have done that for anyone. But he was still the same Arsen.

Victor scowled. "Actually—"

"Good," Arsen said and pulled out a chair for Sal. He sat in the third empty chair. "Someone took a shot at Susan this morning. I want to know where all of you were around eleven-thirty."

Enrique leaned forward, his handsome face creasing with concern. "A shot? Were you injured? What happened?" he asked, his brown eyes soulful. He looked like a poet in his loose white button-up shirt and black jeans.

"She's obviously fine," Victor said.

"But who would shoot at you?" Enrique asked. "Do you think it is connected to Kelsey's death?"

"And Hannah's," Anselm said sharply. He rubbed the tattoo on the back of his neck.

Enrique sighed. "Hannah." He shook himself. "There are too many guns in this country."

"It wasn't a gun," Sal said. "It was an arrow."

The three men looked at each other. Their faces hardened with suspicion.

"But we all know how to shoot," Enrique said. "We were on the archery team."

"Yes," Arsen said. "We know."

"Someone's trying to frame us," Victor said.

"Or one of you did it," Arsen said, his voice tough as iron.

Vida walked to the table. Her ponytail was bound with leather ties. "Can I get you menus?"

Sal leaned forward and pulled her scarf down to speak.

"No thanks," I said before she could respond. If we ordered, we'd have to remove our scarves to eat. Our disguises might be awful, but I wasn't willing to let them go. Not with the pub manager lurking behind the bar. He studied Sal, his mouth pursed.

Vida *must* have recognized us. But if she had, she didn't seem to care. Her hazel eyes lingered on Victor. She shot Victor a last, longing look, then turned and slouched to the bar.

"When's the memorial?" I asked.

"Memorial?" Anselm said blankly.

"For Kelsey and Hannah." There wouldn't be a funeral so soon, not in the midst of coroner's reports and a murder investigation. But you didn't need a body for a memorial.

Enrique shook his head. "Their parents are holding the funeral in Tahoe. That's where they live now. Kelsey loved that lake."

"But their friends are all here in Doyle," I said. A bead of sweat trickled down my neck. It was hot in here with all these clothes on. I itched—literally—to remove the bulky scarf.

"What are you three doing here anyway?" Sal asked.

"Trying to figure out who is responsible for these terrible deaths," Enrique said. "We were the closest to Kelsey. It is our responsibility."

"Have you reached any conclusions?" I asked.

"No," Victor said shortly.

"That's not entirely true," Anselm said. "Vida—"

"Has nothing to do with this," Victor snarled.

"But it is true she did not take it well when you left her," Enrique said mildly.

"Vida has an alibi," I said. "She was working here."

"Which brings us back to your alibis," Arsen said. "Where were you this morning?"

"I was in Sacramento," Victor said. "At a modeling shoot."

Anselm snorted.

"I only returned to Doyle fifteen minutes ago," Victor continued.

"Where were you modeling and for whom?" I asked.

"We were in Old Town," he said. "You can confirm with my agent."

"We will," Arsen growled. "And you two?"

"Alas," Enrique said. "I have no alibi. I was home, working."

"And you?" he asked Anselm.

"The same. I was painting."

"Let's see your shoes." Sal loosened her scarf.

"What?" Enrique asked.

"Your shoes. Show us your shoes."

Expressions perplexed, they shifted their chairs and pulled their feet from beneath the table. They all wore loafers.

"It was a good idea," I told her. Anyone who'd been up on that hill would have had some mud or dirt on their shoes. But the men's shoes were all polished clean. Of course, they could have gone home and changed between eleven-thirty and now. Clean shoes didn't clear them of the attack.

"Yeah," Sal said. "Well, we'll see about this *modeling* shoot."

A shadow fell across our table. The manager's face twisted. "You two again. I told you to stay out and stop harassing my customers."

"Who's harassing?" Sal asked. "We're just having a friendly chat."

"Out!"

"We'll leave," Arsen said hastily and stood. Face burning, I followed him from the pub.

Sal whipped off her scarf, hat, and wig. She shook out her curling red hair. "So Victor's out. That leaves Anselm and Enrique."

"If Victor wasn't lying about being in Sacramento," Arsen said.

"That's easy to check." Sal pulled her phone from the pocket of her thick coat. "I got the number for his talent agent off his website." She winked at me. "And you thought I was taking beefcake pictures. I put the number in my phone book just in case."

"That's great," I said, "but—"

Sal dialed and pressed the phone to her ear. "Hello, is this Marcus Grace...? I'm interested in the whereabouts of one of your clients, Victor Fernheim... Who am I?" She winked at me. "I'm Sheriff McCourt, from Doyle, California."

My stomach bottomed. I shook my head. No, *no, no*.

"Was Victor on a job this morning?" she asked. "Uh, huh. Uh, huh... Have you got any idea when that job ended? Around ten o'clock..? Okay... That helps. Thank you." She hung up. "He's in the clear."

I stared, aghast. "Sal. You impersonated an officer."

She shrugged. "All for a good cause, right?"

"No," I said shrilly. This was a line not to be crossed. "Not good. Sheriff McCourt is going to call him next, and she'll find out."

"But she won't know who called him, because he thinks I'm her." She aimed her finger at me like a gun. "We're golden."

Arsen glanced past my shoulder. "Uh, Sue—"

"No." I ripped off my blue wig. This was so typical. What was *wrong* with her? "We're not golden. If the sheriff finds out—"

"Finds out what?" Sheriff McCourt asked from behind me, and the muscles between my shoulders pinched.

Chapter Twenty-Two

In the pursuit of justice, I've done several questionable things. Impersonating an officer had never been one of them. How could I? You don't betray the trust of a team member, and I was on the sheriff's team.

I bunched the wig in my hands. How much had she overheard? I turned from the pub's green door and smiled brightly. "Hi, Sheriff. What are you doing here?"

Her cornflower eyes narrowed. "What are *you* doing here?" A SUV drove past, snow and water slushing beneath its wheels.

"Not interfering in your investigation," Sal said. "That's for sure."

Arsen's eyes closed. He shook his head slightly.

I jammed the wig in the pocket of my long coat. "Of course not." We were helping, not interfering. "But Anselm, Enrique, Victor and Vida are in there trying to puzzle out the murders, and—"

"You thought you'd interfere in my investigation," the sheriff said.

Sal scowled. "Well, someone had better interfere. Two women are dead, and here Susan and I are doing all the work."

An awkward silence fell. The sheriff drew her hands from the pockets of her near-black jacket.

I had to derail this. Fast. *Talk about something else. Anything else.* "No one's planned a memorial for Kelsey and Hannah here in Doyle," I said. "Her parents are doing everything in Lake Tahoe."

"Yeah," Sal said. "Memorial. Too bad we got thrown out before we could learn more. Total misunderstanding."

"I still don't understand it," Arsen said.

"A memorial in Doyle," the sheriff muttered and removed her wide hat. "That's not a bad idea." She ruffled her blond hair and nodded. "Let me know when it's going to be. Sooner rather than later, if you don't mind. In fact, tomorrow would be best." She nodded and strode into the pub.

"That's..." I trailed off. A memorial in Doyle? I hadn't meant... "What just happened?"

"I think you're planning a memorial service," Arsen said.

My pulse pounded. I couldn't... That was just unreasonable. "I can't pull together a memorial service for tomorrow. It's impossible. I need a venue. Guests. A caterer." I sputtered. "That's just... crazy."

Sal rubbed her chin. "Think the killer will show up?"

"If the killer was someone close to Kelsey and Hannah," I said, "he'd have to or look like a jerk. Or she would."

A memorial *would* give us access to more people who'd known the two women. And talking to others who'd known them might give us a better picture of the two sisters. I still didn't really know much about either, aside from broad and not-very-helpful outlines. *Venue... Venue...*

"It's too cold to hold it in the Wits' End garden," I mused.

"I'll bet Antoine would give us space," Arsen said. "Late afternoons on weekdays usually aren't that crowded at the bar."

I relaxed. Arsen was right. The western bar would be perfect. And they'd be able to take care of the food. I'd been too panicked to think, but Arsen had seen things clearly.

And suddenly the force of him struck me. The lean muscles I knew were beneath his jacket. The strength of his jaw. The warmth of his hazel eyes. I was so lucky to have him in my life, and gratitude swelled my heart.

"You okay?" Sal asked. "You look funny."

My cheeks heated. "I'm fine. I was just thinking... I'd better ask Antoine now."

"That's the western bar?" Sal shook her head. "I'm out. I told you western bars were a jinx for me."

And I could hardly bring her inside after the fight she'd started. I needed to apologize to Antoine for that too. *Honestly.* She was doing more harm than good in this investigation.

"Why don't I get Sal something to eat at Alchemy?" Arsen said. "I can order something for you, and we can meet you there when you're done."

My shoulders unknotted. "Would you order me the eggplant parmesan?"

"You got it." Arsen angled his head toward the south end of the street. "We'll see you there."

He and Sal trooped down Main Street. I crossed the road and hurried down the raised plank sidewalk to Antoine's.

I pushed through the batwing doors. Paper hearts still dangled from the brass chandeliers, but the jukebox was silent. I made my way to the bar.

Antoine pursed his mouth. The older man ambled down the bar to me. "Hi, Susan. Where's your friend?" he asked warily.

"She's a guest, not a friend," I said. "And I'm embarrassed and sorry for what happened the last time we were here. I hope you know—"

He motioned with his hand, cutting me off. "I know you didn't start that fight. Apology accepted."

"Thank you." I grimaced. "And now I have a favor to ask. I'm planning the memorial for Kelsey and Hannah Delaney. Could we hold it here?"

"Sure." He braced an elbow on the wooden bar. "When?"

He'd agreed that easily? My chest lightened. This was why the sheriff relied on me. I was a key part of the local community. "Tomorrow?" I asked, pleased.

He laughed. "Good one. No, seriously. When?"

My gaze flicked toward the beamed ceiling. I *knew* tomorrow had been a ridiculous ask. The sheriff would just have to be flexible. "What about the day after tomorrow, in the late afternoon or early evening?"

His coffee-colored eyes widened. "You *are* serious." He slung his drying cloth over one shoulder. "Huh. Yeah. We could manage that. It's a slow time. You want food?"

Of course I did. What was a memorial without food? But how was I going to pay for all this? I swallowed. "I'll bring the food, if that's okay? The guests can pay for their own drinks."

He nodded. "Sure. I should have thought of the memorial myself. Kelsey was a real firecracker. Terrible thing." He shook his head sadly.

"You knew her?"

He chuckled wryly. "If I'd gotten into Bitcoin when she'd told me to back in 2010, I could retire now."

"Do you want to retire?" Antoine's was an institution. I couldn't imagine the town without it or without him.

"I love this bar, but nothing lasts forever. You've got to grab your joy every day while you can."

I smiled. "Is that bartender wisdom?"

"No, it's getting older wisdom." His expression hardened. "A pleasure Kelsey and her sister won't have now."

I loosened my itchy scarf. "How well did you know them?"

"Kelsey came in once a week for lunch and every Saturday night. And if she didn't bring a new guy in, she left with one. But that's not judgment. She was a kind woman. And there were times when she didn't leave with anyone. She'd just chat with me and the other staff. I think she was lonely."

"Hm." Could it be true? Had she needed all those men around her because she couldn't stand to be by herself? "There's so much we never know about people."

A trio of women in skiwear walked into the bar, and he glanced their way. "I never got to know her sister, Hannah. She was a quiet one. When she did come in with Kelsey—which wasn't often—she pretty much kept to herself. But I never got the feeling Hannah minded. Being by herself, I mean. Tell me more about this memorial. I can put a flyer up here, if you want."

"That would be great. I don't have much time to let people know." And flyers were a good idea. But I'd need to make phone calls too. "I don't know how I'm going to get everything done," I fretted.

He straightened off the bar. "Word will get out. Don't you worry."

We went over the details. There were more than I'd expected, but this wasn't Antoine's first rodeo. I jotted everything down in my planner and walked down the snowy street to Alchemy.

Holding a memorial *was* a good idea. I'd already learned more about the murdered women from Antoine. If I could get more of their friends in a room, I might be able to put together a better picture of the sisters.

I walked inside the restaurant and looked around. Arsen and Sal were seated by the open fireplace. Untouched plates of food sat on the square, tiled table in front of them.

"You're right on time," Arsen said. "The waitress just got here."

"Thanks," I said. Then I sat in the empty chair closest to the fireplace and told them the news.

We ate our lunches and discussed the murders. But Arsen seemed distant. A few times he turned to me with a puzzled look on his face, but then he'd shake his head and say nothing.

Worried, I watched him when he wasn't looking, while Sal chattered on, oblivious. Maybe we weren't okay after all.

We returned to Wits' End. Sal climbed the B&B's stairs to her room.

"Arsen," I said, glancing up the narrow steps. "Can we talk?" My midsection tensed. *Just ask him.*

"Sure," he said. "What's up?"

I drew him closer to the scarred reception desk. "That's what I wanted to ask you." Bailey nudged open the kitchen door and trotted to Arsen's side.

Arsen shifted his weight. "What do you mean?"

"Are we taking each other for granted?" I blurted. "Not you. I mean, have I? Have I taken you for granted? I mean... It just seems like we've each been running around in our own different worlds."

"I don't feel taken for granted. But I guess I was a little surprised you suggested me for a model."

"I'm sorry. I didn't know if you'd want to do it or not."

"Why would you think I would?"

Why would I think he wouldn't? He loved sportswear. "I'm sorry. I guess I wasn't thinking."

His brows drew downward. "No, I wasn't being fair. You've been dealing with these murders on your own. Of course you're— I should have been more involved in the investigation. I just... Things have been kind of crazy."

"I know, but what things?" He knew all about my problems, but I didn't know a thing about his world of high tech security. Shame flushed through my veins. I *should* know. Not to be nosy, but because couples should be sharing. Maybe I could help. Or at least listen.

He took my hands. "Susan, there's something I—"

Sal tromped into the kitchen. "I'll admit to sharing my bed with a sketchy character or two, but I draw the line at squirrels."

The beagle started to his feet and howled. Bailey charged up the stairs, barking wildly.

"Bailey," I shouted, "come—"

"It's okay," Sal chuckled. "I got rid of the little guy myself. Humanely, mind you. Out the window. But he made a real mess in there."

I hung my head. "I'll get the cleaning bucket. Arsen—?"

His smile was lopsided. "It's okay. We can talk later." Broad shoulders slumped, he walked out the front door. The screen doors banged behind him.

Heart bottoming, I stared at the closed door. He seemed... I didn't know what he seemed like, but he didn't seem like Arsen.

And that terrified me.

Chapter Twenty-Three

Arsen scraped back the kitchen chair and stood. "Outstanding breakfast, Sue. The new sign's awesome. And…" He came around the table and took my hands. My insides tensed.

He cleared his throat. "There's—"

The porch door swung open, and Dixie ambled into the kitchen. She peeled off her Army-green parka. She stopped short. "Waffles? Today was supposed to be French toast."

Arsen expelled a breath. "Dixie—"

"Wednesdays are almost always French toast," she said.

He rolled his eyes and kissed my cheek. "I'll see you when I get back from Sacramento." Arsen strode out the porch door, a blast of cold air flooding the kitchen in his wake.

I jabbed my fork into my waffle. *Outstanding breakfast? Awesome sign?* He'd acted as if nothing had happened.

But something *had* happened. Arsen had left with no real explanation yesterday. And what really infuriated me was me. I hadn't pressed him on it.

Maybe I should have written *interrogate Arsen* in my planner. Then I knew it would get done. Bailey gazed hopefully up at me.

Why was Arsen pretending everything was fine this morning? Why hadn't I just asked him what was going on, demanded an explanation? But he had tried to tell me something. And then Dixie had interrupted, and…

I'd been relieved.

I'd been afraid of what he'd say. That we were growing apart. That things had changed. That he just wasn't that into me anymore. At least he'd noticed the STAFF ONLY sign I'd posted on the kitchen door.

Bailey huffed an annoyed breath.

"Fine," Dixie said. "I'll have a waffle."

"They've got pecans inside."

"Not a total loss then," she said.

I fed Bailey a tiny piece of bacon. He wolfed it down and stepped on my foot as if I were a sort of bacon dispensing vending machine.

"No more," I said sternly.

The beagle whined. He dropped into his dog bed beneath the table.

While Dixie ate, I washed up, then opened my planner on the kitchen table. It was time for some memorial planning.

But I couldn't concentrate. Not even my planner could keep me on the straight and narrow.

I stared at its blank planning pages and rehashed our conversation from last night. Worse had been our lack of conversation this morning. What had he wanted to say before Dixie'd interrupted? I drummed my pencil on the kitchen table.

"I talked to all Kelsey and Hannah's friends I know." She took her plate to the dishwasher and slid it inside. "They're coming tomorrow."

"Excellent." I raised my pencil above the planner page. "How many is that?"

"Four."

What? That wasn't enough for a memorial. I swiveled in the wooden chair. "Only four people?"

"That's all I know for sure will make it," Dixie said.

My eyes narrowed. "Those four wouldn't be Enrique, Anselm, Victor and Vida, would they?"

"Yeah. I mean, I wouldn't call Vida a friend of Kelsey's, exactly. But she did like Hannah."

"That isn't—" I sputtered. "We can't have a memorial with only four people plus us." Naturally, I'd managed to talk the editor at the local paper into including the memorial in the morning paper. But we couldn't count on that bringing people in.

"Hannah and Kelsey won't care how big it is," Dixie said.

"You don't know that. And I care." I drummed the eraser end of the pencil on the table. Bailey looked up from his dog bed. "Okay," I said. "I've got to stay here and prep for the memorial. Would you go to the high school and get their yearbook? We need names of everyone from their classes."

"I don't have time. I've got to pack."

I felt my eyelid twitch. "Pack for what?" Where was she going? She hadn't mentioned a trip.

"I'm meeting Steve in Vegas tomorrow night." She leaned one hip against the butcher-block counter. "You know, that guy I mentioned? I'm driving there after the memorial."

Her long-distance romance? He was real? I shook myself. "You mean the memorial? It will take you hours to get to Vegas. You won't get in until after midnight."

Dixie shrugged. "Whatever. I've got to get packed now so I can take off right away. Besides, their contact info won't be in the yearbooks."

"No," I said, "but this is a small town. If we know their names, we can find them. And would you please pick up a copy of the morning paper on the way back? I want to make sure the memorial's in it." Just because the editor had said he'd put it there, didn't mean he'd done it.

"Now?"

"Yes, now," I said, irritated.

"But I've got cleaning to do too, and—"

"I'll take care of your cleaning," I ground out. *Honestly.* She'd known yesterday she was only going to contact four people. Why hadn't she told me then? We were running out of time.

"And while you're in town," I continued, "would you put these flyers up for the memorial?" I nodded to the stack of gray flyers on the butcherblock counter.

"I guess. It's for Kelsey and Hannah."

"Thanks. Ground will take one, and the ice cream parlor owes me a favor. Make sure to put some up at Antoine's and anywhere else that will take them."

Dixie heaved a sigh and grabbed the flyers. "Fine. I'm going." She stomped out the door.

I took five minutes for planning. I had to get a lot of baking prep done today for tomorrow's memorial. I'd also have to clean the rooms. It would be tight, but I could manage it all.

Tackling the former first, I mixed up a batch of sugar cookie dough and formed it into logs. I rolled the logs in the colors of our local high school—blue, yellow, and white. Wrapping them in plastic, I set them in the refrigerator.

That done, I climbed the stairs to the second floor. I collected the cleaning supplies from the closet and knocked on Sal's door. It was the first time since Sal had arrived that the *Do Not Disturb* sign wasn't hanging on the knob.

"Come in," a muffled voice said.

I opened the door and stopped short. Clothing and candy wrappers lay strewn across every available surface. The room was stuffy and had an unpleasant, close smell. Her chalk murder board was a whitish-pinkish-yellowish smear on the wall.

Sal, in tight jeans and a long-sleeved purple tee, lay sprawled face down on the unmade bed. Her face was buried in a pillow.

"Sal?" I asked, concerned. "Are you okay?"

"No."

"What's, er, wrong?"

"It's Bingo."

"Oh." I forced myself not to start scrubbing the wall. But if I was going to get the cleaning and the baking done, I was on a clock. "Did something happen?"

She raised her head and rolled onto her side to face me. "He called."

"Oh. That's good, isn't it?"

"He hadn't even noticed I'd left town!"

"Oh." I shifted the bucket in my hands. "That's not very morale boosting."

"No, it damn well isn't. He *said* he'd wanted to give me my space. But he was just giving me time to cool off so he could weasel his way back into my good graces."

I looked for a free square foot of space to put down the bucket. Finding none, I edged aside a pile of frilly lingerie with my toe and set it on the rug. "Are you sure you don't *want* him to weasel his way back in?"

She sat up. "Not like this. I'm not going to be manipulated by no man."

"Of course not." And since this didn't seem like the time to point out the double negative, I said nothing more.

"He's not like Arsen. He's not one of those honest guys who can never tell a lie. Bingo always finds a way to not tell you what he needs to tell you without lying to you. So I guess he doesn't tell a lie either. But he's sneaky about it. He's like one of those, whatchamacall'ems. Fairies."

Was that why Arsen was acting so weird? Because he couldn't tell me something he was dreading? "Fairies?" I asked, uneasy.

"Yeah, like in your UFO brochure. They can never lie, but they don't always tell you the truth either." Her broad forehead puckered. "I had no idea fairy sightings and UFO sightings were so alike. This trip has been really educational."

"Yes, the similarities are startling," I agreed distractedly. There was a contingent of people who believed aliens were being mistaken for fairies. Others thought fairies through the ages had been mistaken for aliens. "I'll just, ah, clean the other rooms and come back later."

Sal rolled onto her stomach and buried her head in the pillow. "Mmph."

Taking that for: *okay, fine, I want to be alone anyway*, I retrieved my bucket. I backed from the room and closed the door.

The rest of the rooms were in better condition. Brooke's had a *Do Not Disturb* sign on it, so I left that one alone. Still, it took me until two o'clock to finish cleaning them all on my own.

I was unsurprised Dixie hadn't returned yet. If I knew my cousin—and I did—she'd calculated to the second how long it would take me to finish the cleaning. Then she'd added on another hour for good measure. Dixie wouldn't be back for a while.

I knotted my ponytail into a tight bun and began whipping up mini quiches. One good thing about running a B&B—I had plenty of recipes that I could freeze and reheat.

There was a knock at the kitchen door. Frowning, I dried my hands in a dishtowel decorated with pink hearts. I hung it on the stove handle. "Yes? Come in."

A man in a red windbreaker and baseball hat edged into the kitchen. "Uh, I've got takeout for Brooke Nicholson."

"Room nine. Upstairs." I glanced at his empty hands.

"It's all in the van," he said. "I don't suppose you can give me a hand? She ordered the deluxe option."

I bit back an exasperated sigh. I'd had plenty of service jobs when I was in college. They'd been sufficiently terrible that I made a point of being kind to others doing them, even if I *was* trying to throw together a memorial on short notice.

I smiled tightly. "Of course." Throwing on a jacket, I followed him to his red van in the Wits' End driveway.

"That's some UFO you've got there." He opened the van's rear doors and jerked his chin toward our gabled roof. Sunlight glinted off the UFO jutting from its shingles.

"We're a UFO-themed B&B."

"Oh."

"You're not from around here?" I asked.

"Angels Camp." He handed me a picnic basket and a glass vase filled with roses.

I hefted the basket. "What's in here?"

"That's just the decor." He pulled out a large, insulated box. "This is the food."

"Out of curiosity...?"

"Strawberries, balsamic glazed steak rolls, chicken and asparagus crepes, white chocolate raspberry cheesecake, and of course..." He pulled out a green bottle. "...champagne."

Now I knew where Finley was. "How romantic," I said flatly.

He grinned. "Valentine's Day may be over, but the romance never ends, right?"

"They're upstairs." I led him to room nine's closed door and abandoned him there. I just wasn't in the mood. And more importantly, I had food to prepare.

I filled the last mini-quiche crust, and Dixie strolled inside carrying a rolled newspaper. "Got your list," she said.

"Great. Have you called them?"

"Yes. Not all of them. Most have left Doyle. But I got in touch with twenty people, and they're coming. And here's the paper." She dropped it on the counter by my elbow.

"Thanks." I opened it and scanned the obituaries. "It's not here."

"Yes it is. In the crime section."

"What?"

MURDERS REMAIN UNSOLVED

By Tom Tarrant

DOYLE, CA - *The community of Doyle, CA is refusing to give up on finding the killer of Kelsey and Hannah Delaney.*

It's been six days since Kelsey Delaney was murdered in her Doyle ice sculpting studio. Her sister, Hannah, was murdered four days later in her Doyle condominium. To date, no one's been charged.

Only the Doyle Times has continuously investigated the murder. Our recent investigation has brought up questions leading to new action by the Doyle Sheriff's Department.

The Delaney family says our reporting has brought more attention to the case. We urge anyone with information about the murders to contact the Doyle Sheriff's Department.

A memorial service for the sisters will be held at Antoine's Bar on Thursday, February 17th, at 5:30 PM.

I sputtered. "Tom's recent investigation? What investigation? This is just one giant self-pat on the back."

"He does have that true crime podcast," Dixie supplied.

Augh. "How's anyone supposed to read about the memorial? It's buried at the bottom of this crime article. It should be in the obituaries."

"Everyone's going to be reading that article," my cousin said. "The murders are big news."

"I'll bet Tom's going to come and try to interrogate the mourners," I muttered. "And it's totally inappropriate."

"Aren't *you* going to be interrogating the mourners?"

What was her point? I was a part of the sheriff's investigative team. Tom wasn't. "That's different. Besides, I know how to be subtle."

Someone knocked on the kitchen door. I tossed the paper on the counter. "Yes?" I called.

Mrs. Carter stuck her head inside. "I know we're not supposed to be in the kitchen, but oh, isn't it wonderful?" The older woman edged further inside, and her husband followed.

No guests in the kitchen! I had a sign! "What?" I glanced at the mini quiches on their tray, waiting to be put into the oven.

"Brooke and Finley," she said. "Their love has been restored."

"For now." I snatched up the tray and shoved it in the oven.

"I thought it was just a temporary aberration too," she said. "But I think this is for real."

I slammed the oven door shut. The hearts dishtowel slithered to the linoleum floor. "I love romance as much as the next girl, but let's be real. It can't last. It's all just chemicals, and those go away."

Mr. Carter smiled. "True, the romance ebbs and flows, but it's the love beneath it that counts. And the romance is worth the effort."

Scooping up the dishtowel, I pinched my mouth shut. I shouldn't have lost my temper. Just because I was worried about me and Arsen didn't mean I should take it out on others.

"Is everything all right?" Mrs. Carter asked me. "Did Arsen say anything to you about the modeling?"

I forced a smile. "It's fine. I mean, I don't think—he's not interested in the modeling. Sorry, I'm just a little busy preparing food for a memorial service."

She pressed a wrinkled hand to her chest. "Not for the poor Delaney girls? We read about that in the paper. How awful. You poor thing. We'll get out of your hair." They backed from the kitchen.

"They're nice," Dixie said.

"And I'm a horrible person for snapping at them. Yes. I know."

She arched a brow. "What's with you?"

Not Arsen. I had no idea where he was. "I'm just... stressed about this memorial."

"It's being held in a bar. It can't really go wrong."

I jammed my fists on my hips and glared at her. Why would she say something like that? Now she'd just jinxed it.

If I'd known how badly, I might have called the memorial off then and there.

Chapter Twenty-Four

I don't believe in magic. But there's something magical about a planner. Once an idea's in the planner, it just gets *done*.

At the kitchen counter, I studied my planner's pages. The food was on track. My kitchen smelled like baking cheese and sugar. Dixie had posted the flyers, and people we knew to call had been called.

Two poster-sized photos of Hannah and Kelsey stood on easels by the fridge. Beside the portraits, I'd pasted newspaper and yearbook articles about the women.

But something nagged at me that afternoon, something I'd forgotten. And Arsen hadn't called or explained or—

The door swung open, and Sal breezed into the kitchen. "Need help with anything?" Bailey clambered from his dog bed, and she scratched behind his ears.

My jaw spasmed. What I needed was peace and quiet so I could focus. "No," I said, "I think everything's on schedule for tomorrow. But thanks for offering." I returned my attention to the planner. *Did* I have enough food?

"No problem-o. I know how nuts wakes can get." She strolled to the butcher-block counter and plucked a green apple from it.

I turned from the counter. "Nuts?"

"Once people start drinking, anything can happen, and it usually does. I was at one where an Elvis impersonator turned up. And then there was the fistfight. Knocked the coffin right over, and it was an open casket. Big mess. But that was nothing compared to the motorcycle gang." She bit into the apple.

"Gang?" I said weakly.

"They were fine. It was when the *other* gang showed up to make sure the guy was dead that there were problems. Kelsey and Hannah weren't in a gang or anything, were they?"

"Not that I'm aware of."

"They weren't witches either? Because there were a lot of curses flying at the last funeral I attended. I had to take a salt bath afterward just in case I'd been caught in the crossfire." She took another bite.

Witches? How ridiculous. "I didn't see any signs of witchcraft at either of their homes," I said repressively. "This is Doyle, not San Francisco. We don't have witches."

"Then you should be okay." She came to peer at the planner, open on the counter. "Looks pretty comprehensive."

I shut the leather-bound book. "It is." I'd developed a detailed checklist from two I'd found online. For planning purposes, a memorial service was much like any other get-together. Food, drink, music... Okay, maybe not music. Though Antoine's *did* have a jukebox.

"So how are we going to interrogate the guests?" Sal asked. "That's what this is all about, right? The killer will probably be there."

We? If Sal was going to start grilling people, the sheriff would bust her for interfering for sure. I thought fast. "Are you sure you're comfortable attending? It's going to be at the western bar."

She scrunched her face. "I need to face my fears. I mean, I'm not happy about it, but if it's to stop a killer, I'll do it. I'm just not sure about the procedure here."

"There's no procedure. We have to just listen."

"Let the guests talk and see what comes up? Seems a little willy-nilly to me."

I folded my arms, my neck stiffening. "It is not—"

The door to the porch opened, and the sheriff strode in. "Witsend." Her blue eyes narrowed. "Bumpfiss."

"Thanks for the apple." Sal scurried from the room, the door to the foyer swinging behind her.

The sheriff stared after her. "When's the memorial service?"

"Tomorrow at five-thirty."

"I told you to hold it today."

My face tightened. "I couldn't arrange it for today," I snapped. "Do you know what goes into arranging a memorial service? It's a miracle I managed it for tomorrow with all the…" I motioned toward the gently swinging door. "… interruptions."

The sheriff's mouth quirked. "Sal in your hair?"

"You have no idea," I muttered.

"Having an outsider constantly interfering in your investigations?" She removed her broad-brimmed hat and shook out her hair. "I might have some idea."

"Well, I don't know how you put up with it."

"Oh, it's not so bad. Sometimes a different point of view on a case is helpful."

I gnawed my bottom lip. "And I haven't even called their parents yet. I was so focused on inviting locals who knew Kelsey and Hannah, I forgot about their parents until I read that article— I can't *believe* Tom Tarrant is taking credit for aiding your investigation."

"Crazy, huh?" she said dryly.

"I suppose Tom has been the one interfering. It doesn't surprise me one bit." Though I couldn't imagine his point of view would be particularly helpful. *True crime podcast. Huh.*

"Tom's a reporter. It's his job to be a pain in my butt. And don't worry about the parents. They're not going to come."

Of course I was going to worry about the parents. And it was only polite to invite them, even if they weren't interested in coming. "You told them about the memorial?" I asked.

"No, but they made it clear they're done with Doyle. There's a reason they left, and a reason they've stayed away."

"Why?"

She arched a brow in response. "Really?"

"Not those old UFO abductions? We haven't had an abduction in years."

"The *so-called* abductions. And yes. Though I don't think they were afraid of being abducted. They just were tired of living in a punchline." She returned her hat to her head and straightened it. "Thanks for arranging the memorial. I appreciate your interference." She turned and strode outside. Her boots thunked on the porch steps.

I smiled. *Interference. As if.*

My smile faded. Hold on. Was I to Sheriff McCourt as Sal was to me? Was I the sheriff's Sal? Suddenly dizzy, I braced my hands on the small table. It was... But that was...

I shook my head. No. It was impossible. I was *helping*, not interfering.

And maybe Sal was helping too. She had led a very different life than me. Maybe I did need her perspective.

And maybe I needed to stop procrastinating and call Kelsey and Hannah's parents. Sighing, I looked up the number, picked up my phone, and dialed.

After a few moments, a woman picked up. "Hello?"

My heart twisted. "Hello, this is Susan Witsend from Doyle. I knew your daughters, and I just wanted to call, and... I'm so sorry for your loss."

There was a long pause. "Thank you."

I cleared my throat. "We're holding a small, informal memorial for Kelsey and Hannah tomorrow here, and—"

"That's considerate of you, but we won't be able to attend."

I winced. "I understand. I'd be happy to send you photos from the memorial and the guest book."

There was a long silence. "I'd like that. Thank you... Did you... know Hannah and Kelsey well?"

I lowered my head and stared at my open planner on the counter. "Not as well as I would have liked," I said in a low voice. "They were better friends with my cousin, Dixie. I'm just, er, helping out. Her close friends are still in shock."

She laughed harshly. "Kelsey didn't have close friends."

"But there was Enrique, and Victor, and Anselm—"

"Them! I suppose Anselm told you we disinherited Hannah to keep him away from her? We were protecting her. It was obvious he was just after her money."

It didn't seem obvious to me. Not after he'd ended up with the already-disinherited Kelsey. "Oh?"

"You learn to spot it after a time when you reach a certain level. The graspers. The hangers on. But Hannah was naive. She thought they were in *love*." Her tone dripped acid. "And he did go running as soon as we made it clear he wouldn't see a penny from Hannah. We protected her." Her voice caught. "It was all we wanted," she said brokenly. "She had so much potential." The subtext was clear. *Not like Kelsey*. "And then there was Kelsey."

"Kelsey certainly was a free spirit," I said awkwardly.

"Kelsey didn't care about anything or anyone. Here's my address." She rattled it off, and I scrawled it into my planner. "She wasted everything," she continued.

Wasted what, exactly? "When was the last time you spoke with them?"

"Hannah called me after Kelsey... Hannah was such a good girl. Her sister's murder broke her. When I told her we'd have professional movers take care of Kelsey's house, she became hysterical. She insisted on packing everything herself. I'm glad they reconciled before..." Her voice hitched. "I need to go." She hung up.

A damp, cold sadness weighted my chest. It was a shame they hadn't reconciled with their parents. And despite what their mother had said, I didn't think Hannah and Kelsey had reconciled either. And then it had been too late for everyone.

I leaned against the counter and frowned at my planner. Mrs. Delaney hadn't told me anything new. But at least I'd done my duty.

There was a knock on the kitchen door, and Mr. Carter peeked in. Again. Did *nobody* read signs?

"Susan? You have a guest." He pushed the door wider, and Enrique walked into the kitchen.

"I was wandering around your B&B," Enrique said. "This kind gentleman offered to find you for me."

"I'll just, er..." Mr. Carter withdrew, and the door closed softly behind him.

I pushed back my chair and stood. "Enrique. This is a surprise."

He smiled faintly. "Is it, Susan? Is it really?"

Chapter Twenty-Five

My heart thrummed in my chest. Enrique's toothpaste-white smile should have been disarming. But for all I knew, it was the smile of a killer.

Watery sunlight paled the kitchen window curtains. Beneath the table, Bailey watched us, his graying brows furrowed.

I willed my pulse to slow. Odds were Enrique wouldn't hurt me. After all, Mr. Carter had seen him enter the B&B. But I would have felt a lot better if Mr. Carter had stayed with us in the kitchen, despite my new sign.

"Oh?" My voice cracked.

"I want to help with the memorial," he said, his accent lilting.

"Oh. How thoughtful."

"If I had been more thoughtful, I would have planned the memorial myself," he said, rueful. "Is it too late?"

Yes. "No, not at all. There are some friends of Hannah and Kelsey we haven't been able to reach. If you'd like to try calling them...?"

"Of course. Anything to help." His gaze traveled to the two, poster-sized photos of Hannah and Kelsey. He walked to them and studied the articles. "Kelsey was on the school newspaper? I had no idea." He smiled. "You must have learned all sorts of things as you put this memorial together."

"Yes," I said warily. Why was he really here?

He arched a brow. When I didn't continue, he said, "Have you got the list?"

I started. "Right. The list of people to call." I flipped the pages on my planner and pulled out a loose sheet of paper. "All the names that haven't been crossed off were unreachable."

"Then perhaps I shall reach them and learn new things about Kelsey too." He smiled, hesitated, then strode from the kitchen.

I dropped into the kitchen chair. Had it been my imagination, or had his last comment seemed a teeny bit ominous?

The next day, Antoine's jukebox at my back, I stood in my navy dress and cleared my throat. The murmuring crowd quieted and shifted to look at me. The portraits of Kelsey and Hannah gazed, smiling, out at them.

There were at least forty people here. Had Enrique wrangled more guests or had our flyers brought them in? I shook myself. *Not important.* And I was distracting myself from the task ahead.

Sheriff McCourt, also in a navy dress, stood near the batwing doors. It was strange to see her out of her uniform, her curling blond hair in loose tangles. Her gaze lingered on Enrique's broad back. His dark eyes somber and fixed on me, he wore an elegant gray suit.

"Thank you for coming today." I paused and realized what I'd forgotten to do. My mouth went dry. I hadn't prepared a speech.

From the corner of the long bar, Arsen nodded encouragement. At least he hadn't abandoned me today.

But of course he wouldn't. Arsen had his flaws, but a lack of chivalry wasn't one of them. He would never force me to do something like this alone. And he looked devilishly handsome in his navy suit.

I fingered my gold necklace then dropped my hand, embarrassed. "Kelsey used to tell my cousin Dixie we should remember the moment. It was a sort of *momento mori*, to live our best lives, to be in the moment. We wanted to remember the moments we had with Kelsey and Hannah today, to let people speak and share their stories about them. Who would like to come up and say a few words?"

No one spoke. No one moved. *Please someone say a few words.* A few guests at the front edged away from each other and looked around.

"Maybe if people who'd like to speak would line up over there?" I pointed, my stomach churning. No one was going to speak. I should have been more organized.

A ringtone jangled a cheerful tune: *Everything Is Awesome!* Near the front, a youngish, bearded man flushed. He fumbled in his pocket, yanked out the phone, and clapped it to his ear. "Are you kidding me? I'm at a funeral." The man jammed the phone back into his pocket.

Someone barked a nervous laugh and fell silent.

"Anyone?" I asked.

The phone rang again. The man pulled it out again and answered. "I told you not to call again. We're over. Done." He strode from the bar, the batwing doors creaking behind him.

"Ah... Dixie?" I asked, desperate for someone—anyone—to step forward.

My cousin looked around, her pink-tipped hair swinging. "Me?" The chains on her black cotton jacket jingled. She wore a longish black skirt with lots of pockets beneath it. It was as close to mourning clothes as I'd ever seen her wear.

"Maybe you could tell us some memories you have of Kelsey and Hannah? Other memorable things they said?" I prompted.

Dixie folded her arms. "Kelsey had tons of sayings on memory when we went out drinking. She told me not to tell anyone. So thanks for blowing that promise. I wouldn't have told you about the *momento mori* if I hadn't been, like, in shock."

"Oh," I said weakly. "Sorry. Anyone else?"

To my immense relief, half a dozen men and women shuffled forward and lined up. The first was the owner of the local coffeeshop, Jayce Bonheim.

She brushed her mahogany hair off one shoulder of her sapphire top. "I'm ashamed to say I usually get to know people by their coffee orders. Both Kelsey and Hannah were java fanatics. Kelsey, like her coffee, was no frills. She liked the classics—plain, black coffee. That made Kelsey an iconoclast in the age of double mochaccinos and cinnamon lattes. Kelsey did things her own way. She was brave. She didn't care about the things most of us do—money, security, a nice car. She just wanted freedom, and I think she achieved that. Hannah was obsessed with espresso. She was a little more traditional, but she was tougher than she looked. I respected them both, and I'll miss them. Doyle is... emptier for the loss."

Sal, in a black t-shirt that stretched across her ample chest and black jeans, applauded. No one joined in. She flushed, and her hands dropped to her sides.

"Thanks," Jayce said. She stepped aside, her hip bumping the jukebox.

An electronic tone screeched. The crowd winced.

BA-DAH, DAH. BA-DAH, DAH. *Staying Alive* thudded from the bar's high speakers. I covered my face with my hand. Of all the songs for the jukebox to burst into, did it have to be that one?

Reaching behind the jukebox, Jayce yanked out its plug. The song died. "Sorry," she muttered and hurried into the crowd.

A thirty-something blonde in a little black dress, walked to the front. She took a deep breath. "I met Kelsey in high school. She was such a force back then. Truly unique. She didn't care what anyone thought of her. She even got me into juicing. I'm now a part of an amazing company because of her. Some documented benefits of Essence Juice Essentials Juices are detoxification, reduced inflammation, improved immune function, and clearer skin. I'm making over six figures a year. If you're looking to earn extra income, you too can be a part of this amazing opportunity..."

The sheriff caught my eye and made a cutting motion with one hand. My face prickled with embarrassment. But how was I supposed to stop the woman?

Anselm nudged my arm. "Thanks for arranging this," he said in a low voice.

I hadn't arranged for a multilevel marketing presentation. "It's no trouble," I whispered.

"I suspect it was a good deal of trouble." The artist rubbed the tattoo on the back of his neck, ruffling the base of his auburn hair.

"I wanted to ask you something about Kelsey," I said. "That coral pendant she always wore. Did it have some special meaning to her?"

His brow furrowed. "Why would you think so?"

"She wore it a lot. It didn't seem expensive—just a round of gray coral. I thought it must have meant something."

He shook his head and frowned. "I think she got it in Hawaii."

"You two went to Hawaii together?"

His expression darkened. "No."

"And that's why I returned to Doyle," the blonde finished. She smiled and returned to the crowd.

"About time," Anselm muttered and moved off.

The other speakers didn't try to turn the memorial into a sales pitch. So that was one positive. But they didn't reveal anything useful either. I glanced at the frowning sheriff.

When the last speaker stepped from the podium, people migrated to the bar. Antoine pulled the plastic off the food at a long table. The volume in the pub rose. Arsen went to chat with Jayce.

I slumped against a booth. The sheriff had counted on me, and I'd failed. The memorial had only attracted people who hadn't known the victims well. But that's what you got when you didn't leave time for thoughtful planning.

Biting my lip, I glanced at Arsen. This morning had been a replay of yesterday's breakfast. He'd pretended everything was fine, and I hadn't had the nerve to challenge it. Everything was falling apart.

A cold shadow touched my shoulder blade, and I closed my eyes. I was not going to spin up into an anxiety attack. *I am in the present. I am aware.* I breathed slowly.

"Buck up." Sal appeared beside me. "At least no one started a fight."

I folded my arms. "Yet."

"No, seriously. I mean, it *is* a little weird that you got those two songs playing at one memorial. Talk about inappropriate. That guy should have turned his phone off after the first call."

I glanced at Arsen and Jayce. Her heart-shaped face lit, and she touched his arm. And that meant nothing. She was married. I was not jealous. It was stupid to worry...

Who was I kidding? It wasn't stupid at all. Something was definitely going on with Arsen. My breath tightened, my chest rising and falling as I struggled for air.

"Hey, hey." Sal gripped my shoulder. "What's happening here?"

"I don't know," I said wildly. "I have no idea what's going on with Arsen. He's hot. He's cold. He won't talk to me. And I can feel an anxiety attack coming and I don't want to be that person. I don't want to feel this way."

"Well, that's dumb."

"You don't know what it's like," I said, shrill.

"To have an anxiety attack? No. But the way I figure it, anxiety is just a reminder that we're alive. Life is fragile." She motioned toward the two oversized portraits by the jukebox. "Much of our life is out of our control. In fact, if you think about it, it's a miracle we exist at all. Did you know that if the Earth was a teensy bit bigger or smaller, there'd be no life on earth? And don't get me started about the sun and the moon. We're the only planet in the solar system with total solar eclipses. Do you know what that means?"

"Huh?" What did eclipses have to do with anything?

"Of *course* we feel anxiety. So give yourself a break. Things are always going to go wrong. So there's no sense being anxious about being anxious." She clapped my shoulder. I stumbled sideways at the force of the blow, and she moved into the crowd.

I tugged at the collar of my navy dress. Easy for her to say. *Don't be anxious about being anxious.* Ha. My jaw tightened. That was just... just...

Right.

My stomach hardened. I wasn't special. I wasn't the only person who felt anxiety. All normal people felt it at some point. Maybe some more than others, but anxiety was normal.

And in this case, my nerves had accurately heralded disaster. With all the inappropriate things that had happened at this so-called memorial... I looked around.

The noise level in the bar had increased. People chatted with each other, occasionally laughing, remembering. Victor wandered past, his full lips in a male-model pout. At the bar, Vida looked longingly after him.

Maybe the memorial *wasn't* such a disaster. From a detecting perspective, it had been, but it wasn't over. And it was time I started talking to people and doing my own investigating.

I turned and bumped into Tom Tarrant, nemesis and reporter for the *Doyle Times*. He had the good looks of a star high school football player, which he'd once been. "Hey, Susan. You got any comments for the paper?"

I stiffened. He was *not* going to interrogate me. Interrogating people was *my* job. "No."

"Oh, come on. You organized this shindig. Word is you found both bodies. What's up with that?"

"I have to speak with the sheriff." I made my way through the crowd. The sheriff stood talking to Enrique, elegant in a charcoal suit.

Her head was tilted up, her expression speculative. A wistful smile spread across Enrique's face. His gaze was smoldering, and they stood closer than the crowd warranted.

I stopped short and folded my arms. They weren't even being subtle about it. "You have got to be kidding me." *The sheriff and Enrique?* This was a memorial for two murdered women. Who thinks of romance during a memorial?

The sheriff straightened and stepped away from Enrique. Two pink spots darkened her cheeks. "What?"

"At a memorial? Really?" I stomped away into the crowd. Sure the sheriff had been alone for a long time. And sure, Enrique looked like he'd fallen off the pages of one of those old movie magazines. But he was a *suspect*. Plus she was old enough to be his... aunt.

"Hey, Susan." Jayce touched my arm. "Sorry about the jukebox thing."

I smiled at the café owner. "It wasn't your fault."

"Weird *that* song had to come up though," she said.

"Yeah. They're gone, and the rest of us are just staying alive." I laughed hollowly. At least it hadn't been *Dead Man's Party*. "I didn't know you were friends with Kelsey and Hannah."

Jayce cocked her head, her spring-ivy eyes serious. "I don't think Kelsey had many friends. I always thought of myself as a rebel, but Kelsey was a whole other level. Hannah was more of a follower. I'm sorry to say I think Hannah resented it." She shook her head. "But they're both gone now." She studied Anselm, talking to Arsen. "There was a time when I had more than one guy on the hook. But you never really know what's going on."

"It was different for you though. Dating around isn't the same as three serious relationships at once."

"I'm not sure they were all serious. There was something Kelsey always held apart from everyone. Something secret and untouchable. The only person who really knew her was Hannah." She smiled bitterly. "And I'm speculating. Sorry."

Someone jostled my elbow, and I edged sideways into the throng. "No, it's normal after something like this. Everyone's speculating." I furrowed my brow. "Did Kelsey have a secret? I mean, we all have secrets, but did Kelsey have something more?"

"It's strange you should ask that." Jayce cocked her head, her mahogany hair waterfalling over one shoulder. "I know I brought it up, but yes. I got a sense she did. Something in her attitude, her vibe, something that made her feel... I don't know. Powerful?" She grimaced. "Why did I say that?"

"Because it's true, I think," I said slowly.

"They deserved better," Jayce said.

Both women deserved better. And now they deserved justice. My heart hardened. And I was going to make sure they got it.

Chapter Twenty-Six

"Everyone? Hey. Uh, hello." Anselm rapped on his beer mug with a spoon. The artist swayed and grabbed the jukebox. "I'd like to speak," he slurred. His auburn hair had somehow gotten mussed.

I rubbed my arm, realized I'd rumpled the sleeve of my navy dress, and smoothed it. Was Anselm drunk? *Already?* The memorial had only started an hour ago. I was a lightweight, but I'd still have to work at it to get tipsy inside of an hour. Not that I ever would. The idea of losing control like that... I shuddered.

The crowd in the western bar quieted. Stomach writhing, I edged closer. I mean, I *had* asked for speakers. I'd just thought we'd reached the quietly reminiscing-about-the-departed stage of the evening.

Anselm rubbed the back of his tattooed neck. "Kelsey was amazing, but you all know that. But I know... I've heard..." He drew a deep breath and dropped his free hand to his side. "People have been saying things about her, here at the memorial." He scowled. "Don't think I haven't heard people sniggling..." He frowned.

I frowned too. Was *sniggling* a word?

"...about free love," he finished.

A draft gusted through the batwing doors, and they swayed as if haunted. Victor and Enrique moved closer to the jukebox. They glanced at each other, their brows creasing.

Anselm rocked on his heels. "Kelsey was more than that. I asked her to marry me, and she agreed."

The crowd gasped. Victor's nostrils flared.

"We were engaged," Anselm said.

"Liar," Victor shouted. "You don't need to lie to try and make her respectable. She didn't care about what people thought. Neither do we."

"I'm *not* lying," Anselm said mulishly. His jaw jutted forward. "We were engaged. It happened a week before she was killed."

"I do not believe it." Enrique crossed his arms over his charcoal suit. "Kelsey was a free spirit. She would never tie herself down."

"You're calling me a liar?" Anselm's hands clenched.

Enrique shrugged. "Perhaps you did not understand the situation."

"*I'm* calling you a liar." Victor lurched forward. He shoved Anselm against the jukebox.

"Stop," Enrique said.

Victor jerked his arm back for a punch and jabbed Enrique in the chest with his elbow. Enrique staggered backward. Anselm bellowed incoherently and drove his shoulder into Victor's torso.

Arsen stepped between me and the men, blocking my view. But he didn't have to protect me. I was already moving away from the action as fast as I could. I had no illusions I'd be any good at breaking up a fight.

Sheriff McCourt brushed past. "Enough!"

Victor took another swing at Anselm. The sheriff jammed her foot into the back of his knee. His leg buckled, and he dropped to the sawdust floor.

"I said, enough." She pulled out a pair of handcuffs and snapped them onto the unresisting Victor. "You're all coming to the station."

"Yes, ma'am." Enrique promptly held out his wrists, his expression school-boy regret.

"Thanks," she said dryly. "But I'm out of cuffs."

"He started it," Victor said sullenly.

"Arsen," she said. "I'm temporarily deputizing you. Come with me and bring Anselm."

Arsen shot me an apologetic look then angled his head toward the batwing doors. "You heard the lady. Let's go."

Glowering, Anselm stomped from the bar, followed by Arsen. The sheriff marched the other two men out of Antoine's. Vida hesitated, then ran after them, the batwing doors swinging in her wake.

"Huh," Sal said. "There was a fight after all. Who'd of figured?"

I should have figured. Nothing had been going right. Why had I expected the memorial to be any different?

The affair broke up soon after that. Guests drifted from the bar in twos and threes.

I plugged in the jukebox. It stayed mercifully silent. I glanced around the room. Sal collected food trays from the bar, and despite everything, I smiled. Unlike Dixie, Sal didn't have to be asked to help. I frowned. Where *was* Dixie?

"Looking for your cousin?" Antoine asked, picking a crumpled napkin off the floor.

"Yes. Have you seen her?"

"She left ten minutes ago."

That answered that. Dixie was off to Vegas and the mysterious Steve. "Antoine, you said Kelsey suggested you buy Bitcoin. Did she invest in it herself?"

"She said she did. Not a lot—just five hundred bucks. That was back in 2010, when she was just a young thing. I'm surprised she was able to scrape together that much money. I told her not to do it—it was a risk. What an idiot I was." He laughed shortly.

I moved to the bar and helped Sal collect the trays. She popped a mini quiche into her mouth. "Quality grub, Susan. I can't believe people are leaving all this on the table."

"The fistfight may have killed people's appetites."

"Not mine." She tossed a mini quiche into the air and caught it in her mouth. "So which one of them did it?"

I set a tray in a cardboard box on the bar. "Vida and Victor both have alibis. If it's any of them, it has to be either Anselm or Enrique."

"If? You think it's someone else?"

I sighed. "It seems unlikely anyone else would be involved. And they all had motivation—jealousy."

"I dunno. They've been living in that weird love triangle—quadrangle..." She squinted. "Square? Whatever. They've been living like that for nearly a year. Why kill Kelsey now? And if it's jealousy, why not kill one of the other guys instead?"

I grimaced. I'd been so distracted by my love life, this investigation had been less than well organized. "We need more data."

She snapped her fingers. "Idea. Let's go to Enrique's."

"Why? He's not there."

"I know. It's perfect. They're all tied up at the sheriff's. Let's see if there's anything to see at his house. Maybe there's a clue in his backyard or something."

That also seemed unlikely. But Arsen was at the station too, and Dixie was off who knew where, and no one needed me at Wits' End. I might as well go stare at an empty house. Maybe it would give me some inspiration.

We finished packing up the remains of the food and loaded the containers into my Crosstrek. Sal and I drove to Enrique's two-story shingled home, higher in the hills. I parked in the gloom of an ancient pine. Though to be strictly accurate, the evening was well past gloomy and into dark.

"No Tesla today." She hopped from the car. "Told you he'd still be at the cop shop."

I met her on the lawn. Patches of snow gleamed whitely in the darkness.

"Get any brainstorms yet?" she asked.

"No."

"Cool. Let's check the back." She strode around the corner of the house.

"Sal," I hissed. "Don't." I looked around. The wooded street was silent. I shivered and hurried after her into the back yard. Pines crowded a snow-covered lawn.

Sal straightened away from a French door. Lights streamed from inside. "Hey, it's unlocked. Could be burglars. We should check." She opened it and stepped inside.

My heart jumped unpleasantly. "Wait." What were we supposed to do if there *were* burglars inside?

I trotted up the steps and stuck my head inside what looked like a martial arts dojo. Soft white mats and weapons hung from the walls. Why were the lights on? Had Enrique forgotten to turn them off, or was there a more sinister explanation? *Like burglars?*

Sal picked up a trophy and whistled. "Enrique's judo skills didn't do him much good at the memorial today, did they? He went down like a sack of potatoes."

"He didn't really go down. He just sort of staggered a bit," I said, glancing around. We shouldn't be here. This was trespassing, even if his door *had* been unlocked. "We should—"

"That, or the dude was faking it." She set down the trophy and walked through a squarish entrance to the hall. "Oh my God!"

Heart jamming in my throat, I hurried into the empty hallway. "What? Where are you?"

She stuck her head from an open doorway. "He's got a music room."

I walked inside. In front of a glassed-in fireplace sat a drum set. A Spanish guitar on a stand rested on a leopard-print rug.

She picked up the guitar. "Now *this* I could be serenaded with."

I stiffened. "Not everyone can play the guitar."

"That wasn't a knock on Arsen. At least he went retro with that boombox. And everyone knows it's the thought that counts."

If I knew what Arsen had been thinking, I might agree with that sentiment. "There aren't any burglars. We should get out of here. We can look for clues outside."

She returned the guitar to its stand. "Don't need to. It's obvious Anselm did it."

"How is that obvious?"

"Enrique's too perfect to be a killer." She gestured toward the guitar. "What kind of killer plays Flamenco?"

"I'm sure at least once in the history of the world, there's been a Flamenco-playing murderer."

"You may be right." She put her hands on her hips and looked around. "Yeah. This dude's too perfect. Enrique did it all right."

I managed not to roll my eyes. Sal's enthusiasm for truth and justice was admirable. But this was not how one solved crimes. "Check his medicine cabinet for drugs."

"I thought you said we needed to go outside?"

"Well, we're in here now," I said, flustered. "We may as well—" Why was I arguing? "I'm going to find his home office."

Enrique's office was as modern as the rest of his house. Bookshelves displayed books and more African art. The computer on his sleek white table desk required a password I didn't know. His leather day planner seemed innocuous enough, if a little thin. It was only a calendar, and nowhere near as useful as mine. But I photographed the last two months of calendar pages anyway.

"No drugs," Sal said from the doorway. "But he's got chocolate covered goji berries in the kitchen. Want some? They're organic." She held out her hand.

Never in my life had I raided a suspect's kitchen. At least not for snacks. "No. Thank you."

She tossed the chocolates into her mouth. One missed, bounced off her cheek, and rattled across the wood floor. It vanished beneath a bookcase. "Find anything?" she asked.

I closed the planner. "No." I dropped my phone into my purse. "And we should get out of here before a neighbor sees my car and gets suspicious." Or before Sal made a noticeable dent in Enrique's goji berry supply. "We've already been here too long."

"Right. Let's check out that other dude's place."

Because this foray had been so successful. *Ha.* A dozen excuses rose and fell in my mind. But in the end, Arsen wasn't around, and Dixie was driving to Vegas, and I...

My jaw tightened. I met Sal's gaze. "Let's do it."

Chapter Twenty-Seven

In my annals as a detective, I've engaged in some bizarre investigations. Cruising suspect's houses like a lovesick stalker had to be the most hairbrained of them all.

But we drove to Anselm's house anyway. As Sal said, there was no harm in trying. Besides, Anselm would likely still be busy with Sheriff McCourt too.

I parked in front of the shingled Craftsman. The bungalow's porch lights gleamed, illuminating the porch but not much beyond it.

My fingers drummed on the wheel. Arsen *had* to be finished by now. So why hadn't he called? Had he gone home? If he'd gone to Wits' End and found me not there, he definitely would have called. So he obviously hadn't gone to Wits' End.

The Crosstrek's headlights switched off, bathing the street in darkness.

"You coming?" Sal stepped from the car and slammed the Crosstrek's door, rattling my teeth. Her bulky shadow vanished into the darkness.

I exhaled sharply. Arsen was fine, and there was no sense worrying about things I couldn't control. Like Arsen. And Sal. Unfortunately, anxiety was pretty much my default mode.

Grabbing my purse, I stepped from the car and fumbled my way across the lawn. One hand on the shingled side, I made my way around the corner of the house. The porch light illuminated a slender strip of lawn. It vanished beneath thick pines.

Sal straightened away from the wood-framed glass door and pulled it open. "Whadaya know? This one's open too."

I gaped. "That's not…" No. No *way*. My face tightened. "You broke in. You broke into both houses." I glanced through the glass into the elegant dining room.

"I didn't break anything," she said. "I picked the lock." She slid a slim leather case into the pocket of her bulky parka.

"We can't break in," I hissed. "It's illegal."

"Only if we get caught. I can teach you how, if you want."

"How to evade the police?"

"How to pick locks."

"I know how to pick locks." My parents had taught me. Though it had been ages since I'd practiced. Not to mention the most critical point, that housebreaking was wrong and illegal.

"Well the door's open. Are we going in, or not?"

I hesitated. It just seemed wasteful not to go inside now. "Fine. Let's go."

Sal stepped inside. Cautiously, I followed her into the dining room. Using the flashlights on our phones, we moved past the stained glass doors.

At the junction of a hallway, Sal stopped. "You go that way." She pointed. "I'll go this way."

I nodded, definitely not irritated that Sal was giving orders now. It was important to be proactive, and I could give her this. Even if I had been planning to go this way anyway. I made my way down the hall.

"No drugs in the medicine cabinet," Sal called out.

"That's good." I stopped inside the doorway to his bedroom and sighed. "In for a penny, in for a pound."

"What?" Sal called.

"Nothing." I scanned the room with my phone light. Its glow picked out a bank of computer monitors atop a desk. I'd always found one monitor sufficient, but all I did was run a B&B.

And Anselm was an artist. Maybe he'd moved into digital art?

I edged into the bedroom, my footsteps hollow on the wooden floor. My shin banged against the bed's footboard, and I bit back a curse.

I moved more slowly toward the desk. An envelope from the electric company made a bookmark in a dictionary. I flipped it open to *Aardvark* and extracted the envelope. It was addressed to Charles Holmes and at this house. Did Anselm have an alias or a roommate? Hoping it wasn't the latter, I snapped a picture of the envelope.

"Susan?" Sal asked from the doorway.

I turned toward her, and a flashlight shone in my eyes. Wincing, I looked away. "What?"

"We gotta go," she said. "We've got company."

My stomach bottomed. "The sheriff?" I hurried toward her.

"Nope. Anselm. Come on."

Even worse. If he caught us, he could have us arrested. And I couldn't exactly blame him. I *knew* we shouldn't have broken into the house. We jogged across a short hall and into the kitchen.

The front door snicked open. The kitchen brightened.

Sal and I froze. The light from the front hallway backlit the stained-glass doors. Geometric slivers of colored light flowed from them into the dining room and kitchen.

I swallowed. Our exit was through the dining room. We were trapped.

Sal pressed a finger to her lips, and I exhaled slowly. *Patience.* I should be encouraging Sal in her transition from scofflaw to crime fighter. But what did she think I was going to do here? Burst into the chorus of *Oklahoma*?

Footsteps made their way down the hallway toward the bedroom we'd just left. We tiptoed past the refrigerator and toward the dining room.

In the hallway, the footsteps stopped.

I froze, one hand hovering above the tile counter. Had he heard us? We were so close to escape, and my hands jittered. All we had to do was cross the dining room and we'd be free.

The glass door on the opposite side of the dining table creaked open. Cold air wafted across my skin, turning the sweat on my forehead clammy. We hadn't closed the door properly when we'd come in. If he heard the door, felt the draft, he'd know someone had broken in.

The footsteps retreated. Anselm's lean shadow passed behind the stained glass sliding doors. The front door clicked open. After a moment again, it closed. Anselm's silhouette, head bent, passed behind the stained glass.

I hurried through the dining room and out its glass door to the yard. Sal followed behind me.

Noiselessly, I shut the door, and we jogged around the corner of the house. I raced across the lawn. A tree root tripped me up, but I managed to catch my balance and make it to my Crosstrek unscathed. We hopped inside and quietly closed the doors.

"That was close," Sal said. "Find anything?"

I willed my heart to stop beating like a bongo drum. "An electric bill for Charles Holmes."

"I thought this guy's name was Anselm."

"It is." I pulled out my phone and typed CHARLES HOLMES DOYLE CALIFORNIA into the search engine. The screen glowed white. "I can't get any reception here." And we shouldn't be waiting outside Anselm's house like a pair of idiot criminals.

I started the SUV. Headlights flared in my windscreen. A black and white SUV pulled up beside us. My stomach rolled queasily. The SUV's driver's window hummed downward. Smiling like a madwoman, I cranked down my own.

Deputy Owen Denton peered out. His blue eyes narrowed. "Susan? What are you doing here?"

"I just, ah, was checking something on my phone. Don't want to surf the internet while driving."

"That would be dangerous," Sal agreed.

"And you just happened to stop here," he said flatly.

"Is this a bad place to stop?" I asked.

He lifted a blond brow. "Yes."

"Then I'll just, er, go?" I asked.

"Please do," he said.

I let the car drift forward and pulled from the curb. I glanced in my rearview.

The sheriff's department SUV made a U-turn, and I tensed. It parked on the opposite side of the street, and its lights dimmed.

We made it home without further incident, and I opened up the laptop on my kitchen table. Sal scratched Bailey behind his ears.

Once again, I looked up Charles Holmes online. "Oh."

"What is it?" Sal asked.

"Charles Holmes is Anselm Holmes's father." So, not an alias. But why was his father's name on Anselm's electric bill?

"So that's that," Sal said. "No alias. No drugs. If we had more time, we might find something incriminating. But we can always go back tomorrow."

Was she out of her mind? We'd barely made it out tonight. "No. We can't. If one of those two killed Kelsey and Hannah—"

"If?"

"If," I said firmly. "There needs to be a clean chain of evidence, or they won't go to jail for the murders. And if we break in, we'll be messing that chain up. In fact, we may already have."

The phone rang in the pocket of her parka, dropped over a kitchen chair. She pulled it out and scowled. "Bingo again."

"Why don't you answer?" I hoped her interest in my murders wasn't a way for her to evade her ex. Crime solving could be a critical piece in her transition from jail.

But if it was the former, I sympathized. I knew firsthand that a murder investigation could be a pleasant distraction.

She dropped the phone on the table, and Bailey looked up in alarm. "I don't want to talk to him." She sniffed. "There's nothing he could say that I'd have any interest in."

Uh, huh. Returning my attention to the laptop, I web surfed some more. A pop-up window displaying diamond necklaces blocked my view of Victor's social media page.

"Buying your own Valentine's Day present?" Sal asked. "That's not a bad idea. No sense in waiting on a man to make you happy."

I closed the page. "It's not really my style." *Or my budget.*

"Buying your own jewelry or that stuff in particular?"

"The diamonds," I said. "They're ridiculous. They lose value as soon as they leave the jewelry store. The only reason they're expensive is because of the diamond cartel. Diamonds are common stones, in fact, they're some of the most common. And I'm perfectly capable of buying things for myself." When I had the money. But right now I was saving for a new roof for Wits' End.

She gusted a breath and leaned against the butcher-block counter. "I hear you. We're just two independent women making our way in a cold, cruel world. It ain't fair."

"The world's not that bad." But I confess, I said it more because I was in the mood to contradict her than because I believed it right now. With Arsen acting so oddly, the whole world seemed off its axis.

"Says the woman who's up to her neck in bodies."

"Some people are awful, yes," I said. "But I'd rather focus on the good and on fixing what I can."

"I don't know if there's any fixing what's happened here."

I glanced again at Victor's social page. My hand flattened on the kitchen table. Actually... I was starting to think there might be. Not a way to fix things—that was impossible—but a way to see justice done.

Chapter Twenty-Eight

I studied the window. But all I saw was black, thanks to the reflection of the kitchen's overhead lights. Bailey rested against my foot. "Sal," I said, "what do you know about Bitcoin?"

She dropped into the chair opposite me and rested her elbows on the small, round table. "It's a cryptocurrency that allows peer-to-peer exchange of value through the use of a decentralized protocol. Its exchange value is based on a blockchain, which in the case of Bitcoin is just a publicly updated ledger. Why?"

"Uh... a what now?"

"Which part?"

My face warmed. "All of it."

She shifted, leaning forward. "Okay, a cryptocurrency is a digital currency where the transactions are recorded on a decentralized system using cryptography."

I still only understood about half of that. "How do you know all this?"

"From Bingo. I told you, he's a money guy."

I shook my head. How Bitcoin worked didn't matter. "What if—?"

The kitchen door swung open. Arsen, still in his suit from the memorial, strode into the room. He stopped short, his broad chest heaving, his tie askew. "Oh. Hi, Sal. Do you mind if I have a word with Susan? Alone?"

My stomach knotted. Suddenly, I didn't want to be alone with Arsen. I was afraid of what he might say.

She winked, pushed back her chair, and rose. "No problem-o. I'll give you two lovebirds some privacy."

"Thanks," he said.

She ambled from the kitchen. The door swung shut behind her.

I swallowed. "Did everything go okay at the sheriff's station?"

"Yeah." He paced the kitchen's linoleum floor. Bailey watched him, his doggy head swiveling back and forth beneath the table. "It was fine."

"Are you still a deputy?"

"No, she de-deputized me." He shrugged out of his suit jacket and dropped it over the back of a kitchen chair.

"That's too bad."

He stopped and stared earnestly at me. "Not really."

"What took you so long to get back?"

"Vida showed up at the sheriff's station."

"She's still in love with Victor," I said sadly.

"And he's still got a thing for her. He just doesn't know it yet."

Good for them. It wasn't exactly a happy ending, but it was a break from the awfulness. "I hope they can work it out."

"I really don't care. Susan, we've been together a long time."

The knot tightened and grew, throttling my chest and throat. This was it. He was breaking up with me. "What do you know about Bitcoin?" I blurted.

He blinked. "Just what I told you before. I mean, I own some, but I basically treat it like a casino. Forget Bitcoin. We've been together a long time. And it's been great. Really great. But things have changed between us."

Oh God. He *was* breaking up with me.

My cellphone rang on the table. I snatched it up, my hands shaking. "It's the sheriff. I'd better take this." Before he could respond, I answered. "Hello, Sheriff."

"What were you doing at Anselm's house tonight?"

"The, ah, side door was open, and we were worried about burglars—"

"How would you know the side door was open? Why were you prowling around his yard?"

I glanced at Arsen. His brow furrowed. My breath squeezed from my chest. This was happening. This was happening, and I couldn't stop it. My eyes burned. But at least I could delay it. "What do you know about Bitcoin?" I asked her.

"It's a decentralized digital currency that uses blockchain to maintain an open ledger," she said. "Why?"

Why did everyone seem to understand Bitcoin but me? "Because according to Antoine, Kelsey bought into Bitcoin back in 2010."

There was a long silence. "How much?" she asked.

"Five hundred dollars."

"Good God. And she held it?"

"I don't know. But it might explain why she was so blasé about her parents disinheriting her. And she had some very expensive kitchen equipment." I avoided Arsen's gaze.

"Kitchen—?" The sheriff barked a laugh. "Forget the copper pots. Do you know what a five hundred dollar investment in Bitcoin back then would be worth?"

"A lot, I'd imagine," I said.

"Yeah," she said. "Like over a hundred million."

It was one of those numbers that didn't really mean anything, it was so big. Arsen might not have been the richest person in Doyle after all. "If she kept it in a digital wallet, that might explain what Hannah was digging for in her yard. Everyone said Kelsey didn't trust banks. I'd presume that would extend to safe deposit boxes."

"It would also make it impossible for us to track it. The whole point of Bitcoin is it can't be tracked, and if it's on a wallet..."

"It might speak to motive." My pulse thumped unevenly in my head. I didn't look at Arsen. With my fingertip, I pushed a rubber band around the kitchen table. The rubber twisted and curled beneath my finger.

"It would," the sheriff said, "if we could prove any of it. And without that wallet... Hell, even *with* that wallet I'm not sure I could prove it was Kelsey's. And it could look like anything. A USB drive—"

"A piece of jewelry?" I asked, throat aching. I couldn't do this. I couldn't lose him. But I couldn't keep him either if he wanted to go.

"We'll do another search of their homes," she said grimly.

"I doubt you'll find the wallet." My voice cracked on the last word.

"I think you're right." She hung up.

"Kelsey was into Bitcoin?" Arsen asked. "Back when it started?"

I stared at my hands, flat upon the table. "That's what Antoine told me. I think someone else mentioned it, too. She may have been a very wealthy woman."

Nausea churned my gut. *Another night, just one more night as a couple.* If I could keep him interested in the murder, he might get distracted. He might forget telling me, just for the night.

"If she got in at the beginning," he said, "very wealthy doesn't begin to cover it."

"It's amazing she was able to keep it quiet."

"Not really. Not if you want to have friends and a peaceful life."

Looking up from the table, I studied him. I had no idea how much Arsen was worth, but I knew he came from money. And he didn't talk about that much, or act like a particularly wealthy person. The money just seemed to appear when he needed it, and he didn't discuss how.

The ache at the back of my throat swelled, choking. None of that mattered anymore. It was a mystery I'd never solve.

He shook his head. "But if Kelsey was worth that much—"

The kitchen door burst open. A lean, handsome man in a business suit and glasses stormed into the room.

"Oh, my God," I burst out. "I've got a *sign*." Beneath the table, Bailey lumbered to his feet and barked.

"I'm looking for Sal," the man said. "I've been ringing the damn desk bell, and no one answered." His cocoa-colored hair stuck up in short spikes, as if he'd come through a windstorm.

Arsen straightened. "Sorry about that, but this is a private room. Let's go to the desk, and we'll talk."

I studied the newcomer's polished shoes, his red tie. "Bingo?" I asked. "I mean, Bernard?"

The man shot me an impatient glance. "I know Sal's here. I saw her car out front, but she's not answering my calls."

"There's probably a reason for that, buddy," Arsen said, voice hard.

Bingo raked his hand through his hair, and it stood up even straighter. "I know what the reason is," he said wildly. "It's a misunderstanding. I just need to talk to her."

The door flew open and banged against the cupboard. Sal stormed into the kitchen. "What are you doing here bothering my friends? We got nothing to talk about."

"I thought the gummies were expired." Bingo extended his hands in a plaintive gesture. "I was going to get you more."

"Huh." She folded her arms. "A likely story."

"It's true," Bingo insisted.

Her mouth trembled. "And the girl?"

"What girl?" Bingo's brow creased.

"That girl I saw you with at La Strada."

He blinked. "Edie?"

"You said La Strada was *our* special place."

"It is, but she's my cousin from Tallahassee. I wanted to take her somewhere nice."

She folded her arms over her ample chest. "Then why didn't you invite me to go with you two?"

"You said you thought it was creepy when guys dragged girls to meet their family too soon."

"Why'd you think it was too soon?"

"I didn't think so," he said. "I thought *you* did. I love you."

She blinked. Her hands dropped to her sides. "You... what?"

"I love you, Sal. My life isn't the same without you in it." He took her hands. "Please come back."

Arsen steered me into the sitting room. "Let's give them some privacy."

"Why not?" I said, stunned. I dropped onto the black velvet sofa. It was the cycle of life, I thought bitterly. One romance was ending, and another was being brought back from the dead.

He jammed his hands in the pockets of his navy slacks. "So that was..."

"A shocking turn of events?"

"I was going to say romantic."

I shifted on the soft couch. Now we were alone again, we'd have to talk. "You realize we can't leave here until they do. The only way out of Wits' End is through that kitchen."

"Do you have to go anywhere?"

"No," I admitted. "Do you?" I asked, hopeful.

"No."

We stood there for a long moment. Light from the chandelier glinted off Arsen's whiskey-colored hair. His handsome face looked tense, his jaw tight. One corner of his shirt collar was turned up. I wanted to go to him and smooth it down. But I didn't.

Instead I groped for the right thing to say, the thing that would fix everything. But that was ridiculous. There were no right words, only the truth. And I couldn't avoid that forever.

Arsen pulled his hands from his pockets. "Susan, this is ridiculous. I've been trying to tell you—"

The parlor door burst open. A pink-faced Sal stood in the entry. "Susan, I'm sorry to leave you in the lurch, but I've got to go. I've had it all wrong. Bingo and I are good. Better than good. I've got to go with him."

I smiled, my mouth dry. "That's wonderful. I mean, I'm sorry you won't be able to help anymore. But love is more important."

"Are you sure? I have this feeling." She pressed a hand to her stomach. "It seems like things are coming to a head, you know?"

"You've already done so much work on this," I said. "You've done enough."

"Yeah," she said, her tone uncertain. "But if you want me to stay, I can stay."

The parlor was too hot. I needed to open a window. Or just run. "No, no, no. You and Bingo deserve this."

"Okay," she said. "If you're sure. Um, I guess I need to check out."

"I've got your credit card info. I'll take care of it." *Just go. Let me get this over with. I'd been stupid to think I could prolong it. This was agony.* I blinked rapidly.

Bingo appeared behind her shoulder, Sal's light blue suitcase under his arm. "You ready, Sal?"

"Yeah." She rushed into the room and pulled me off the couch and into a smothering hug. "Come see me in Nowhere sometime."

"Or we can come back here," Bingo said, and she released me.

Save me. I gasped a breath and forced a smile. "That would be great."

Arsen and I saw them to the front door. Their two cars backed from the driveway, and they were gone.

I stood beneath the porch light with Arsen. A strange hollowness emptied my chest. "I'm going to miss Sal," I said.

"That's because you like challenging people." His head brushed against a hanging fern.

"I wouldn't say that." I smiled, rueful. "I like you." I tried and failed to swallow. No matter what he had to say, nothing would change that.

I raised my chin. "Let's talk."

Chapter Twenty-Nine

Soberly, Arsen followed me into the kitchen. The beagle glanced up from beneath the table, then closed his eyes. Fear seized my throat. All my resolutions to stay strong fled. *Let's talk?* Why the hell had I said that?

Arsen touched my shoulder. "Susan—"

"If I was going to steal a digital wallet," I interrupted, "how would it work?"

Whatever he had to say would happen, I knew. I could only put it off for so long. Then I'd have to face what was coming. But for now, for this moment beneath the kitchen lights, I didn't want to face it. I couldn't face it.

I rubbed my wrist, twisting my watch. And yes, I *knew* I was vacillating between delay and getting it over with. And yes, I also knew how unattractive that was. But it was hard to be consistent when facing total devastation.

Arsen hesitated, then leaned against the counter. He folded his arms. His muscles swelled against the rolled-up cuffs of his dress shirt. "Stealing the wallet would be easy enough. It's getting the Bitcoin off of it that would be a challenge."

"The wallet requires a password?"

"Two sets, usually. Mine has a pin code just to open it. There's also a sequence of twenty-four random words to access the Bitcoin."

"That's... not the sort of thing you memorize," I said.

"I memorized the pin code, but no, not the twenty-four passwords. It's recommended you keep your password list in a separate place from the wallet."

"Like a safe, if you were wearing the wallet." And Kelsey's safe had been emptied.

He nodded. "Kelsey was keeping her Bitcoin on a digital wallet?"

I pulled out my phone. "I have an idea she might have been wearing it." I called Enrique.

After three rings, he answered. "Yes?"

"Enrique, this is Susan Witsend," I said rapidly. "I have a question for you. That coral necklace Kelsey wore, did she get it when she was with you in Hawaii?"

"Uh, I do not think so. No. She had it before then. She's had it as long as I've known her. She said it was her lucky charm. Why?"

"Just curious. Thanks." I hung up before he could ask any more questions and turned to Arsen. "Kelsey wore a round disk that looked like gray coral around her neck. She wasn't wearing it when I found her body."

Arsen pursed his lips. "Something inexpensive-looking tracks. It's less likely to be a target for robbers. But even if it was stolen, as long as Kelsey had the correct sequence of twenty-four words, she should be able to get her Bitcoin back."

A muscle jumped beneath the skin on my neck. Arsen and I were so good at this. I'd *missed* him on this investigation. And we'd never do it again.

"I think she was killed for her money," I said. "I think that's what Hannah was looking for, not a lockbox with gold in it. She wanted the passwords. If someone stole that Bitcoin, it would be untraceable, wouldn't it?"

"Yes. We'd need her passwords to get into her online account. That would prove the Bitcoin had once been hers. It should include her trading history."

I opened the photo album on my phone. "Twenty-four words..." I swiped to the picture of the envelope in the dictionary from Anselm's desk. "I found this at Anselm's. There's a line drawn through *Aardvark*."

"Like he's trying out words."

My eyes burned. This felt so right. Arsen and I figuring things out together, like we always had. Was it really ending? Were we ending? "He can't believe he can figure out the correct order for all twenty-four words. Can he? He'd need a supercomputer or something."

His tanned brow furrowed. "When I bought my wallet, it came with cards to record the passwords on. I put half the words on one card and half on the other and keep them in separate places."

"Kelsey might have done the same," I breathed. "Maybe he only has one card."

"Even if he only has to figure out twelve words, he's screwed. There's no way."

"Good. I hope he suffers." I dialed the phone. "I'm calling Sheriff McCourt."

She answered on the first ring. Being friends with the sheriff had its benefits. "What now, Witsend?"

"I think Anselm is missing some passwords for Kelsey's Bitcoin wallet."

"And why would you think that?"

I hesitated. It wasn't that I didn't want to admit breaking into Anselm's house. The sheriff would understand. I was an instrumental part of her investigative team. But I didn't want to get Sal into trouble. "When I accidentally, purely by chance found myself inside Anselm's house—"

"You went inside his house?"

I paced the linoleum floor. "The door was open." *After Sal picked the lock.* "Anyway, I found an open dictionary beside his computer.

Words were crossed through in order, like he was ticking them off. He may be missing some words."

"That's a big jump," she said.

"Who crosses off words in a dictionary? There's no point unless he's trying to build his vocabulary. But he's only on *aardvark*, so if he's on a self-improvement kick, it's a recent one."

The sheriff grunted. "I'll ask him about it." She hung up.

Arsen shook his head. "Too much money attracts trouble. It's hard to know who to trust."

"Is that why you don't like to talk about yours?"

"That, and money's not very interesting." He smiled. "But I trust you." He took my hands. "And now that you're on a solution-to-a-murder high, there's something I need to say."

He was going to dump me when I was in a good mood. It's what I would do to make it easier on him. Not that I'd ever be able to dump Arsen. My jaw trembled. "Arsen—"

He got on one knee. "Marry me." The clock on the range ticked. The kitchen's overhead lights glinted off his hair, cast shadows across his chiseled face. The refrigerator hummed.

The tension in Arsen's face was expectant, uncertain, un-Arsen-like. I was used to devil-may-care Arsen, to Arsen bulling his way into trouble. This was a new part to him. There were still parts to him I didn't know, and my heart cracked open. Beneath the kitchen table, Bailey snorted.

And then I realized what he'd said. "What?" I asked.

"I wanted to do something big and romantic, but the timing was always off. And then I realized the right time is always now. I should have said it earlier. But I can't go back, so I'm asking you now. I've been in love with you since we were kids. You ground me. You keep me focused and moving forward. You're never boring. I want to build a life with you. I mean, we are building a life, but I want to build it together. Will you marry me?"

I swayed. *Married?* "You've been acting so... You want to get married?"

Arsen's forehead puckered. He drew away slightly. "You mean you don't? If you don't, that's—"

"No! I mean, yes." I laughed, my eyes hot. "Yes, I do want to marry you." I stepped closer, and he stood. My arms slipped around his waist. He tilted my head back and kissed me, and my heart hammered like it had the first time we'd kissed.

He pulled away and blinked. "Oh. Hold on." He pulled a blue velvet box from his pocket. "I have a ring."

I laughed and wiped my eyes. Arsen had never been strong on organizational skills. He opened the ring box, displaying a ring with a rectangular diamond that made me gasp. It was *huge*.

"If you don't like it, I can get another," he said anxiously.

"I love it," I said quickly. "It's perfect." I can't believe I thought diamonds were gaudy. How silly. Of course they weren't a waste of money.

He slipped it on my finger. "Your parents know," he said. "I went to San Francisco last week to get their permission."

I leaned against him and sighed into his dress shirt. "You thought of everything."

"I had a little trouble with the ring. There was a mix-up at the jeweler and a delay and... I'm sorry I've been acting weird this last week."

"Weird?" I looked up at him and a laugh burbled from my chest. "I didn't notice a thing."

We kissed again. And again. And finally, I sighed and rested my head against his chest. "This is the perfect moment."

"Any moment with you is perfect," he rumbled. "I should have realized that sooner."

I jerked away from him. "Remember the moment."

"Don't worry, I'll never forget this."

"No," I said excitedly. "Kelsey's saying that she told to Dixie. She told Dixie not to tell anyone."

"Okay. Dixie said Kelsey did that when she had a few glasses, but..."

"The words were secret. Like a password. And she told Dixie other secret sayings too."

His expression flattened. "Oh, boy."

I grabbed my phone off the kitchen table and called my cousin. The phone rang once, twice.

"Come on," I muttered. My cousin was probably driving and couldn't answer. I shook my head. "She's—"

"Yeah?" Dixie answered. "I can't believe it," she burst out. "He told me not to come, he couldn't make it. I've been catfished. *Me*. He's probably a woman or a scammer or worse, he's a Fed."

"What?"

"Steve! If that's really his name. I never should have dated someone into UFOs. They're all weirdos."

"So, you're not going to Vegas?" I asked slowly.

"Why would I go to Vegas?"

My heart tightened. *Poor Dixie*. My cousin deserved better. And this Steve person deserved... something much worse than I could think of right now. "I'm so sorry things didn't work out."

"Valentine's Day," she spat. "I held our meeting off until afterward so he wouldn't think I was putting pressure on him. And he dumped me anyway. What a creep."

"Ah..." Talk about bad timing. But maybe this would distract Dixie from the breakup. Or whatever it had been. "Those sayings Kelsey told you, what were they?"

"Who cares? They were just dumb sayings."

"Yes, but what were they?"

"She told me not to tell anyone."

Come on. "And Kelsey's dead now," I said, frustrated. "It shouldn't matter. And since when did you do what anyone told you to do?"

"That's a good— Hold on. Someone's at the door."

"Wait," I said. "Dixie?"

There was a cry, a scuffling sound.

My hand turned clammy on the phone. "Dixie? Dixie?" I asked, shrill.

The line went dead.

Chapter Thirty

Gripping the phone to my chest, I stared at Arsen in horror. "Dixie," I breathed. "He's at Dixie's now."

"Call the sheriff." He bolted for the porch door.

Beneath the kitchen table, Bailey staggered to his feet and woofed.

Pressing the sheriff's number, I raced outside. I hurtled down the porch steps, the phone clapped to my ear.

Arsen's muscular figure bulleted across the dark lawn. He hurdled the picket fence. I raced to the driveway, my heels skidding on the gravel. Why was I still wearing this stupid dress?

"What now?" the sheriff said in my ear.

"Anselm's at Dixie's trailer. I think he's done something to her." A shiver wracked my body. The night was cold, and I'd left my blazer in the kitchen.

"Where are you?"

"We were on the phone." I panted. "And then someone came to her trailer door. She screamed, and we were disconnected." I tottered around the picket fence and jogged toward the end of the court.

"Where *are* you?" she repeated.

"Chasing after Arsen in heels."

She swore and hung up. I jammed the phone into my pocket. A car swung onto the court, its headlights illuminating Arsen. He vanished into the trailhead between two ranch houses.

As the crow flies, Dixie's trailer was only a few blocks away. But by car, it was a winding mile and a half down twisty, residential streets. Running would get us there faster. Or at least it would get Arsen there faster.

Muscles tight, I plunged down the narrow trail. Thin branches lashed my dress in the darkness.

Arsen's footsteps thudded ahead of me. I turned on my phone's flashlight, and a fence rose before me. I turned sharply, racing along its high, wooden pickets, and stumbled over something. I slewed forward, and my fingers scraped against earth. Then I found my footing, straightened. I kept running, my heart battering against my ribs.

Dixie. Anselm wouldn't hurt my cousin. Not if he thought she had the passwords he needed. And Dixie wasn't stupid. She'd stall, delay out of sheer cussedness if nothing else. But if he was hurting her... My heart, aching from the sudden sprint, hardened to something cold and tight.

I couldn't see Arsen ahead, but I didn't call out. We were getting close to Dixie's trailer. We couldn't give Anselm any warning.

A branch whipped my arm. Arsen would save her. Arsen would save her, and he wouldn't get hurt. Another shudder rippled through me, but this time not from the cold. Arsen couldn't get hurt.

I slowed at the clearing around Dixie's Airstream. Moonlight glinted off the trailer's metal sides. Lights shone through its high, narrow windows. A dark SUV was parked in the silent clearing.

I looked around, my heart thudding in my throat. Where was Arsen? He couldn't be inside. He would have left the door open, wouldn't he?

I crept toward the trailer, my hands clenching and unclenching. Despite my attempts at stealth, I stepped on every twig and pinecone in the clearing. Every move I made cracked like a gunshot. But I couldn't hear Arsen. That worried me.

That familiar, cold shadow touched my shoulder. I shrugged the panic away. Arsen knew what he was doing. And he knew I was behind him. And he knew what I would have to do.

I knocked on the trailer door. "Dixie? It's Susan." My voice trembled, and I hoped no one noticed.

Stars gleamed, brittle above the mountain's silhouette. The trailer's metal hitch groaned. "I'm busy," my cousin shouted.

"Mr. Carlson is missing his wallet," I said. "He thought you might have seen it when you were cleaning." *Keep talking*. If Dixie was talking, she was alive, and Anselm hasn't done anything to her. *Stall, stall, stall.*

"No," she said through the door.

"He's desperate to find it." I swallowed. "Can you come back with me to help look?"

"No."

"Honestly, Dixie, I don't know why you're always so… bullheaded. I'm not leaving until you come out."

The door opened outward, and I sprang away. My ankle turned in its heel, and I straightened before I could do any serious damage. Dixie's slender form stood silhouetted in the doorway. "I'm busy. I can't help you."

"The thing is…" *What?* What was the thing? "Mr. Carlson called the police."

"What?" she said.

"The police are on their way." Dixie would understand what I meant. She'd *have* to understand. "Arsen tried to put them off, but Mr. Carlson couldn't be stopped." Where *was* Arsen?

Anselm came to stand beside my cousin in the doorway. Casually, he slung his arm around her neck. "Well, damn," he said. "That's inconvenient." The trailer's overhead light turned his auburn hair to fire.

I swallowed. "Hi, Anselm," I said. "What are you doing here?"

"Just reminiscing with Dixie about Kelsey. The memorial brought up all sorts of memories." Behind him, a trailer window slid open.

"I'm glad the sheriff let you go," I lied. Why the devil couldn't she have kept him overnight? "That was so unfair."

"We all declined to press charges after the fight," he said. "Feelings were running high."

Arsen's head and shoulders appeared in the narrow window. Light, quick energy jolted through my body. "That's understandable," I said. "It was a rough night for everyone. Look, I'm sorry I interrupted. I thought Dixie was here alone."

"Did you?" He reached behind him and pulled a handgun from the waistband of his charcoal slacks. The breath stoppered my throat. "I thought you'd figured it all out," he continued.

Behind him, Arsen froze. Then, moving like liquid, he slithered inside the trailer. He dropped onto the narrow couch beneath the window.

"Don't, Arsen," Anselm said without looking behind him. "I'll shoot Susan. I'm very aware. Aware enough to evade your video cameras when I left that Valentine at your house."

My hands went limp at my sides. He knew. But it didn't matter. The sheriff was on her way.

"We called the sheriff." Arsen straightened, rising to his feet. "She knows about the Bitcoin."

"You don't have all the passwords," I said. "But you're wrong. Dixie doesn't have them either."

Anselm pivoted sideways in the doorway. Whipping Dixie around, he positioned her between him and Arsen. He kept the gun aimed at me. "*Moment* is one of the words," he said. "I tried it when I got home. It's in there. It's funny, but Kelsey never quoted odd sayings around me. It seems Dixie was the sole recipient of her wisdom."

"Kelsey trusted Dixie," I said, my arms tight. "She knew Dixie didn't have an agenda. And like Kelsey, Dixie's always been self-sufficient. Unlike you. Did Kelsey find out your parents were supporting you? She couldn't have respected that. Not after she broke with her own wealthy parents."

A muscle twitched beneath his neck tattoo. "How did you find out?"

"They're paying your utility bills," I said. "And you lied about being engaged to Kelsey. Did you think it would divert suspicion if people believed you'd be marrying the wealth?"

"Sit down," Anselm told Arsen.

Slowly, Arsen sat on the narrow couch.

"Put your hands beneath you," Anselm continued.

Arsen slipped his hands beneath his thighs, straining against his navy slacks. "Put the gun down and let Susan and Dixie go," Arsen said. "The sheriff's on her way."

"I don't think so." Anselm climbed from the trailer, pulling Dixie along with him. "Dixie and I are going to have a private chat. Susan, get in the trailer." He and Dixie edged awkwardly across the clearing toward his SUV.

Blood pounded in my ears. He'd kill my cousin once he got what he wanted. "No," I said. "Take me instead." It was a silly offer. I didn't know the passcodes. But I had to keep him focused on me.

"Don't be dumb," Dixie said. "I've got the passwords, not you."

My hands clenched. I didn't need for her to point out that detail.

"Get in the trailer before I shoot you," he ground out.

A shadow moved at the edge of the clearing. *The sheriff.* "Okay," I said. "I'm moving."

I walked backward toward the trailer door. A second shadow moved behind the SUV. I forced my breathing to even. This would be fine. The sheriff knew how to handle this. Dixie would be okay.

Sal popped up from behind the SUV and waved. My heart plummeted to my toes. What was *she* doing here?

"Move," Anselm barked.

I took another step backward, and my heel hit the base of the metal stairs. Fumbling, I found the trailer door behind me. "Are you sure you don't want to take me instead? I'm excellent at puzzles. I suppose you killed Hannah because she knew about the Bitcoin? She was digging in Kelsey's yard for the wallet, wasn't she?"

"Once Hannah blabbed," he said, "the cops would be looking for the wallet. I couldn't let that happen."

"And you knew Hannah had a weakness for chocolate," I said, "since you two dated. How did you find out about Kelsey's Bitcoin though? Did Hannah tell you?"

"She let it slip." He backed toward his car. "She was always jealous of her sister."

"Even more so when you dumped her for Kelsey." My fingers touched the cold metal of the trailer door. "Hannah couldn't have known Kelsey kept the wallet around her neck. It was that coral necklace. You ripped it off Kelsey so fast you cut your finger." I climbed onto the first step. "I'm assuming you'd gotten Kelsey's safe combination at that point. You thought you could steal her passwords. What you didn't know was that she hadn't written all the passwords down. It must have been a shock. So many words in the English language—"

"Get in," he said. "Close the door behind you. And Arsen, I can see you. Don't move."

"Dixie," I said, "just tell him the phrases now, and he'll let you go."

Her lips peeled into a snarl. "I'm not telling this jackass anything."

Something thumped on the other side of the clearing. Anselm swiveled, aiming the gun at the spot. Sal hurtled over the hood of the SUV toward Dixie and Anselm.

Anselm stepped aside. She landed flat on the ground between them.

"Oof." She grunted.

Strong hands grabbed me and yanked me backward. I fell into the trailer. Arsen leapt over me.

Dixie's arm whipped out. She struck Anselm in the neck. Dropping the gun, he gagged and fell to the ground and clutched his throat. Arsen was on him in a flash, rolling him onto his stomach and pinning his arms behind him.

Dixie kicked the gun away. "Jerk."

Bingo raced across the lot. "Sal! Are you okay?"

She sat up. "Huh. That didn't go like I'd expected." She brushed off her parka.

I braced myself on my elbow. Aches flamed up and down my back along the spots I'd landed on the stairs. "Not for me either. What are you doing here?"

"We saw you and Arsen running into the bushes and figured something was up," she said. "I *told* you Anselm was the killer."

I clutched the top of my head with both hands. She'd thought they'd *all* been the killer. "But what are you doing back here at all?"

"We couldn't abandon you in your hour of need," Sal said stoutly.

"Uh, he needs a doctor." Arsen looked up from Anselm. "And maybe a tracheotomy."

"Good," Dixie said.

Flashlight beams scanned the clearing. "Everybody freeze," the sheriff shouted. "Police."

Sal flopped onto her back. "Never around when you need 'em."

Chapter Thirty-One

Arsen was right. Anselm *did* need a tracheotomy. It turns out, a karate chop to the neck can be deadly. But Anselm had killed two people. He would probably have killed Dixie too if he'd had the chance. So I was short on sympathy.

Fortunately, a paramedic arrived on the scene. She performed the procedure beneath Sal and Bingo's fascinated gazes. Anselm was taken to the hospital under guard. We drove to the sheriff's station in separate cars to make statements.

I was a little surprised Sal and Bingo actually showed up to make their statements. I'd gotten the impression she wasn't a big fan of sheriff's stations.

The five of us left the station together. We stopped beside Bingo's Tesla in the parking area. The lot's amber lights dimmed the stars above, but not enough to forget you were in the mountains. I rubbed the new ring on my finger with my thumb. It felt strange and lovely and exciting.

"I get it," Sal said. "Why you like to solve murders, I mean. It gives me a sort of satisfied feeling, you know? Like all's right with the world."

"It's all an illusion," Dixie grumped.

"But seriously," Sal said. "Maybe I should do this more often. Use my powers for good."

A shudder pebbled my flesh. Sal? An unsupervised amateur detective? "I don't think—"

"I didn't know you were going to try and tackle that guy," Bingo told her severely. "We were only supposed to cause a distraction."

"It was a spur of the moment thing," Sal said. "And hey, all's well that ends well. A*nd* at least I got the guy who spiked my chocolates. Right?" She grasped my hand and pumped it, jarring my shoulder.

I grimaced, my arm feeling like it was about to break loose from its socket. Anselm hadn't explained why he'd tampered with those chocolates. Had he been trying to take me out?

"We'll see you when we see you." Releasing my hand, Sal turned toward the Tesla, and Bingo opened the door for her.

"Sal," I said helplessly. "You saved Dixie's life."

"Nah." Dixie examined her nails. "I was just waiting for my moment."

"Yeah," Sal said. "Dix would have been okay. We just sped up the timeline. Right?" She punched Dixie on the shoulder, and my cousin staggered.

We watched the couple get into Bingo's Tesla and roll out of the parking lot.

Dixie yawned. "Stick a fork in me, I'm done."

The three of us trooped toward Arsen's Jeep Commander. "Did you and the sheriff figure out the rest of the passwords?" I asked her.

"Yeah. Her parents are going to be even richer than they are now."

But if they were richer, it was only in goodwill. We learned months later their parents had donated Kelsey's millions to a non-profit for artists.

I buckled my seatbelt. "So, ah, Dixie, we have something to tell you." It seemed churlish to tell her after her recent disappointment in love. But she'd find out soon enough.

"You and Arsen are tying the knot?"

Arsen pulled from the parking spot. He grinned and laid a hand on my knee.

"How'd you know?" I asked, twisting in my seat. The car lurched over a speed bump.

She shrugged. "It was obvious he was working up to it. Plus the ring's hard to miss. Especially the way you've been flashing it around. So when's the big day?"

Embarrassed, I dropped my hand to my lap. "I don't know. We haven't gotten that far. But soon, I hope."

I took Arsen's hand, and he squeezed it lightly. Nearly losing Dixie was a painful reminder of how short life could be. I didn't want to waste a second.

"A wedding's a lot of planning," Dixie warned.

I felt the blood drain from my face. We'd hosted weddings at Wits' End, and they *were* a lot of planning. I fingered the engagement ring. I didn't care how much trouble it was. Arsen was worth it.

"Hey, Dix, would you reach under my seat?" Arsen asked. "There's something for Susan there."

Her head disappeared behind the seat. She straightened and handed a white box wrapped in a red bow to me.

"What is it?" I asked.

Arsen glanced at me and grinned. "Open it and find out."

I tugged on the ribbon, and it easily fell off the box. I pried off the lid. A stack of paper inserts, the top page reading WEDDING PLANNER, stared up at me. "You knew I'd say *yes*."

"The way I screwed up this proposal," he said, "I didn't know anything. But I hoped."

Dixie leaned over the seat between us. "What was with that boom box?"

He sighed. "It was supposed to be the song Susan and I first danced to. I screwed up the music." He shot me a sideways glance, then turned the Jeep onto the mountain highway. "I screwed up a lot."

Dixie wrinkled her nose. "Holy crap. You remember the name of the song you and Susan first danced to? What's wrong with you?"

"I made a point of it." He squeezed my thigh. "Susan's worth it."

"Blech." Dixie slouched back against her seat.

We drove Dixie to her trailer, and then Arsen took me home. And what happened next was a night I'll never forget either, but I'll draw a veil over it. It was between Arsen and me.

He helped me with breakfast the next morning, carrying the chafing dishes into the breakfast room. The Carters wandered into the octagonal room. The heating vents in the wood floor fluttered the blue curtains.

Arsen flushed. "Mrs. Carter," he said, "I—"

"That's all right." She motioned toward me airily. "Susan told us you couldn't model, and I quite understand. Bigfoot erotica isn't for everyone."

My eyes bulged. "Bigfoot... What?"

"You'd make an excellent Bigfoot." Mrs. Carter opened a chafing dish. "And no one would know it was you beneath all the fur. But I understand why you wouldn't want a bunch of romance readers ogling you."

"You wanted him for a cover model?" Heat raced to my face. "For Bigfoot..." There was such a thing as Bigfoot erotica? And I'd volunteered Arsen for it?

"Of course." She speared a piece of bacon with a serving fork. "What did you think we wanted him for?"

"For your outdoors wear company," I said. I owed Arsen *such* a big apology. He grinned and lit a candle beneath a chafing dish.

Mr. Carter laughed. "Oh, we don't use models anymore. Much better if people can visualize *themselves* in the clothing."

Brooke and Finley edged into the blue room, their faces pink. Though Finley had always had a bit of a burnt look to him.

"Morning," Brooke said and smoothed her frosted hair.

"Good morning." I shook myself, trying not to think about what Bigfoot erotica might entail. But of course the more I tried not to, the more I thought about it. I swallowed. "I hope you're hungry. I went a little overboard with breakfast today since you're all checking out."

"We're starving." Finley lifted a lid on a chafing dish. The scent of scrambled eggs and cheese flooded the room. His stomach gave a Bigfoot-sized rumble.

"Finley..." I trailed off, speculative.

His gaze met mine, his brown eyes guileless. "Yeah?"

"Is there something you want to tell me? About those chocolates on the front desk?"

Brooke nudged him and scowled. "I told you that you'd have to fess up. You should have come clean from the start."

"I'm sorry," he blurted. "It was an accident. They were for Bigfoot. That woman who spotted him told us he loved chocolates. Then Brooke was talking about tranquilizer guns—"

"This is my fault?" She arched a brow.

His shoulders sagged. "No. I take full responsibility. I just left them there for a minute, and then they were gone. I didn't know what to do. I thought someone from the group had taken them. I didn't realize until too late that your other guest had. Do you think she'll press charges?"

I wrinkled my nose. "I don't think she's the type."

Brooke glanced shyly at him. "We were actually wondering, thinking, I mean, we might come back here someday soon."

"For a wedding." Finley adjusted his sling. "You do weddings here, don't you?"

Arsen slung his arm over my shoulder, and I leaned against him. "Yeah," he said. "In fact, there's going to be one this June."

"It'll be simple," Brooke said. "This is our second time around, after all."

"Maybe we'll actually find Bigfoot next time," Finley said, rueful.

Brooke smiled up at him. "We found something much more important."

They embraced, and Arsen and I discreetly returned to the kitchen. I stopped short in the doorway, and Arsen bumped into me. Sheriff McCourt sat at the round table and fed a small piece of bacon to Bailey.

"Bribery," I said. "And with my own bacon."

"I got tired of him growling at me." She shoved aside the broad-brimmed hat on the table. "I'm going to tell you this only so you don't try to ransack Anselm's house—"

"I would never," I said loftily. There was no point after he'd been arrested.

She quirked a blond brow. "We found Kelsey's digital wallet at Anselm's house. It was that necklace, like you thought. Enrique told me she never took it off."

"Enrique?" I asked.

Spots of color appeared in her cheeks. "He's a witness," she said roughly.

Hm. "He's an interesting guy. Travel. Martial arts. A self-made man." And rumor had it the sheriff had been seen sharing a drink with Enrique at Antoine's. Mrs. Steinberg had told me.

"A witness," she repeated. "And that's all."

"Sure," I said. "That's all."

"What do you mean repeating *that's all*? That's all." The sheriff rose and snatched her hat off the table. Bailey made a disappointed noise. "Anyway, I just came to tell you Anselm's done. You three will need to testify whenever they get around to having a trial. FYI, that could be years from now. His lawyer's tying things up in knots, but he won't get him off."

"We knew you'd get your man." I widened my eyes innocently.

Sheriff McCourt glared and jammed her hat on her head. "That's right." She strode out the porch door.

"The sheriff and Enrique?" Arsen asked.

"It's been a very weird Valentine's season."

He wrapped his arms around my waist and pulled me close. "Valentine's has a whole season now?"

"Maybe a month."

He kissed me. "Let's say forever."

More Kirsten Weiss

The Perfectly Proper Paranormal Museum Mysteries

When highflying Maddie Kosloski is railroaded into managing her small-town's paranormal museum, she tells herself it's only temporary... until a corpse in the museum embroils her in murders past and present.

If you love quirky characters and cats with attitude, you'll love this laugh-out-loud cozy mystery series with a light paranormal twist. It's perfect for fans of Jana DeLeon, Laura Childs, and Juliet Blackwell. Start with book 1, *The Perfectly Proper Paranormal Museum*, and experience these charming wine-country whodunits today.

The Tea & Tarot Cozy Mysteries

Welcome to Beanblossom's Tea and Tarot, where each and every cozy mystery brews up hilarious trouble.

Abigail Beanblossom's dream of owning a tearoom is about to come true. She's got the lease, the start-up funds, and the recipes. But Abigail's out of a tearoom and into hot water when her realtor turns out to be a conman... and then turns up dead.

Take a whimsical journey with Abigail and her partner Hyperion through the seaside town of San Borromeo (patron saint of heartburn sufferers). And be sure to check out the easy tearoom recipes in the back of each book! Start the adventure with book 1, *Steeped in Murder*.

The Wits' End Cozy Mysteries

Cozy mysteries that are out of this world...

Running the best little UFO-themed B&B in the Sierras takes organization, breakfasting chops, and a talent for turning up trouble.

The truth is out there... Way out there in these hilarious whodunits. Start the series and beam up book 1, *At Wits' End*, today!

Pie Town Cozy Mysteries

When Val followed her fiancé to coastal San Nicholas, she had ambitions of starting a new life and a pie shop. One broken engagement later, at least her dream of opening a pie shop has come true.... Until one of her regulars keels over at the counter.

Welcome to Pie Town, where Val and pie-crust specialist Charlene are baking up hilarious trouble. Start this laugh-out-loud cozy mystery series with book 1, *The Quiche and the Dead*.

A Big Murder Mystery Series

Small Town. Big Murder.

The number one secret to my success as a bodyguard? Staying under the radar. But when a wildly public disaster blew up my career and reputation, it turned my perfect, solitary life upside down.

I thought my tiny hometown of Nowhere would be the ideal out-of-the-way refuge to wait out the media storm.

It wasn't.

My little brother had moved into a treehouse. The obscure mountain town had decided to attract tourists with the world's largest collection of big things... Yes, Nowhere now has the world's largest pizza cutter. And lawn flamingo. And ball of yarn...

And then I stumbled over a dead body.

All the evidence points to my brother being the bad guy. I may have been out of his life for a while—okay, five years—but I know he's no killer. Can I clear my brother before he becomes Nowhere's next Big Fatality?

A fast-paced and funny cozy mystery series, start with Big Shot.

The Doyle Witch Mysteries

In a mountain town where magic lies hidden in its foundations and forests, three witchy sisters must master their powers and shatter a curse before it destroys them and the home they love.

This thrilling witch mystery series is perfect for fans of Annabel Chase, Adele Abbot, and Amanda Lee. If you love stories rich with packed with magic, mystery, and murder, you'll love the Witches of Doyle. Follow the magic with the Doyle Witch trilogy, starting with book 1, *Bound*.

The Riga Hayworth Paranormal Mysteries

Her gargoyle's got an attitude.

Her magic's on the blink.

Alchemy might be the cure... if Riga can survive long enough to puzzle out its mysteries.

All Riga wants is to solve her own personal mystery—how to rebuild her magical life. But her new talent for unearthing murder keeps getting in the way...

If you're looking for a magical page-turner with a complicated, 40-something heroine, read the paranormal mystery series that fans of Patricia Briggs and Ilona Andrews call AMAZING! Start your next adventure with book 1, *The Alchemical Detective*.

Sensibility Grey Steampunk Suspense

California Territory, 1848.

Steam-powered technology is still in its infancy.

Gold has been discovered, emptying the village of San Francisco of its male population.

And newly arrived immigrant, Englishwoman Sensibility Grey, is alone.

The territory may hold more dangers than Sensibility can manage. Pursued by government agents and a secret society, Sensibility must decipher her father's clockwork secrets, before time runs out.

If you love over-the-top characters, twisty mysteries, and complicated heroines, you'll love the Sensibility Grey series of steampunk suspense. Start this steampunk adventure with book 1, *Steam and Sensibility*.

Get Kirsten's Mobile App

Keep up with the latest book news, and get free short stories, scone recipes and more by downloading Kirsten's mobile app. Just click HERE to get started or use the QR code below.
Or make sure you're on Kirsten's email list to get your free copy of the Tea & Tarot mystery, *Fortune Favors the Grave*.
You can do that here: KirstenWeiss.com or use the QR code below:

Connect with Kirsten

You can download my free app here:
https://kirstenweissbooks.beezer.com
Or sign up for my newsletter and get a special digital prize pack for joining, including an exclusive Tea & Tarot novella, *Fortune Favors the Grave.*
https://kirstenweiss.com
Or maybe you'd like to chat with other whimsical mystery fans? Come join Kirsten's reader page on Facebook:
https://www.facebook.com/kirsten.weiss
Or... sign up for my read and review team on Booksprout: https://booksprout.co/author/8142/kirsten-weiss

About the Author

I write laugh-out-loud, page-turning mysteries for people who want to escape with real, complex, and flawed but likable characters. If there's magic in the story, it must work consistently within the world's rules and be based in history or the reality of current magical practices.

I'm best known for my cozy mystery and witch mystery novels, though I've written some steampunk mystery as well. So if you like funny, action-packed mysteries with complicated heroines, just turn the page...

Learn more, grab my **free app**, or sign up for my **newsletter** for exclusive stories and book updates. I also have a read-and-review tea via **Booksprout** and is looking for honest and thoughtful reviews! If you're interested, download the **Booksprout app**, follow me on Booksprout, and opt-in for email notifications.

- bookbub.com/profile/kirsten-weiss
- goodreads.com/author/show/5346143.Kirsten_Weiss
- facebook.com/kirsten.weiss
- instagram.com/kirstenweissauthor/

Made in United States
North Haven, CT
15 June 2023